# HOLLYWOOD KILLS

# HOLLYWOOD KILLS

## AN ANTHOLOGY

### EDITED BY
### ADAM MEYER & ALAN ORLOFF

*To my mother, who inspired me with her love of movies — AM*

*To desperate dreamers everywhere — AO*

# Contents

# Introduction

The morning of Tuesday, January 7th, I saw a cloud formation unlike anything I'd ever seen before. It hovered over the entire city of Los Angeles, giant and ominously gray. The formation freaked me out so much I posted photos of it online, joking that I wouldn't be surprised if the colossal cloud parted and a spaceship landed.

Instead, the fires came.

The world watched in absolute horror as flames driven by hurricane-force winds flattened entire neighborhoods. My daughter made the apt and very L.A. observation that huge swaths of the city looked like a scene from the movie, *Independence Day*. Being a Tulane University alum with strong ties to New Orleans, for me, it brought back memories of what my NOLA friends endured after the disaster that was Hurricane Katrina laid waste to so much of their city.

The fires knew no class distinction. The Eaton Fire tore through the incredibly diverse neighborhood of Altadena, home to generations of Black, Brown, and Asian homeowners. The Palisades Fire decimated an entire neighborhood, ranging from apartment dwellers to seniors who'd spent decades in their homes to the very wealthy. I texted a friend who's a successful showrunner. She wrote back, "We lost our beloved home of thirty years. Every nonliving thing that was precious to me is gone." Initially, the media focused on celebrities who lost their houses, leading to an appalling lack of sympathy on the part of way too many people. Grief doesn't discriminate. Billy Crystal said that when he saw the incinerated remnants of the home where his family lived for thirty-six years, he fell to his knees and wailed in a way he hadn't since he was fifteen and learned his father had died.

I've had a fractured relationship with Los Angeles. It can be a very lonely place. It can be hard to build a community here. But I *have*. Several of them. A community of television writers and crews I worked with. The mom friends I made while our daughter was growing up. My wonderful circle of local mystery pals. And our neighbors here in Studio City. I love our home. I love the hills I walk almost daily, often witnessing glorious sunsets in the mountains to the west and north of us. I can hike trails in the Hollywood Hills and catch an intoxicating view of the Pacific Ocean glistening in the distance. Hard as it can be to love the City of Angels, love it I do.

*Hollywood Kills* reflects that passion for this city. My story, "Billy Wilder's Ghost," was inspired by the five seasons I worked on shows in the Paramount building, named after the film comedy legend. A friend of mine is head of production at the studio, and he got me back onto the lot to revisit my old haunts as research. I was happy to see that the offices where I wrote sitcoms like *Wings* now host the writing and production staff of *Only Murders in the Building*.

Over half the authors represented in *Hollywood Kills* also live in the Los Angeles area. We're the fortunate ones. None of us lost our homes. But we all know people who did, or who won't be able to return to their damaged homes for months, years, or perhaps ever. The authors in this anthology have agreed to donate all proceeds from the anthology's sales to recovery efforts from the fire.

Recovery from a disaster of this magnitude has a long tail. It will take years. Decades. But Los Angeles *will* recover. We will show the world our strength and resilience. We will support and hold up our neighbors in their arduous journey forward. The bright lights of America's second biggest city will shine again. Until then, we are…

\#LASTRONG

Ellen Byron
  Studio City, CA

# The Second Act Twist

by Matt Goldman

Hollywood soundstages have padded walls to dampen the acoustics, but the similarity to padded cells should not be overlooked. "It's a crazy business," says almost everyone working on any soundstage at one time or the other, "but it's the business we chose." Shake of the head. Wry smile. Sometimes tears. Then a heavy sigh and right back to it.

Jude Abramov chose show business through one of its famed back doors. He married into it. Now he's an executive producer and principal in ASP—Abramov Shalit Productions. His wife, Rachel Shalit, has created and run two hit television shows. She's made Jude wealthy. Eight-figures wealthy. Rachel works seventy-hour weeks overseeing writing and production. Jude flits about doing what he thinks needs to be done.

"You know," he says in his heavy Brooklyn accent as he stands over the craft services table. Jude's fifty years old, wears three-hundred-dollar Air Jordans and cashmere-hooded sweatshirts. He picks up a coffee stir stick from a box of thousands and shakes it to make his point. "Stir sticks can be reused. It's wasteful to throw them out after one stirring."

"Okay…" says Chelsea, a production assistant who has nothing to do with craft services but just happens to be getting a cup of tea. "I'll mention that to Mariana."

"'Cause it ain't like these sticks grow on trees," says Jude. He's not joking. Even though the stir stick is made of wood. "Production costs are killing us. These runaway expenses we incur…" He puts his hands on his hips as if he's looking over his kingdom. "…I want this situation turned around 360 degrees."

Chelsea, a twenty-three-year-old who has a B.A. from Dartmouth, clenches her jaw to prevent herself from laughing in her boss's face. She also makes a point of memorizing his exact words so she can relay them to other members of the crew the minute Jude leaves the soundstage to go wherever he disappears to for hours at a time. "Got it," says Chelsea. "I'll spread the word."

"Yeah," says Jude. "Good." Then someone catches his eye and he says, "Hey, Shannon. I need to see the looks for Day One." He heads in Shannon's direction.

Shannon is the second assistant in wardrobe. Her long auburn hair falls to the middle of her back. She was the prettiest girl at her high school in Dubuque, Iowa. Voted most likely to become a movie star. She certainly has a face and body worthy of the big screen. But most feel that her acting talent belongs behind the camera. Assistant to the Head Costumer is a temporary job, thinks Shannon. A stepping stone. She's taking two acting classes, scene study and improv, and is confident her true talent will be recognized soon.

Chelsea watches Jude chase after Shannon and says, "Jude really should be more discreet." This to Miles, who drives for transportation and has just helped himself to a cinnamon roll. He has long blond hair, and his skin is covered in more ink than *War and Peace*.

"He don't got the brains for discreet," says Miles.

Chelsea chuckles and says, "Hey, Miles. I'm just finishing up a spec script. One of the main characters is an ex-con. Would you mind glancing at it for a reality check?" Miles smiles, exhales, and doesn't say a word. Chelsea expected this. Nearly everyone in the department asks Miles for favors. As the head of transpo, he has access to trucks and muscle, dollies and padded blankets. Anyone who's moved, bought an antique at a swap meat, or needed an old treadmill hauled out of their house has hit up Miles, who's always willing to help. For a price. Chelsea meets his smile and says, "For a hundy?"

"Sure," says Miles. "Happy to. My email's in the staff directory. Send it anytime."

***

On the far end of the soundstage, Jude's wife, Rachel, stands with script in hand. She's forty years old and lives in floppy dresses that are more comfortable than adorable. There's something childlike about her appearance. Big eyes and smooth skin, the latter more from spending most daylight hours indoors than due to any creams or dermatologists. Rachel stands in the living room set as her lead actress sits on the couch next to the director. They're discussing the blue pages that just came down to set.

"I hate to say this…" says the actress. She looks around to make sure no one else is in earshot. She also checks the overhead boom mics to make sure they're not hovering within listening distance. "The guest actor this week who's playing my old roommate…she's not great. I really feel bad saying that about a fellow actor, but she's giving me nothing."

The director, whose job depends on both the approval of the showrunner—Rachel—and being liked by the lead actor, conspicuously avoids eye contact with either.

"Yeah," says Rachel. "I've noticed. The network really pushed her on us. She's the it girl this week. We'll do some rewrites for her tonight. See if we can help her in the pinks." The pinks refers to the pink pages, the next color revision that will arrive to set tomorrow after tonight's rewrite. It won't be a small rewrite, thinks Rachel, but that's the job. "And if she's not better tomorrow…" Now it's Rachel's turn to look around and make sure no one is eavesdropping. "…I've asked casting to start putting together a list of possible replacements. Just so we're not blindsided."

"You're the best, Rachel," says the actress. "Thank you."

Rachel's number two approaches and says, "Hey Rachel. Sorry to interrupt. But we got that thing."

Rachel turns toward Stephan with impatience for his intrusion until she sees in his eyes what *that thing* means. Then she turns back to her actor and director and says, "Excuse me a minute. I have to deal with the network.

You'll see those changes in tomorrow's script. And good work today."

* * *

Jude stands among racks of clothing, each rack tagged with the name of the character who may or may not wear those clothes in the upcoming episode. Wardrobe approval is one of Jude's official duties. Not because he's great at it but because his wife, Rachel, hates it. "I can barely dress myself," says Rachel, "I'm not going to waste everyone's time trying to dress an entire cast."

Of course, the head costumer dresses the actors. She just needs final approval from an executive producer, and unfortunately for the costumer, that executive producer is Jude. Jude subscribes to *GQ* and *Vogue*, but that's the extent of his expertise. What he's more of an expert in is Shannon's clothing. At least getting her to take it off.

As the second assistant in wardrobe, Shannon's job mostly involves shopping for clothing and then returning all the options that aren't used. It's a lot of driving around in LA traffic, using the production credit card, and taking one-hour sojourns to meet Jude at her apartment, a hotel, or sometimes even at Jude and Rachel's Hollywood Hills home.

But right now they're tucked into the back corner of the soundstage in a makeshift room of plywood walls and no ceiling. You can see straight up to the soundstage ceiling and the pipes and catwalk that hang from it.

"No, Jude," says Shannon. She sits on her desk with her arms crossed. "This has gone on long enough. Tell Rachel about us, or I will."

"Oh come on, Shannon," says Jude. "You know I can't do that. We'd both be out of a job."

"Why do either of us need a job?" says Shannon. "You're rich. Take half the money and we'll run off to New York or London. Who cares as long as we're together?" Then she crosses her legs to reinforce her crossed arms and adds, "Unless all you want me for is sex. And if that's the case, Jude, you can go straight to hell." Shannon keeps her eyes on Jude as she twirls a lock of hair around her sparkly press-on nail. "I'm serious, Jude. If you don't tell

Rachel, I will."

Jude Abramov is not her first married man. There was that producer at Paramount who did get her a guest spot on *Star Trek*, but her voice was digitized to sound like a machine's, and her alien costume made it impossible for anyone to recognize her. And there was the director of that indie movie that was accepted into the Cedar Rapids film festival. And that D-list actor who snagged her a non-speaking juror role in *Law & Order*.

But Jude Abramov is Shannon's last married man. Enough is enough.

"All right," says Jude. "Yeah. You're right. It's time." He sits on the couch next to a pile labeled CATTIE, the wise-beyond-her-years adolescent who plays the lead's daughter. "I'll tell Rachel tonight when she gets home. That means you and I will be persona non grata around here tomorrow. Rachel should be in a rewrite until at least ten P.M., so meet me at the boat around seven and we'll make our getaway plan."

"Really?" says Shannon. "You mean it?"

"You're my one true love," says Jude. "Of course I mean it."

Shannon uncrosses her arms and legs and practically leaps into Jude's arms.

* * *

Rachel Shalit walks out the soundstage elephant door with Stephan. They each have one AirPod from a pair. Rachel has the left one stuck in her left ear. Stephan has the right one stuck in his ear. The sound is crystal clear.

* * *

"So how late do you think you'll be?" says Jude. He stands in the writer's room talking to his wife, Rachel, who sits at the head of a conference table, a script open before her. Stephan sits at the opposite end of the table, and half a dozen other writers sit between them. A writer's assistant occupies a small desk and types away at the script, which is projected on one full wall of the room.

"Late," says Rachel.

"How late?"

"Well, the longer you prevent us from starting, the later it will be."

"I'm just asking 'cause—"

"Why?" says Rachel. "Why are you asking? What does it matter, Jude? I'll get home when I get home. You saw the run-through today. The second-act twist didn't work so we have to come up with a new one. My guess is I won't be home until midnight at the soonest."

Jude can feel the room's eyes on him. They're laughing at him. He knows they are. He's used to it. But they wouldn't be laughing if they saw his financial statements. Because Jude has something they don't have. Fuck you money. "Right," says Jude. "See you later."

* * *

Jude pulls out of the Radford lot in his Tesla Plaid and takes a right on Laurel Canyon to head north into the San Fernando Valley. He wishes that he'd had more time to plan. If he'd known, he could have bought a burner phone and called Mikey, who still lives in the old neighborhood. Mikey would take a week to drive cross country. Pay for gas and hotels with cash. But Jude doesn't have a week. It has to be done tonight.

The Home Depot on Saticoy has everything Jude needs. Plastic sheeting, duct tape, concrete blocks, bulk chain, and carabiners for holding it all together. Jude changes into a pair of boat shoes he keeps in his trunk. He ditches his cashmere hoodie for an old, gray sweatshirt. He wears sunglasses and a baseball cap into the store and pays with cash. It's just after six P.M., and the store is crowded with DIYers stopping in after work to supply themselves for their evening project. No one will remember him. No one will even notice him. Of that he's sure.

Jude takes Coldwater Canyon up the valley side to Mullholland, then starts down Benedict Canyon to the house. He turns off the alarm, turns on the TV, orders dinner from DoorDash, plugs in his phone, then leaves the house without taking his phone or resetting the alarm. He leaves the Tesla in the driveway because he's sure a satellite knows its every location.

He hops on his '72 Harley instead, drops down to Wilshire, and weaves through traffic heading west. Jude gets to Marina Del Rey just after seven o'clock. The boat is a dual-engined forty-footer that his wife, Rachel, does not know exists. Nor is she aware of the hundred thousand dollars in cash he stores in the cabin. Getaway money. Just in case. Jude's buddy Kevin from the old neighborhood holds the title and pays the slip rental. Jude loads the goods from Home Depot into the cabin and remains below deck waiting for Shannon. When he hears footsteps on the deck just after 7:30, he goes up to greet her.

* * *

The writer's PA enters the room carrying take-out bags from Mistral, Rachel's favorite French restaurant in the Valley. Dinner orders are distributed, and the writer's assistant disappears into the kitchen and returns with several bottles of wine. Good food and good wine make for a good rewrite. That's what Rachel always says.

They put away their scripts and take half an hour to eat like civilized people. The conversation ping-pongs around the room, writers talking about their home lives and latest exercise fads and upcoming vacations. Claire, an executive story editor who's four months pregnant, informs the room that her doctor has put her on vaginal rest, so she doesn't care how late they work tonight. There's a brief lull, and Rachel jumps in.

"I know everyone thinks I married an idiot," says Rachel. "And that Jude gets a fat paycheck for doing nothing. And that it's ridiculous his name comes first in our production company. But when I was twenty-two years old and fresh out of college with no money and no confidence, working temp jobs in New York and hoping to find a way to break into the business, he took me under his wing."

The other writers don't say a word. They barely keep eating and instead choose to empty their wine glasses as they listen to this rare glimpse into their boss's personal life. Stephan doesn't take his eyes off Rachel. He nibbles on a piece of baguette as she continues.

"He was ten years older and had a nice apartment on the Upper West Side. He gave me a safe and secure place to become what I've become. And when I finally broke into the business and was out working long hours, he was nothing but supportive. SNL was the worst. Six days a week. Sometimes we'd sleep there. But on Sunday, my one day off, he would pamper me like I was a queen. Extravagant meals. A drawn bath with candlelight and Vivaldi. He'd hire a masseuse to come to the apartment. I didn't lift a finger all day. And by Monday morning, I was reenergized to go back to work."

Rachel cuts into her half a chicken and forks some breast meat into her mouth. She sips her chardonnay, sets down her glass, and adds, "I wish he were still like that, but time and success have taken their toll. Still, I don't begrudge Jude his success. He made an investment in me, and now I'm making one in him. And he deserves it. He deserves everything he has and everything he'll get." And then, knowing it's always best to close with a joke, Rachel turns to Claire and says, "Vaginal rest. How do I get put on that?"

The room laughs. Dinners are finished. More wine is poured. Profiteroles are distributed. And the scripts reappear on the table.

* * *

Shannon pours two glasses of champagne from a bottle of Cristal. She hands one to Jude and says, "We've never gone out this far before."

"It's a beautiful night," says Jude, sitting behind the captain's wheel. "And we have plenty of time."

He takes his glass, offers Shannon a smile and a clink of rims. The Pacific Ocean is quiet and calm. Los Angeles shrinks and twinkles as the sky and sea darken. Faint wisps of pink and purple hang in the western sky as the evening's first stars mock the lights of LA. Catalina looms to the south as the marine layer moves in to swallow it.

"I don't care if we go all the way to Japan," says Shannon. "As long as we're together."

"I don't think we have enough fuel for that," says Jude. He kills the engine and lets the boat drift. It's dead quiet other than the lapping of small waves against the hull. No wind. No city noise. The chem trail of a jet hangs high in the sky, which is still lit by the sun that has dropped below the horizon.

"So where are we going?" says Shannon. "Where shall we start anew?"

"I thought maybe we'd head up to Santa Barbara," says Jude. "Spend the night at The Biltmore. And plot our course from there."

"Our course?" says Shannon. "I think you mean our lives. Our lives and our love. What do you think of having children? We've never discussed that."

"I don't know," says Jude. "Rachel never wanted them, so it was never an option. I'd be an old dad. But maybe better late than never."

"Really?" says Shannon.

"Why not?" says Jude. "I think I'd be a good dad. And you'd be a hell of a mom."

"That turns me on," Shannon puts a hand on Jude's shoulder and says, "I'm going down to the cabin if you want to join me." She kisses him on the cheek, then disappears below deck.

Jude remains at the helm. He restarts the engines and puts the boat on autopilot. He sets it to maintain the current position, then double-checks the running lights. All good. In fact, all great. Shannon is making this easy on him. He has no qualms about killing her. He's not going to let a pretty face and fit body cut off his gravy train. In fact, killing Shannon is the first productive thing he'll have done in some time. Sure, he keeps himself busy on the show. He oversees little things like the procurement of office machines and ordering the cast's Christmas gifts and approving wardrobe. They don't let him handle anything really important like budgets or schedules. Jude knows he could handle it. He can handle any undertaking if he has to.

At least he used to think he could. Over the years, self-doubt has crept in. Maybe Jude doesn't contribute to the success of Abramov Shalit Productions. Maybe Rachel would be a multi-millionaire, Emmy Award winner without him. But now he has his own production. A solo act. A one-man show. That's what killing Shannon is. He'll get no accolades. No awards night.

No silencing his doubters. But he will silence his own doubt. Kill Shannon. Dispose of her body. Get on with life. Act one. Act two. Act three. This episode will prove to himself he still has what it takes to thrive in this town.

Jude Abramov takes one more sip of champagne then leaves the wheel to go below deck. When he enters the cabin, he finds Shannon reclining on the bed, wearing nothing but her underwear, lowering her glass of champagne from her lips.

* * *

"Anything on page thirty-nine?" says Rachel.

"Thirty-nine is thirty-fine," says Stephan.

Rachel keeps her eyes on the script and says, "You know…I think we may have overreacted to the run-through. Our second act twist isn't the problem. The actress we cast to play the old college roommate…she never gave it a chance. I want to see it again tomorrow before we rewrite it."

The other writers sit expressionless. Gleeful but expressionless. No one wants to appear eager to go home, even though they're all eager to go home. They might even make it in time to tuck their kids in. Rare for a Tuesday night.

Stephan says, "Are you sure? We can rewrite the scene and hold it. Send the script out tonight stet and give it another shot. And if it doesn't work, we'll have the new pages ready to go in the morning."

Rachel sighs. "Yeah, I'm sure. The scene should work as written. I'll text casting and tell them to have a few options ready if we recast."

"What about what's-her-face? The one we didn't cast because she's blond. We could put her in a wig."

Rachel taps her pencil against the table and says, "What do you all think of Shannon from wardrobe? At the beginning of the season, she pulled me aside and, in a very nice way, said if there's ever a guest role that might be right for her, she'd like a shot at it."

"Can she act?" says Stephan.

"She's done guest spots on other shows. And a lot of theater before she moved to L.A. Her look is great. And she can't be worse than who we have now."

"Let's read her in the morning," says Stephan. "Can't hurt."

* * *

Jude hears the motors whirring as the autopilot holds the boat's position. He's not only produced and directed this production, but he's acting in it as well. Shannon was especially passionate tonight. She really believes they're going to head to Santa Barbara come daybreak. And that's all thanks to Jude's stellar performance. Now he's just waiting for her to fall asleep. The duct tape and plastic are stowed in the drawers under the bed. It shouldn't take longer than a few minutes. He'll be back to the slip by ten o'clock and home by 10:30. In bed watching the news when Rachel gets home. Another ho-hum night for Jude Abramov.

He hears Shannon's slow, steady breathing. He places a hand on her naked back. Her breathing does not change. She's asleep. Jude picks up his pillow and holds it toward Shannon's face. That's when he hears the closet door open.

Jude turns and sees Miles from transportation. It is such an unexpected sight. Miles is so out of context here on Jude's secret boat that Jude is still searching for the words to express his shock when Miles's right arm swings toward him, holding something metallic. The speeding glint of light is the last thing Jude Abramov will ever see.

Shannon hears Jude's skull crack and his body fall back down onto the bed. She wraps the sheet around herself, swings her feet onto the floor, and stands. "Is it over?"

"It's not over-over," says Miles. "But he's out." Miles opens the drawer under the bed and removes the duct tape. "He went to Home Depot after leaving the lot. Bought everything I need."

"I'd rather not watch when you do it," says Shannon. She reaches for her champagne glass and empties it.

"No need," says Miles. He pulls a length of duct tape from the roll and starts on Jude's legs. "He'll be on the bottom of the ocean in five."

Shannon looks at the duct tape and plastic and shakes her head. "The son-of-a-bitch was really going to do it."

"Yeah," says Miles, now wrapping tape around Jude's torso, securing his arms to his body. "And you know why? Because you're a damn good actress. You really had him believing you were going to tell Rachel about the affair."

"Thanks," says Shannon. She can't hide her smile. She's been waiting to hear words like that for a long time. Then she adds, "But I got to give credit to my executive producer. Rachel wrote me one hell of a script."

# Type

by Phoef Sutton

Percy Fielder was a type. He always knew that. He was short, balding, often wore glasses, and had a distinctive piping voice. If you needed an officious bureaucrat or an annoying boss, Percy was your man. Or he could also play a pathetic cuckold or a whining innocent bystander, if that was what your script called for.

And, since a lot of scripts seemed to call for that, Percy made a good, if not spectacular, living filling those roles in episodic TV and film. True, he never got that big payday job—a regular role as the intrusive neighbor or the infuriating upper-management type on a hit sit-com—but he made do. People recognized him at the grocery store, even if they never knew his name. Sometimes, they called him John Helton.

John Helton was also an actor. He was short, balding, often wore glasses, and had a distinctive piping voice, though it piped in a different key. Percy didn't know John well, but they crossed paths in the old days of "in-person" casting calls. Often, they sat opposite each other in the casting director's waiting room, and one would acknowledge the other with a smile and a nod, knowing they had to be up for the same small role.

Career-wise, they split the difference. About half the time Percy would get the role. Half the time, it would go to John.

Did Percy resent John? Did John resent Percy? Not really. Not for the first twenty years, anyway. True, they each made only half of what they would have made had the other not been around, but half of a reasonably good living was enough for them. John was gay, and Percy was straight, but neither of them were married. Their careers, each of them said, were their whole lives.

About five years ago, that started to change. From the age of thirty, they had both looked like fifty-year-old men, so the passage of time didn't affect their casting opportunities, but changes in the "industry" did. The "industry" was what they and everyone they knew called show business, as if they were engaged in making automobiles or digging for coal or running a smelting furnace. The term had seemed funny to Percy when he first heard it, but after a few years, he felt it captured the profession perfectly. Except coal miners and auto makers and smelters had some sense of job security. Actors worked from gig to gig, never knowing when the gigs would stop forever.

These changes in the industry were gradual and, like the proverbial frog in the boiling pot, neither Percy nor John noticed them at first. The wages stopped keeping up with the cost of living, and the production companies grew tougher to bargain with. Percy was used to getting "top of show"—meaning the highest price a given show will pay for a guest actor who isn't a "name." Then Percy's agent told him no one was doing that anymore. The most they would offer was "scale"—the lowest salary the union would allow. His agent told him not to take this personally. It was happening to everyone. It was the evolution of the business. Still, enough jobs were coming through that Percy could get by. True, days of taking vacations were gone, but he could keep his house. For now.

Then came Covid. Not only did the coronavirus shut down all production for almost a year, but when things started up again, the entire world of auditioning had changed.

B.C. (Before Covid), auditioning meant driving to the casting director's office, chatting with the other actors in the waiting room, exchanging pleasantries with the casting director or, if you were lucky, possibly the producer or director. After that you'd read the "sides" with an assistant (provided by the casting director), you would do the scene once or twice in different ways, responding to thoughts from the room, engaging all the people involved, making sure they remembered you, so that even if they didn't hire you for the current job they'd be sure to call you in again for another. Because you know each other. You're all in the game together.

A.C. (After Covid) came the era of Self Taping. To Self-Tape meant that you had to record an audition on your own, reading a few pages of a script which was sent to you via email, and send the taped audition back to them. That meant that you were not only responsible for providing a quality recording, you also had to come up with a scene partner to read with. And that scene partner must be good enough to give you someone to bounce off of, but not so good as to upstage you. It was a tough role to fill.

At first, the most rudimentary taping was fine. As long as they could see and hear you, that was all that mattered. As time went on, though, producers expected more. Better production quality. A more expensive backdrop for the tapings. Better clothing. Even make-up. And period costumes, if appropriate. After a time, businesses popped up that were dedicated to Self-Taping, providing everything for a fee. As Percy said, self-tape auditioning was getting to be a very expensive way to get rejected.

It was clearly the wave of the future, so both Percy and John put up with it. As long as they got the work, it was worth it. When Percy didn't get a role, he figured John had gotten lucky. When John didn't get one, he knew that Percy had a payday. It all evened out.

But then Percy started losing jobs more and more often. Parts he was sure were his were going to someone else. Choice roles like a befuddled witness in *NCIS* and an overzealous administrator in *911* didn't come his way. Neither did a featured part as a suspected pedophile on *Chicago PD*—an audition Percy felt he had *nailed*. It was as if John Helton was really coming into his own; as if he was scoring two-thirds of the roles available, not just half of them.

On top of that, production here in Los Angeles was slow. Fewer and fewer TV shows and movies were being made at all, and those that were had moved production to Atlanta or Vancouver or Prague, for goodness sake. Los Angeles was starting to feel like a ghost town, with all the unemployed supporting actors wandering through it like wraiths searching vainly for houses to haunt.

The episode of *Chicago PD* that Percy had missed out on was aired on the day that he missed a payment on his mortgage. He'd always prided himself on paying right on time or perhaps even early, so that delinquent payment weighed heavily on his mind. He sat alone in his house that night, a glass of bourbon in his hand, checking his email reflexively, again and again, to see if the bank was going to swoop down on him right away and throw him out to live on the street. He knew it was silly to think Bank of America would act that fast, but he knew it was coming, sooner or later.

He could picture himself living in a one-room apartment in Lancaster, juggling nights as a bartender with dayshifts on the cash register of a Jack in the Box. It would be like he was twenty-one again. Except he was fifty-eight now.

To get his mind out of this downward spiral, he decided to switch on the TV and see how John Helton did in the pedo role that should have been his. That should add to his pain nicely, he thought, letting the bourbon burn down his throat.

But, when the Chicago detectives interrogated the mild-mannered child molester, Percy was surprised to see that he wasn't played by John Helton, but by another actor who was short, balding, wore glasses, and had a distinctive piping voice. As the credits rolled by at the end, he could just catch the actor's name.

Kyle Sampson.

Looking him up on IMDB, Percy saw that Kyle was thirty-three and had only five credits to his name.

So, there was a new gun in town.

* * *

As the months passed and Percy *did* have to move to a one-bedroom apartment (in Santa Clarita, not Lancaster), Kyle Sampson started getting more and more credits. And Percy and John were getting fewer and fewer.

One day, Percy did the unthinkable. He contacted John Helton and asked him for coffee. He didn't have John's cell number, but they were both over fifty, so he got in touch with him through Facebook. He asked to meet John at Priscilla's Coffee Shop on Riverside.

At the coffee shop, Percy ordered a Cortado, and John had a Café Breve. They'd never really talked before, apart from chatting in casting directors' offices, but in no time, they found themselves talking with the easy rapport of old friends. It wasn't until he got home that it occurred to Percy why he had been so at ease with John. It was like he was talking to himself.

"I guess I know what prompted you to get in touch with me," John said, sipping his Café.

Percy nodded. "Kyle Sampson."

John nodded too. "Kyle fucking Sampson."

"I lost my health insurance."

"I had to stop seeing my therapist."

"I had to sell my house."

"My boyfriend left me."

"My agent dropped me."

"No? Really?" That was just too much.

"Well, he turned me over to a junior partner," Percy said. "Same thing."

"That's going to happen to me soon."

"Things can't keep going on this way."

"No, they can't."

"We have to do something."

It was agreed.

Kyle Sampson was in his thirties, so he wasn't on Facebook, which made getting in contact with him a little more difficult. John suggested looking him up on IMDbPro to find out who handled him. It turned out that Kyle was a client of Percy's old agent, the one who'd handed him off to a junior partner. Percy thought of calling Ari up and giving him a piece of his mind. What did he mean by handling an actor who filled the exact same niche as Percy did? But he decided that would draw undue attention to this competition. Let that be Percy's little secret.

In the end, he got Kyle's contact number from the First Assistant Director on *Abbott Elementary*, where Kyle had played the sort of meddlesome county official that Percy and John had excelled in. Percy knew the A.D. from her days on *Brooklyn 99*, and since Percy had always been professional and pleasant on a set, she was more than happy to give him Kyle's phone number. Percy knew it always paid to be nice to the little people, especially when you were little yourself.

Percy and John FaceTimed Kyle together, since they'd learned a long time ago that more people recognized them by face than by name. They introduced themselves as The Milquetoast Brothers, welcoming him to their fraternity. Since he was a Millennial, Kyle was unfamiliar with the term "milquetoast," so Percy had to explain that it meant a timid or feeble person; the "type" they all played. And, since Kyle was fairly new to the industry, they invited him to come to dinner and offer some pointers on navigating this crazy business. Kyle accepted, though he objected somewhat to being called a "milk toast."

They met at John's place. John made a delicious Spanish Paella, and they drank white wine and traded funny stories of bad auditions and worse directors. Kyle was a trifle reserved at first, but by the time they unscrewed the second bottle of River Road, he opened up and told them a hilarious story about a missed cue during a college production of *A Man For All Seasons*.

Wiping tears of laughter from his eyes, Percy got down to the point. "How long have you been in town, Kyle?"

"Three years this September."

"You've done very well in a very short time," John said.

"I know," Kyle said, proudly.

"What did you do before you moved out here?"

"I worked in a bank. Made a good living, but I wanted more."

"And you went and got it," Percy said.

"You seized the day," John said.

"I did. You see, I believe in positive thinking. When I was working in the bank, I used to say to myself, 'You're not here. You're on the set of a major production. A TV show or a movie. You're an actor.' I just kept saying that. And, lo and behold, it happened."

Percy and John looked at him.

"And you think that 'positive thinking' is the key to your success?" John asked.

"I know it is."

"That's fine. But what you have to remember is," Percy leaned forward intently, "it's a marathon, not a race."

"What does that mean?"

"It means it's a long haul. And as hard as it is to get into this business, it's even harder to *stay* in it."

"I'm sure that's true," Kyle said.

"No, really," John insisted. "Right now, you're the new face in town. When they say, 'We need a young John Helton,' you're it." Kyle gave an embarrassed chuckle. "That won't last long," John went on. "You have to have a strategy."

"A strategy?"

"Yes," Percy said. "Positive thinking won't take care of everything."

"We're already on our way out," John said.

"It's been a good ride," Percy agreed with a nod.

"But it's almost done."

"What are you talking about?" Kyle asked. "You guys aren't done. You're still working."

"For now," John said.

"But the writing's on the wall."

"We're on our way out."

"Why do you say that?" Kyle asked.

"Because of you," Percy said.

Kyle looked at Percy. He looked at John. He started to smile, as if he thought they were joking. But the smile died before it could form. "Because of me?"

Percy nodded. "The business these days can only support two of a type."

"A type?" Kyle was confused.

"A type. You know. There can only be two bearded stoner guys," John said.

"Or two cheerful muscular black jocks," Percy said.

"Or two mousey Midwestern women."

"Or two middle-aged milquetoasts," Percy concluded.

"The economy just can't maintain three of us anymore."

Kyle looked like he didn't quite know how to respond to this. "I'm sorry."

"Are you? Why?" John asked.

"Well, I mean…that I'm taking work from you guys."

"Don't be. Somebody has to get the jobs. You're doing well."

"Of course," Percy piped up, "you'd do better if there wasn't so much competition."

Kyle looked confused.

"If there were only two of us, you'd get more work," Percy explained.

"I'm doing okay."

"Are you really? As well as you did working in that bank?"

"I don't make as much money, but it's more fulfilling."

"Fulfilling? Really?" John said.

"I remember when it was fulfilling," Percy said.

"So do I," John said.

"Now it's a living," Percy said.

"But, if one of us were to step out of the game," John said. "It would be more of a living."

"And more fulfilling," Percy said.

"For the rest," John said.

Kyle looked at them, one to other, not comprehending.

"Do you understand why we brought you here, Kyle?" Percy asked. Kyle just stared at them. Percy sighed and went on. "It is in the best interest of everyone concerned if we go back to the regular quota. Two milquetoasts to choose from."

Kyle's head swiveled from Percy to John.

John had to explain. "We think one of us should retire. Step aside. For the good of everyone."

Slowly, it seemed to dawn on Kyle. "You don't expect me…"

"No, no," Percy assured him. "We're not saying that. Not necessarily. Just that one of us should leave the business."

"Now, I could leave," John said. "I'm fifty-three. I could retire, I guess. Go into some other line of work. But what? Before I got into acting, I was a clerk in a video store. That job doesn't exist anymore. Still, I'm sure I'll find something to do with the last thirty or forty years of my life."

"Or, *I* could quit," Percy said. "I was a bartender. You can always get work doing that. I'm twenty years sober, so it would be an awful temptation for me, but I could do it. People in recovery can work in bars. Look at Sam Malone in *Cheers*. Of course, he was just a character in a TV show. But you can learn a lot from characters."

Kyle nodded, but his expression was still uncertain.

"Then there's you," John said, looking at Kyle. "You were a banker. It wouldn't be too hard to pick that up again. Or to get a similar job. Isn't that right?"

"I suppose not."

Percy and John looked at Kyle, expectantly. Kyle seemed to think awhile before he could speak. "I...I can see how it would seem like it's easier for me to go back to my old way of living. And maybe it would be. But—and don't take this the wrong way—I don't see my career going the way yours did. I can picture so much more."

"Really? And how do you see your career going?" John asked.

"I mean, I can see myself in twenty years. I'm not still going to be playing the little parts..."

"That we play?" Percy asked.

"Yeah. I mean, there's nothing wrong with...what you've done. Just being a character actor, doing little parts for years and years. That's cool. I admire that."

"Thank you," John said.

"But I don't limit myself that way. I see myself playing bigger roles. And writing. And producing."

"And, eventually, you want to direct," Percy said.

"Exactly. I mean, I know everybody *says* that, but I can really picture it. I mean, look at Taylor Sheridan or Billy Bob Thornton. It can happen."

"It can," John said.

"You can also win the lottery. That can happen," Percy said.

"I think positively. I can *manifest* it. It's going to happen for me. So, I'm sorry, but I can't give this up. It's just one step on a tall, tall ladder."

Percy and John looked at each other.

"Okay," John said. "We didn't know you had such lofty goals."

"I do," Kyle said, firmly.

"Well, then. That lays that to rest."

"We'll have to come up with some other answer."

Kyle stood and walked to the door. "I should probably go now. I have an audition tape I have to get done for tomorrow. It's for one of the *Law &* *Orders*. You're probably up for it, too, huh?"

"No," John said.

"I didn't get that offer," Percy said.

"Oh," Kyle said, embarrassed. "Well, anyway, I need to get going."

"Of course," John said, getting up

"And we'll figure out how to deal with this problem," Percy said, also getting up.

John laughed. "Who knows? Maybe one of us will just kill himself."

Kyle laughed nervously. "Oh, come on, don't say that." But when he glanced back at the two men, he saw the gun in John's hand.

"Don't worry about it," John said. "Go, go. This is between us now. No problem."

Kyle hung back by the door. "You're not serious?"

"It's not your problem," Percy said. "You have big plans."

"We're just character actors," John said.

"I never said that," Kyle protested. "This is crazy. You're not really going to…"

"Of course not," Percy said.

"It's just a joke," John said.

"That's a real gun, isn't it? That's not funny," Kyle said. "You shouldn't joke about something like that. No one is going to kill themselves."

Both men sat down wearily at the dinner table. "You're right," John said.

"We could never do it," Percy said. Then he looked up at Kyle as if an idea had just struck him. "But you could."

John looked up, too. "That's right. You could."

"I could what?" Kyle was appalled. "I'm not going to kill myself."

"No, of course not."

"You have too many plans."

"It's ridiculous to even think you would kill yourself," John said.

"Then what?"

"We were thinking you could kill one of us," Percy said.

Kyle gave them a long look. "You're fucking with me, and I don't appreciate it."

John turned the gun on Kyle. "What makes you think we're fucking with you?"

"We could kill you right here, and it would solve all our problems," Percy said.

Kyle seemed to think that over. "Um...I don't think it would. For one thing, someone knows I'm here. I sent the address to my Accountability Partner."

Percy turned to John. "I might have known he'd have an Accountability Partner, whatever that is."

John looked it up on his Android. "Apparently, it's a thing. 'Someone who supports you to keep a commitment to a desired goal.'"

"Who's your Accountability Partner?" Percy asked.

"I'm not going to tell you," Kyle said.

"And what's your desired goal?" John asked.

"At the moment? Staying alive," Kyle answered.

Percy nodded. "Sounds like we could use an Accountability Partner, John."

"I think you're my Accountability Partner, Percy."

"Thank you, John."

"I'm going," Kyle said, moving toward the door.

"Take another step and I'll shoot you and worry about the consequences later."

Kyle hesitated. Then he turned, walked to the table, and sat down. "I don't believe you, but I can't take a chance."

"So you believe me a little bit?"

"I guess. Look, if you were going to kill me, you already would have. At least I think that's how it works. What is it you want?"

John flipped the gun around and held the handle toward Kyle. "We told you. Shoot one of us."

"Either one. It doesn't matter which," Percy said.

Kyle reached to grab the gun. He stopped. "I know what you're doing, and I'm not falling for it. You want me to get my fingerprints on the gun, and then you'll frame me for something, and I'll get sent to prison."

"Now, that would have been very smart," John said.

"Why didn't we think of that?" Percy asked.

"We're just not as clever as Kyle is."

Kyle went on. "Or, if I do shoot one of you, the other one turns me in, I get arrested, and he gets the town all to himself."

Percy frowned. "I don't know about that one."

"It's hard to see how we'd agree to that," John said. "I mean, one of us would be getting shot."

"You want me to shoot one of you now?" Kyle said.

"Yeah, but that's not some trick. That's a real sacrifice."

"Don't belittle it."

"Or," Kyle continued, "I could fire the gun, but maybe it's boobytrapped, so it explodes in my face. Or shoots backwards at me or something."

"Well, that's a little too James Bond for me," John said.

"Yeah, where would we get a fancy trick gun like that?" Percy asked.

"It just doesn't track, Kyle."

"Well, either way," Kyle said, "I'm not shooting anybody. I don't see myself as a convicted murderer."

"Who said anything about convicted? You and…whoever is left, will clean up, dispose of the gun and the body. We have it all worked out. Easy-peasy."

"Well, I don't care. I'm leaving. And you know what I'm going to do? I'm not just going to leave. I'm going straight to the police and tell them all about this crazy game you're playing. What do you think of that?" Kyle got up and headed for the door. He was clearly going to leave this time. John didn't have a choice. He picked up the gun, aimed, and fired.

The gun exploded.

Black shrapnel from the barrel flew backward and blew off John's ear and most of his face. His head rocked from the impact, and he slumped in his chair, lifeless.

Kyle turned around and looked at John's body. He grimaced. "That was kind of messy."

"Yeah," Percy said. "I thought it would be neater."

"I guess that's what you get when you blind-order something from the Dark Web and pay with bitcoin."

"I just about shit myself when you came up with that trick gun theory," Percy said.

"I like to add a little reality to my improvs. It makes them ring true."

Percy looked at what remained of John. "Will it still look like suicide?"

"I guess. He's holding the gun. He fired it," Kyle said.

"But, I don't know. He wasn't pointing it at himself. He was pointing it at the door."

Kyle shrugged. "Maybe he knew it was a trick gun."

"Helluva way to kill yourself," Percy said.

"Maybe somebody broke in and he grabbed a gun, and it blew up in his face."

"But who broke in?"

"Somebody who wanted to kill him," Kyle said. "A jealous actor, maybe?"

With that, Kyle seized Percy by the back of his neck and slammed his head into the corner of the dining table. Percy went limp. "See, when the gun exploded, you got startled and you tripped and hit your head against the table."

He touched Percy's wrist and felt a faint pulse. Percy's eyes were open, and the pupils had rolled back so far that they looked almost pure white.

"You're not dead yet, but you will be by the time they find you in the morning. Severe head injuries, if left untreated, are fatal." Kyle stood and looked down at Percy. "Yep, you're going to die, I'm positive. And you know I *believe* in positive thinking. If you just concentrate on the good things in life, they'll come your way. If you focus on the negative, that's what you'll get. Well, I choose to concentrate on success. And if the price of success is eliminating the competition, so be it. As of tomorrow, I'll have the milquetoast lane all to myself, Percy. 'Bye now."

* * *

At Burbank airport, the passengers of flight 4555 from Kansas City, Missouri, were deplaning. Among them was Logan Swanson, a man with a dream. A dream of being an actor. A real *actor* in film and television. People back home said he was crazy. He didn't look like a TV star. He was short and balding, wore thick-rimmed glasses, and spoke with a piping voice that sounded like a cartoon character. But Logan didn't see these things as disadvantages. He saw them as assets. He was a *character,* and every TV show or movie needed a *character.*

He was a type, he told himself. And there was always room for a type.

# The Cutting Room Floor

by Eric Beetner

It was meant as an inside joke. No way the producers would go for it, but it might make them all laugh. After a full season, they needed a chuckle. One episode away from the finale, and everyone was running on fumes. The shooting always went by in a blur, but post seemed to drag. A new network exec hadn't helped. He needed to get his fingerprints all over the show like a toddler eating spaghetti with his hands.

Scott downloaded the song and dropped in it rough cut one, expecting it would go no further than the EP, the executive producer. When you finally lost the main villain on the show, the breakout name being talked about on social media and in the tabloids, you needed to add a little extra sauce. So when Scott cut together the scene where Violet finally got eliminated, he cued up *Ding Dong The Witch Is Dead* and let that play under her exit.

It made him laugh, anyway. The composer would come in with a custom cue in the end and make this moment a rare score-to-picture piece. Something they rarely had the time or budget for. But this was huge.

The network liked to call this a "social experiment" rather than a reality show. Everyone working on the series knew better. It was cut from the same mold as every other dating/competition/lifestyle show out there. A Frankenstein's monster of ideas that combined bits and pieces of at least six other successful reality franchises.

And it was a hit. A big reason why? Violet.

She was blunt, rude, short-tempered. She "didn't come here to make friends." She was "a bad bitch and I know it, honey." She was ratings gold.

She made life miserable for everyone on set, a six-week shoot that Scott, thankfully, didn't have to endure. But as soon as he started cutting the footage together, he found himself trapped in the edit bay with her shrill voice, her faux-urban millennial affectation, her spray tan and fake nails, her camera-hogging, fourth-wall-breaking, irritating behavior. All day. Every day.

Then she finally fell one episode away from the half-million-dollar prize. She was stunned, and her exit was an epic tantrum of expletives, accusations, and outright lies. In the end, two security guards who looked like they could take down a grizzly bear with one arm and an armed terrorist with the other, had to escort this hundred-and-ten-pound diva off the set.

The network, of course, loved her. They wanted her to stay as long as possible. There was even a small controversy about the judging of a competition that took place in the pool of the mansion where the contestants all lived. When Scott played back the footage, it became clear Violet had cheated in the game.

By the time he brought this up to Alison, the EP, shooting was long over. Alison admitted they had a sidebar meeting on set with the network when questions arose over her behavior, but the two junior network execs pushed hard to keep Violet, and they won out.

"Just cut around it," she told him.

He hadn't argued. He had done his job and did what he was told.

*　*　*

When Alison watched Scott's first cut, she called him directly, a rarity.

"Oh my god, I love it. We have to license that song."

"Really?" Scott said. "I just threw it in as a joke. I figured Edwin would score something there."

"No. I'm gonna show this to the network. They'll love it. We have to. It's too good."

It would be a viral moment for sure. The new standard for what made a hit show. Early in Scott's career, it was all about Nielsen ratings. Waiting for the overnights was a nerve-wracking time. A few points here or there could make or break your show. Now it was about your social media engagement. How many people were making reaction videos on YouTube to your episodes.

As long as the checks kept clearing and he kept up his union insurance, it didn't matter much to Scott, who watched the damn shows. They weren't making art here. Most viewers probably wouldn't even get the reference, he figured. But hey, it wasn't his money. Let the network fork over a metric ton of cash for an 85-year-old song.

Of the twelve episodes, eight had aired. They were cutting it close. Nine and ten were locked and in mix, eleven and the finale still needed work. He hated when they were this close to air and the show wasn't locked. But when a series started gaining traction, everyone at the network needed to get their hands on it so they could claim some part of a hit. Scott had worked on plenty of shows where the network acted as if they'd never seen their own show. Those were the one-and-done series. No season two for them. This one, however, could go for a while.

As long as they cast another Violet next season. But characters like that were hard to find. That particular brand of crazy and telegenic was like mining for diamonds in the casting trade.

Scott set down his laptop bag and his coffee mug. He read the night report from the assistant and woke up his AVID. He had until tomorrow to work through the rest of Alison's notes before the show went to network. Shouldn't be too hard.

Behind him, he heard a voice. He knew immediately who it was.

"Well, I wanna see him!"

He turned in his chair to see her shape move past his edit bay door. It was a blur of pink, bleach blonde, and hoop earrings. Following close behind was the girl from reception.

"You can't be back here," she said.

"Why not? What are you trying to hide?"

She reversed course and appeared in the doorway to Scott's bay. Violet, in the flesh.

It was always weird to see people you'd cut footage of in real life. Scott watched as the receptionist tried to get Violet to leave.

"You can't be here, ma'am."

Violet swirled and faced her. "Ma'am? Do you know who the fuck I am?"

Yeah, this was her all right. The same two-dimensional collection of pixels and sound bites he'd been watching for months was now in his doorway, suddenly thrust into 3-D.

"I'm the reason you have a show, honey," Violet said. "Now, fuck off." She shoved with both hands, and the receptionist hit the wall hard. Violet stepped inside with Scott and shut the door. She turned the lock.

"Umm…" Scott said.

Violet faced him. She'd brought in a cloud of off-brand perfume laid on way too thick. The kind of smell you get at an airport duty-free shop.

"They said you're the one editing this bullshit."

"I'm the senior editor, yeah."

"Well, quit making me look like such a fucking bitch."

He didn't know what to say. He'd never been confronted by anyone he'd edited before. They were always just anonymous cyphers, happy to be on TV in any form.

"I'm sorry, but—"

"I have feelings, you know."

"Well, it's not really up to me how you look."

"You edit the show?"

"Yeah, but—"

She drew a straight razor from the small pink purse around her wrist.

"I want you to fix it."

Scott looked at the edge of the blade. She moved it side to side like a snake looking for an opening to strike.

"Hey, hey. I don't…I don't…"

"Make me look good," she said.

"It's not that easy."

"It's just cutting, right?" She lashed out, slicing the razor across his arm. "Seems easy to me."

Scott clamped a hand over his wound. Blood leaked out between his fingers. The pain was unbelievable.

"Now fix it."

* * *

The first person who came to the door was one of the story producers. She knocked gently and tried to reason with Violet.

"You tell them you're gonna fix it," she said to Scott.

He yelled through the door. "She wants me to recut the episode. She has a razor. I think I need stitches."

The pain had gone from blinding white to a constant throb, counting out his pulse. The wound had to be six inches long and who knew how deep. He'd found some napkins in his computer bag and pressed them to the wound.

The story producer went away from the door, and the line producer was next. The money man who made the logistics happen, Gary, was the one you called when any on-set emergency came up. Scott felt slightly better with him on the other side of the door.

"Violet? It's Gary, remember me?"

"No, I don't fucking remember you. You ain't on TV. I am. And this motherfucker is making me look like a bitch. It's slander. I'm gonna sue your asses, all of you. Ruin my fucking life."

"Violet, it's not Scott's fault. He just cuts it how the executives tell him to."

It wasn't true. He had quite a lot of latitude to cut the show the way he wanted, but he wasn't going to argue the point right then.

"Then get me an executive! The one who decides!"

There was a long pause. Gary must've realized he had miscalculated and dragged Alison into this now.

"Gary?" Scott said. "Can you get a first aid kit in here? I've lost a lot of blood."

Violet turned and held out the razor. "Shut the fuck up." Turning to the door, she added, "He doesn't get any help until I talk to someone who can fix this shit."

"Scott, you sit tight," Gary said, his voice projecting calm. "And Violet, let me see what I can do."

A faint murmur of voices from the other side of the door, then silence.

Violet gestured to the twin screens on Scott's desk. "So how does this thing work?"

"Well, all the footage is ingested, and I have clips of everything. Then I put it all together, cut it to time, score it with music."

"Sounds easy."

"I mean, not really, it's—"

"Why'd you make me look like such a bitch?"

Scott tried to choose his words carefully. He shifted in his chair, keeping pressure on his wound. The blood around his hand had started to dry and harden.

"I just cut what's there. I can't make you say things you didn't say or do."

"Bullshit. You got that, like, AI or shit."

"No, no, we don't."

"Show me."

Violet sat behind him, like a producer poised to give notes, some of which often hurt as much as a razor cut.

He looked at what was loaded into the timeline. Shit. Not what he wanted to show her, but he had little choice. He wanted another cut from her blade even less. Scott pressed play. The opening notes of *Ding Dong The Witch Is Dead* started, and Scott waited for the razor to cross his neck.

Violet watched in silence for five minutes until the act break arrived and the screen went black. Scott's arm had stopped bleeding, but he was afraid to move his hand in case it started up again. He swiveled his chair to look at her.

She gave him a stare that could crack glass.

"Change it," she said.

"Well, the network has to approve—"

"Change it."

"Okay. Whatever you say."

* * *

They worked together for the next hour, removing anything Violet called objectionable, which was most of it. It wasn't the worst notes session he'd ever been in.

He tore a strip of fabric from the lining of his jacket, the one they'd given out on premiere night with the show logo on the front. He tied it tight around his cut to staunch the bleeding. The editing went slower than usual since he was using mostly only one hand, but he got the job done.

From the hallway, he heard voices. A few moments later, there was a knock at the door.

"Violet?"

It was Alison.

"Can we talk?"

Violet nodded at Scott, who stood and unlocked the door. When Alison saw him, she gasped. He opened the door further and saw the hallway filled with the story team, the AEs, and several field producers all lined up like they were watching a show about a staged situation, not a real one. When Alison was in, he closed and relocked the door. She'd brought a first aid kit with her, and she handed it off to Scott, who greedily dug in and took out gauze and alcohol wipes.

"Violet, what's going on here?"

Scott had heard that Alison had a contentious relationship with Violet in the field. Her antics usually ran counter to getting the scenes they needed in a timely fashion, and it was on Alison to avoid running long and sending the union crew into meal penalties. But Violet didn't care. In her mind, the whole production revolved around her.

"Y'all lied to me," Violet said. "You said I could be a star from this. You said I'd be famous."

"You are famous," Alison said. "You're all over the place."

"As a bitch. Who the fuck wants that? People hate me."

Alison grinned and tried to sell it. "They *love* to hate you."

"They still hate me. And all because of the way you put me on TV. You make me say shit…ooh, it ain't right."

"Have we made you say anything you didn't say?"

Violet opened her mouth to protest and dispute the charge, but she couldn't think of any concrete examples.

Scott sucked air through his teeth as he pressed an alcohol wipe to the open wound. The sting hurt almost as much as the razor blade.

"Look," Alison said. "Sometimes when we see ourselves as others see us, it's hard. The same way that nobody likes the sound of their own voice, you know?"

"We're fixing it." Violet pointed to the monitors with the razor, still crusted with Scott's blood.

"You changed the cut?"

"Yeah. Made it so I don't go home. I can come back, and I can win this shit."

Scott wanted to add the caveat that the cuts were Violet's, not his. The new edit was clunky and didn't make much sense. He hadn't had time to recut the music, either.

"Violet, we're wrapped. There's already a winner. Chad won."

"Fuck that dude."

Scott raised a finger on his good hand. "Can I just…have you called the police? Can we end this? I need a doctor."

Alison held out a flat palm to him. "Hold that thought. Violet," she rested her elbows on her knees and leaned in. "The network will never air a cut they didn't approve. I know you think because Scott is the one with the keyboard and the monitors that he makes the decisions, but that's not the case. He just pushes the buttons. It's me and, above that, the network who make the choices."

Scott tried to hold in the insult he felt. He made hundreds of choices every day and was far more than a button pusher.

"So it ain't even you who did this shit?" Violet said. Scott could see her hand tighten on the razor. "Get the network people on the phone."

"I can't do that, Violet. They're in New York."

"New York ain't got phones?"

"They do, but I can't call them and say one of our contestants is holding my editor hostage with a knife."

"Well then, what fuckin' good are you?"

"Violet…"

"Nah, look, we're makin' cuts here. That's what we're doing. Making cuts. Ain't that what you call it?"

It was a strange sound he'd never heard before. A blade cutting flesh. He hadn't been paying attention when the razor slashed his own arm, but he was looking at Alison when Violet's arm swung through the air. The blade caught Alison under the chin. The sound was dull and flat, then came the rush of liquid spilling. Blood, like an overturned bucket. The cut went deep. Veins, arteries, important structures that live below the surface in the neck—all severed. All spilling out. All at once.

Scott pushed back in his chair until it hit the desk and knocked over his coffee. More spillage.

Violet turned on Scott, who kept his eyes on Alison. Her wide-eyed shock. The slow slide as she flopped off the couch onto the floor. The short gasps for air through a cut windpipe.

"Get the network on the phone," she said to Scott.

Scott picked up his phone and dialed reception. He got connected to Joe, the co-executive producer. He explained, as calmly as possible, the situation. He tried not to panic, not to raise his voice or say anything like, "This crazy bitch just killed Alison, and she's gonna kill me with a fucking razor if you don't get a SWAT team in here to bust in and shoot her in the face."

Violet watched him closely while he talked. Joe said he'd get back to them shortly and hung up. Scott turned.

"He's going to call the network."

"Why didn't you do it?"

"I don't deal with the network directly. I just get their notes sent to me."

"I don't understand this job at all."

"Sometimes, neither do I."

Scott tried not to look at Alison. Luckily, her body was mostly blocked by the small table in front of the couch. He did notice the dark stain on the carpet from the blood seeping through in a growing pool. Violet kept pacing the tiny room.

"Why the fuck you make me look so bad in that pool scene?"

"In episode four?" he asked.

"I don't know! You made me look crazy."

"I...I just cut what was there."

"Bullshit."

Scott used his cursor to open a bin of the locked cut of episode four. He loaded the sequence, then matched back to the raw footage from the day. He set the monitor to a quad split so four cameras all displayed at once. He looked to her to make sure she was paying attention, then pressed play.

Violet stopped her pacing as she watched the unedited footage play out. Four cameras captured her rant at Julie, one of the other contestants who she'd had multiple fights with. The curse words were un-bleeped. The frantic zoom and focus-finding on camera B could be seen, where Scott had cut around it for the final version. Violet watched with rapt attention as she saw herself as the others saw her.

The phone rang. Scott stopped the footage and put the phone on speaker.

"This is Joe here. What the hell's going on?"

"You're on speaker," Scott said.

"So, Violet, Joe Coleman. We met on set."

"Yeah?" she said.

"I talked to the network."

Scott leaned forward. "Not the police?"

Joe ignored Scott. "They can't recut anything. Not after they've aired."

"What the fuck is—"

"But!" Joe blurted out. "But, they are loving this twist."

Scott was confused. "What?"

"They want this covered. Scott, can you start with some cell phone footage? Are you Apple or Android? Ten-eighty HD is fine, but if you have 4K that's better, obviously."

"Wait, hold on."

"And we're dropping off some GoPros to your office to get some lock-off coverage."

There was a knock at the door. Violet opened it, and a PA timidly handed over a small stack of three boxes with brand-new GoPro cameras in them. He peered around her to Alison's body on the floor. Violet slammed the door in the PA's face and locked it again.

Scott leaned closer to the phone. "Joe, this is crazy!"

"We'll need a signed release, Scott, but we can get that after."

"After what? I'll be fucking dead. After that?"

Violet set down the boxes and held the razor toward Scott. "Hey! I never said I was gonna kill you."

"You killed her. You already cut me. What else am I supposed to think?"

"If you would just do the notes I had, then we wouldn't be having this problem."

Scott stood up. Holding it in wasn't an option anymore.

"Your notes? Fuck your notes. You don't know how to cut the show better than I do. Nobody does. Not you, not him," He pointed to the phone with his wounded arm, which had started leaking blood again now that he waved it around. He pointed at Alison's body. "Not her! Definitely not the network. So I need all of you to stop fucking giving me stupid notes. Did I make you look like a bitch? Yes, I did. Wanna know why? Because you are a fucking bitch. You're crazy. This show is not gonna make you famous. Nobody liked you on the show. The people who are writing articles *about* you don't *like* you. The people who follow you on Instagram don't like you. I don't like you. So no, I'm not doing your fucking notes."

Violet curled her face into a scowl that would frighten an MMA fighter. She lifted the razor to throat-level.

"You'll do my goddamn notes, because that's all you're good for. A monkey could do this job. You'll probably be replaced with AI any day now. That or some kid in India who can press buttons. So make the changes I want, or I *will* fucking kill you."

She took a step closer to him, set the razor against his cheek.

"You'll cut."

She flicked her wrist, and the razor sliced open the skin.

"You'll trim."

She flicked the other direction, slashing the opposite cheek.

"And you'll—"

Scott head-butted her on the bridge of her nose. Violet reeled backward. Scott kicked out with his leg and swept her ankles. Violet fell, landing with a squish in a pool of Alison's blood. Scott went to one knee and grabbed the razor from Violet's hand. He put it to her throat.

"I'll make a cut, all right. That's what I do. It's my job."

He jerked his arm to the right like he was flinging a Frisbee. A spray of blood shot from her neck. She tried to scream, but her vocal cords were severed.

Scott stood, stumbled back, and sat down on his desk, his backside slamming into the keyboard and pressing play. The sounds of *Ding Dong The Witch Is Dead* started up.

Over the song, Scott could hear Joe on the speakerphone.

"Did you get any of that? Were you rolling? Please tell me you got that."

Scott dropped the razor to the carpet. He wondered what the union rule was on defending yourself in the edit bay while on company time.

He went to the door and opened it. Lining the hall were every member of the post team, and many from production who were still on staff. They watched him walk out, the blood on him fresh and not entirely his own. Everyone stood in silence as he shuffle-stepped toward reception.

Joe continued to shout over the speakerphone. "Scott? Did you get it? What can I tell the network?"

Scott headed for the elevator and pressed the button. "Tell them I made some cuts."

# Billy Wilder's Ghost

by Ellen Byron

## COLD OPEN

There was a legend on the Paramount Studios lot that the ghost of Billy Wilder occasionally visited the building named in his honor. The man behind such hilarious film classics as *Some Like it Hot* would sprinkle his comedy magic on a troubled script, gifting a sitcom staff toiling on a rewrite with a much-needed joke.

The disastrous table read for "Bathroom Break," episode ten of *On the John*, was proof Wilder's ghost never showed up to help out the show's beleaguered writers.

## ACT ONE

No one said much on the death march from the stage back to the writers' room in the Wilder Building. Showrunner Gary Hovac had stayed behind to get studio and network notes. He told his staff to start brainstorming ways to fix the script. Instead, each writer disappeared into their office, pulling the door shut behind them. Dee Stern, the sole woman on the writing staff, knew exactly what they were doing: calling their agents with desperate pleas to get them off *On the John* and onto a show without trainwreck vibes.

Dee didn't have that option. During staffing season, every time she'd brought up a sitcom she'd heard was meeting with writers, she got the same response from her agent: "They have their woman." Only *On the John*, a new mid-season show with a thirteen-episode order, hadn't had their woman. At least, not until showrunner Hovac bowed to pressure from the network and hired Dee.

Dee's cell phone rang, alerting her to an incoming FaceTime. She answered, and Allie Gould, the show's costume designer, appeared on the screen. Hovac had tasked Dee with handling Wardrobe, assuming it was a good job for a woman and clueless to the fact that Dee's own wardrobe consisted of three pair of jeans and a rotating assortment of t-shirts.

"Hi, Allie," Dee said, knowing exactly what was coming.

"Please say you're not cursing me with an entirely new script. Or you're at least going to keep the scene in the flooded banquet bathroom. Do you know how hard it was to dig up multiple tuxes that fit John?" John Franco, the star of the eponymously named sitcom, was an ex-pro wrestler who still sported the bulky build of his former career.

"I have no idea what we're doing," Dee said. "Gary's not back from notes."

Allie released a frustrated grunt. "Do me a favor and fight for that scene. If you don't, the cast will be acting in their underwear for the rest of the order because my budget will be toast. Also, I've got a couple of wedding gown options for the bride who's stuck in the bathroom stall. Can you run down and take a look?"

"I can't. We have to start the rewrite as soon as Gary's back."

Allie let out another grunt. "We've got a block-and-shoot for the scene on Thursday, if it lives. I need to move fast on the gowns. I'll send Lucy up with sketches and fabric samples."

"Do you have to?" Dee couldn't help blurting this. Like a huge percentage of the staff, Lucy, Allie's perky twentysomething production assistant, was an aspiring writer. She was also a gossip, and time spent with her meant being peppered with pleas to read her latest spec script, interspersed with dirt on the actors and crew. All TMI for Dee.

"Yes, I have to. Lucy will be up soon. Like it or not." Allie signed off, pre-empting a response.

Dee inhaled a calming breath, then opened a file on the ancient PC that came with her equally ancient office, furnished in lot warehouse hand-me-downs that had seen better days and better series. The pilot Dee had been crafting in her all-too-rare off hours popped up on the screen. Selling it would raise her profile in town. Getting it produced would give her a leap up the ladder from lowly story editor to vaunted showrunner. Having it picked up to series…this was a dream Dee dared not dream. Still, stranger things had happened in Hollywood. Like a sitcom titled *On the John* starring a lunk of a wrestler getting a network order.

Dee lifted her hands and was about to place them on the keyboard when there was a knock on the door. "Gary's back," his assistant Sarah reported from the other side. "We're gathering."

"Be right there." Dee sighed and closed the file, putting her own ticket off the show on hold.

She joined the other writers gathered around the writers' room's long wooden table, taking her designated seat farthest from the power center that was showrunner Hovac. Marc Wittenberg slipped into the seat next to her. Not even thirty years old, Marc was a rising star. His spec pilot—basically *Friends* on the space station—was the *Damn, why didn't I think of that?* of the writer world. Marc was only on *John* because the job came with a multi-year, multi-million-dollar studio deal. He refused the title of co-executive producer, instead opting for consulting producer, which telegraphed to the town, "I'm only here because the studio made it part of my deal." His choice of a seat next to Dee was a physical way of distancing himself from the show.

"All the dwarfs are here," Marc whispered to Dee, eyeing the rest of the writing staff.

"Doughy, Pasty, Chubby, Handsy, Brown-Nosy, Bossy," she whispered back. "And we're all Cranky."

Marc stifled a laugh. "Truth." He pushed his rolling office chair back to stretch his legs, revealing the worn cowboy boots he wore every day, as opposed to the Hoka-clad feet of the other writers. Another thing that set him apart, purposefully or not.

Gary ran a hand over his thinning medium-brown hair. "Network and studio notes were useless, as usual. Lip flap about John's drive, what's at stake, blah blah blah. All the crap the execs learned in the USC Cinematic Arts Department." He mimed air quotes with disdain. "We're on our own. So, phones down and metaphorical pencils up. Olivia, hup to."

Olivia, the writer's assistant on duty, took a seat at the computer. She pressed a button, and the large screen above Gary's head illuminated. He pushed back to see it. "Page one—"

One of the room's two doors flew open, interrupting him. A giant sheet cake, its candles flickering, was pushed into the room on a rolling cart by Sarah. Various production assistants, along with Chris Tobert, the obsequious line producer, followed, crowding the doorway. "Happy birthday, my man," Chris declared, addressing Gary with one of his patented hail-fellow-well-met smiles.

"Nothing sadder than a page one birthday cake," Marc whispered to Dee.

She responded with a vigorous nod. "Same cake every time," she said under her breath. "Now comes the birthday song, sung like a dirge."

Right on cue, Chris led the group in a funereal version of the song. Gary rolled his eyes, but it was obvious he liked the attention. "Thanks, work wife," he said to Sarah with a rare smile when the song mercifully ended. She blushed and returned the smile. Given that Gary spent about ninety-five percent of his life running *On the John*, his moniker for Sarah was more reality than joke.

Chris maneuvered Sarah out of the way to cut the cake. He was about to hand the first piece to Gary, but Dee piped up, "Not the yellow rose. We always save that for Lucy."

"Lucy?" Gary appeared puzzled.

"Allie's assistant in Wardrobe," she said. Gary wasn't the kind of showrunner who knew the names of anyone below the line on the call sheet. Dee had to remind him who Lucy was with every birthday cake. "When we had a cake for Marc's birthday the first week of pre-production, she asked us to save her the yellow rose because she's from Texas, and we've been doing it ever since."

"Being from Texas is nothing to brag about these days," Marc said, earning a couple of nods and chuckles.

Sarah glared at Dee. "It's a ridiculous custom. Gary's the showrunner. If he wants the yellow rose, *he* gets it and not some dim bulb below-the-line assistant whose goal in life is to gossip and flirt."

She grabbed the plate from Chris's hand and held it out to Gary. He waved her off. "I don't care who gets the yellow rose. We're going to be here all night with this rewrite. Give cake to everyone on this floor and take the rest down to the stage."

"You can leave Lucy's piece in the kitchen," Dee said. "She's on her way up to show me sketches."

The cake and all who'd shown up with it backed out of the room. Gary faced the screen again. "Say a prayer Wilder's ghost shows up, or we're screwed. Page one…"

Whether or not the credit could go to the Paramount poltergeist, the writers made faster progress than Dee expected. She even got a couple of fresh jokes into the script and managed to save the bathroom scene when Gary brought it up for debate. Feeling more confident than she ever had on the show, Dee elbowed her way to the front of the lunch line when the production assistants delivered tins of El Pollo Loco. She loaded up her plate…and then instantly dropped it when a piercing scream came from the hallway, startling her and everyone else in the room.

Rob—the writer Dee had secretly nicknamed Doughy—clutched his heart. The stent correcting an eighty-percent blockage in the thirty-nine-year-old's widowmaker artery was only a few months old. "What the fuck?"

Gary stormed to the door and threw it open, almost colliding with Olivia, who was shaking with panic and fear.

"It's Lucy." Olivia's teeth chattered as she said this. "I-I-I went to get a Le Croix in the kitchen, and she's on the floor. There's…there's…foam on her mouth. I think she's dead."

## ACT TWO

"I've never seen a dead body before."

This came from Brandon, also known as Brown-Nosy to Dee and Marc. The small, slight supervising producer looked ill as he hovered by the entrance to the kitchen with the rest of the writing and production staff.

Dee had never seen a dead body before, either. She stared at Lucy, gray and lifeless, blonde hair splayed out on the floor, yellow frosting crusted in the foam around her lips. Unnerved, Dee glanced away. She heard the unpleasant sound of someone retching in the women's room next to the kitchen and looked around. Of the female staffers who worked on the floor, only Sarah was missing.

"Everyone, back where you were," Chris said. "The police are on their way." He began herding the staff away from the kitchen, his line producer skills coming in handy for protecting what looked like a crime scene to Dee. At least the crime scenes staged on her favorite guilty pleasure viewing, *Law & Order* reruns.

The writers trooped back to the writers' room and dropped into their seats. An awkward silence permeated the air, which was scented with chicken and fermenting salsa. "Poor Lucy," Dee finally said, desperate to break the silence and acknowledge the young woman in some way. Not sure what else to say, she lamely repeated, "Poor, poor Lucy."

"What do you think happened?" Rob asked. He nervously massaged the area around his heart, a tick he'd developed post-stent.

"It sure looks like—" Marc began.

Gary held up a hand. "I don't think we should talk about this. The police will want to interview all of us. We don't want to give them the impression we colluded on our stories." The way Gary put this made Dee wonder if she wasn't the only one in the room who unwound with *Law & Order*.

"What are we supposed to do, park our asses in these seats and keep our traps shut for hours?" Pauly Kapp—Chubby, to Dee and Marc—barked this at Gary. Pauly was "the joke guy," a comedian who came in for the table read and network run-through solely to pitch one-liners. In his sixties, he was almost a couple of decades older than the oldest writers in the room. The Borscht Belt, long gone from the Catskills, lived on in Pauly's personality and occasionally his pitches. Pauly was the first to get antsy during a long rewrite, and Dee usually appreciated his attempts to speed up the process. But not today. Not when a coworker lay moldering on the production staff kitchen floor, her death a chilling mystery.

"We don't have to 'keep our traps shut,'" Gary shot back at Paul. "We can keep going with the rewrite."

Dee's jaw dropped. She snapped it shut but saw with relief that she wasn't alone in her reaction. All the other writers were exchanging looks of dismay. "I don't think that's a good idea," Marc said, his response measured but more serious than Dee had ever heard him sound. "For one thing, I don't think Olivia is in any shape to type."

"Of course not," Gary said. Dee thought he was backtracking, but then he added, "I can do it."

"The point is for us to be funny, right?" Pauly looked around the room to the other writers. "I gotta say, I'm not feeling it right now. Not with a corpse lying in the next room."

"Please don't call Lucy a corpse." Dee felt a surge of emotion well up and batted it back. She'd sworn to herself on her first show that no matter how miserable the circumstances, she'd never be reduced to tears in the room. And while she couldn't imagine more miserable circumstances than these, she refused to break the promise. She swallowed and said, "Just…don't."

"Sorry," Pauly said. Dee appreciated that he looked genuinely chastened.

Chris stuck his head in the room. "The police are here."

"Praise Jesus," Marc muttered, his roots from whatever southern state he hailed from showing. Dee was too rattled by the current circumstances to remember which one.

A tall, attractive woman stepped into the room, followed by her equivalent in male form. Both wore jeans and blazers, his navy, hers black with a tiny plaid of charcoal and lighter gray woven in. She wore her black hair pulled back in a tight bun. His hair was also black but threaded with silver. Dee briefly wondered if they were actors filming on the lot who'd wandered into the wrong building. The delusion was dispelled by brief greetings, followed by introductions.

"I'm Detective Jennifer Rick." The detective motioned to the man standing a foot behind her. "And this is my partner, Detective Jim Gutierrez."

"Detectives, huh? So she was murdered, wasn't she?" Pauly asked the question on everyone's minds.

"It's too soon to determine how the decedent passed," the detective responded. "This is standard procedure for any death that falls under the category of unusual circumstances."

"For 'unusual circumstances,' read 'murder,'" Brandon said.

"Shut up," Gary snapped. Dee noticed the showrunner had broken out in a sweat. Beads of perspiration dripped from his forehead, making the journey down his face to his pale blue button-down shirt, where stains had sprouted under his arms.

"We have officers talking to the deceased's coworkers down on the stage." Detective Rick tucked a strand of hair that had come loose behind her ear. "But since the death occurred in this building and on this floor, we'd like to talk to each of you to get an idea of what happened. No pressure. Just to get a timeline of events."

Despite the detective's easy tone and disclaimer about the cause of death, Dee couldn't shake the feeling they were all suspects. She stole a surreptitious look at her fellow writers. Since most of them were perspiring as profusely as Gary, Dee assumed she wasn't alone in sensing this.

"Is there a contact list we can work from?" Detective Gutierrez asked.

"I'd have my assistant get you one," Gary said, "but I texted her a while ago to bring a couple of aspirin and she still hasn't gotten back to me." He winced and rubbed his forehead.

"I think there's a printout on the table somewhere," Dee said. She hunted through a pile of papers in the table's center, ignoring the stray M&Ms and other errant snack food remnants rolling off the stack. She located the crew sheet and handed it to Gutierrez. "Here you go."

"Thanks." He snapped a photo of the front page where the writers and a few others, like line producer Chris, were listed, then handed the printout to his partner. "We'll need two offices."

"You can use Dee's across the hall," Gary said without asking the office's occupant if it was okay with her, "and the empty one next to it." Dee panicked, worried she'd left her pilot open on her computer for all to see. Then she remembered the screen was set to sleep after five minutes and relaxed.

Detective Rick tapped one of her fingernails on the printout. "Okay then. We'll start at the top and work our way down."

*Story of my career*, Dee thought to herself ruefully as she settled in for the long wait to the bottom of the writer list.

The afternoon dragged on into evening. Pasta and pizza replaced the lunch spread, the pizza ice-cold before it hit the table. The detectives forbade texting and placing calls but allowed use of phones for other purposes, which is how Dee learned Lucy's death was the lead story on the entertainment site Deadline.com but nowhere else…yet. She knew that would change if Lucy's death was classified as a homicide. She chafed at not being able to return any of the texts popping up on her phone from people who'd seen the story, especially the one from her agent Lexi Chase, who texted a terse *Call me*. Finally…blessedly…Detective Rick appeared in the doorway and motioned for Dee to join her in Dee's own office.

The detective took the office chair, leaving Dee to claim the couch. She sank into its lumpy cushions and heard a spring *boing* from its innards.

Rick crossed one leg over the other. She removed a small notebook from her jacket's inside pocket. "One of my colleagues talked to Ms. Gould, the costume designer. Help me create a timeline of Lucy Neubling's movements, starting with your conversation about the wedding gown sketches."

"I wish I had something useful to tell you," Dee said. "But I have no idea where Lucy was when I talked to Allie or where she was afterwards. Allie said Lucy would come up to the production offices to show me the sketches. The next thing I knew, she was lying on the floor…deceased."

"Uh huh." Rick scribbled something in her pad. Dee found the use of pen and paper disarmingly old-timey. The detective looked up from her notes. "Ms. Gould said you didn't like Ms. Neubling."

"Did she now?" Pissed off, Dee considered reversing course on the bathroom scene, recommending Gary cut it purely to get back at blabbermouth Allie. "I didn't like or dislike Lucy. I barely knew her. I did find it annoying when she badgered me about reading her latest spec script or bent my ear with gossip. I don't have time for either. Being a writer on a TV show is incredibly demanding."

"I bet. But regarding show gossip, what do you think about Gary and Lucy's affair?"

Dee stared at her. "Affair? *What?!* Where did you hear that?"

"Does it matter?"

"I don't know. Maybe." Dee shook her head emphatically. "Sorry, but I don't believe it for a minute. Gary's a snob. I don't see him commingling with anyone below the line. I had to constantly remind him who Lucy even was."

"He could have been acting that way to throw people off."

Dee scoffed at the notion. "Please. Gary? He likes to fill in for guest stars who can't make it to the table read, and he's *terrible.*"

Detective Rick opened her mouth to pose another question, and Dee tensed. Suddenly, footsteps pounded down the hall in a run. Detective Gutierrez threw open the door. "We got someone on the roof," he said, out of breath.

"A sniper?" Rick responded, confused by the new development.

"No. A jumper."

## ACT THREE

Dee stood with the other writers, watching in horror as Sarah paced the edge of the Wilder Building roof. The police had cordoned off the street. The lights on a phalanx of patrol cars cast an ominous red glow as they blinked on and off. An ambulance stood waiting in case law enforcement failed to coax Sarah down. Judging by the woman's distraught state, Dee gave them a fifty-fifty chance.

"So this is what a psychotic break looks like," Brandon said, transfixed. "I should take notes for my therapist."

Sarah pointed an accusing finger at Gary from her rooftop perch. "You were going to leave me for her!" she screamed.

Gary pulled on what was left of his hair with both hands. "I have no idea what you're talking about!" he yelled back.

Sarah released a guttural moan that turned Dee's stomach.

"I can't watch this," Dee said. "It's cruel. I'm going inside."

Dee hurried away. She yanked open the building door and took the stairs up to her office two at a time. Once inside, she collapsed onto her chair. Her heart hammered so hard she feared she might be the one loaded into the ambulance instead of Sarah. She closed her eyes and fought to calm herself. Once her heart returned to a close-to-normal beat, she opened them. Unsure what to do, Dee sat facing the wall in front of her, waiting for an update.

She was still in this frozen position when Pauly came into her office a half hour later.

"It's over," he said, somber. Seeing the expression on Dee's face, he hastened to add, "Sarah is okay. Detective Rick literally talked her off the ledge."

Dee released a long exhale. "Phew. Huge relief."

"You know it. Crazy shit, huh?" Pauly parked himself on the arm of Dee's couch. "Is it too soon for me to say Hot Lady Detective can slam me against a wall and frisk me any time she wants?"

Dee laughed, a release of tension as much as anything else. "Not too soon. I needed that."

Pauly looked at her with concern. "You okay?"

This simple touch of humanity, more than she'd known in the months she'd been on the show, almost broke Dee. *Never let them see you cry, never let them see you cry.* She nodded and cleared her throat. "Where's everyone else?"

"Gary went to the police station where they took Sarah and Brown-Nosy went with him, and yes, I know you call him that, just like I know you call me Chubby." He patted his stomach. "The others all went back to their offices, probably to call their agents and see if they can force majeure themselves the hell out of here. You can bet Marc jumped right on that. The kid is a born operator."

"So...I guess we go home?" Dee hoped so. She was emotionally and physically drained.

"Until we hear otherwise."

"They'll probably cancel the rest of the order."

"Because a low-level assistant was offed by another low-level assistant? You wish. Our meatball of a star, John Franco, is hot right now. Believe it or not, there's buzz on the show." Pauly stood up. "I'm gonna go home and day drink. You need anything, call me."

"Thanks, Pauly. Will do."

Shortly after he left, Dee did the same. As she made the drive from the studio to her San Fernando Valley apartment, something about the conversation with the comic nagged at her, but Dee couldn't land on exactly what. She forced herself to focus, but the connection proved elusive, flitting in and out over the next week of a forced hiatus. Dee finally gave up, instead devoting the break to working on her pilot while she waited for updates on when to report back to *John*. Her own agent made it clear there were no other jobs available. All the shows currently in production had their woman.

It took a six a.m. notification from Deadline.com announcing the new showrunner for *On the John* to trigger the memory spurred by Dee's conversation with Pauly.

She met Marc at the Starbucks near her apartment. "Coffee's on me," she said, handing him a grande black, his drink of choice when PAs made coffee runs for the writers. "To congratulate you on the new gig."

"Thanks." Marc took the coffee. He smiled a self-deprecating smile. "I guess no one else in town wanted the job."

"Being a showrunner is a big deal. I knew you'd eventually be one, but I never thought it'd be at *On the John*."

"Neither did I. But like my grandfather used to say, ya dance with the one who brung ya."

"Sounds like something they'd say in Texas." Dee took a sip of her tea. She hated coffee, another thing that made her an outlier in writers' rooms. "You *are* from Texas, right? I didn't remember until they mentioned it in the Deadline post."

"Yeah, from outside Dallas." The self-deprecating smile disappeared, replaced by a wary expression.

"So was Lucy. Did you know she had a website?"

"No. Why would I?"

"She was an aspiring novelist as well as a TV writer, so she set one up for herself," Dee continued. "I did an online search and found it. In her bio, Lucy name-dropped taking a writing workshop with you in Dallas. You taught them before you moved here. The two of you obviously knew each other but pretended you didn't, which made me remember something else. At the block-and-shoot for the 'In the Toilet' episode a few weeks ago, you ruined a shot because the director heard you yelling at someone. You came out of the hallway behind the sets, really angry. Lucy came out a few minutes later, but I didn't connect the two of you until yesterday." Dee took another sip of tea, adopting a casual attitude she didn't feel. "Was she blackmailing you or something?"

Marc looked down at his coffee. Then he looked up, sat back in his chair, and smirked. "Busted. Lucy's gone, so I guess it doesn't matter anymore. I didn't write *Spaced Out*. That's not completely true. I did rewrite it, but the manuscript came from one of my students, an old guy who was a retired high school English teacher. He was in the early stages of dementia, so I offered to buy the script from him, and he agreed. He knew he could never follow through on it. Lucy was my key student in that particular workshop. She helped me organize it and communicate with the students in exchange for free attendance."

"So she knew about the deal."

"She was the only one who did. *Spaced Out* was the perfect pilot to get the town's attention. It was 'noisy,' in exec speak. 'Noisy.' Puhleeze." Marc released a derisive snort. "I bet some executive gave himself a boner coming up with that bullshit description. Anyway, to keep Lucy quiet, I helped her get a job on *John* without ever revealing to Gary we knew each other. But she always wanted more. 'Read my script' became 'read my script or else,' which became 'get me a writing job or else.'"

"I get it," Dee said, nodding. "What I don't understand is how you dragged Sarah into it."

"She and Gary have been having an affair for years. You didn't know?"

"No," Dee said, embarrassed. She'd been so in her own world she'd missed the obvious signs.

"I could see Gary was losing interest, which was freaking out Sarah. Her whole life was about him. And she was getting up there in age."

"We had a cake for her a month ago," Dee said, appalled. "She just turned thirty-six."

"I know, right?" the twenty-eight-year-old said, clueless. "I encouraged Lucy to flirt with Gary as a way of getting him to hire her as a staff writer. When we had a couple of those sad birthdays, I joked to Sarah you could hide cyanide in frosting and kill off anyone who was bugging you because they'd just think the frosting tasted like it was made with almond flavor. I figured eventually Sarah would lose it, Gary would be fired for sexual misconduct, and I'd be in line to run the show."

"Wow, you really are an operator."

Marc chuckled. "You've been talking to Pauly. Jealous, jealous Pauly."

"The thing is, I thought you weren't interested in running the show."

Marc's cocky façade faded. "I need the credit," he admitted. "I'm realistic about my own work. My show scripts are decent. My pilots are fine, but not stand-out. No one is ever going to make *Spaced Out*. It works as a spec, but people stuck together on the space station? Where's the ongoing series? There are only a few *John* episodes left to shoot. I just have to power through those, and I'll always be a showrunner." The smirk returned. "I came up with the perfect plot. I got everything I wanted without getting my own hands dirty."

"Too bad you can't come up with a plot that good for one of your own pilots."

Dee regretted the retort the minute it came out of her mouth, but Marc responded with a wry, "Truth." He lifted his shoulders in an *Oh well, what can you do?* shrug, then leaned forward and spoke in a low voice. "Anyway, now that I've agreed to run *John*, I could use a strong co-EP. We're friends. We work well together. I can promise you a bump from story editor to co-executive producer. Nobody makes that leap. And how many co-EPs are women? You'll be a star, Dee."

"Wow. Co-EP. We're talking about a…" Dee counted in her head. "…five credit bump. That is a *lot*."

"I know." Marc flashed a conspiratorial smile. "It's a good offer. Think about it."

Dee rested her back against the coffee shop's hard metal chair, evaluating her options. Allie wasn't wrong when she told Detective Rick that Dee disliked Lucy. And Marc's offer was more than good. A five-credit bump was epic. Dee imagined herself skipping past the other writers on staff, working side-by-side with Marc as his second, blowing through the last few episodes of *On the John.*

She returned his smile.

The next morning, Deadline shared breaking news that the studio had fired Marc Wittenberg after discovering he'd plagiarized the pilot that landed him his fat deal. There was no mention of the devious machinations that led to Lucy's death, Sarah's arrest, and the breakup of Gary's marriage when the affair with his assistant went public. The fact that LAPD was looking at the now ex-rising writing star as an accessory to murder also went unreported…at least until Marc was officially charged with the crime.

*On the John* was on its third showrunner in two weeks. This time, the honor went to brown noser Brandon.

That same morning, Dee sat outside the office of Ashley Woods, the studio's VP of Current Programming on the show. Ashley's assistant opened the door and gestured to Dee. "Ashley's ready for you."

"Great."

Dee stood up. A large black-and-white photograph of Billy Wilder held a place of honor on the wall next to the door, and Dee touched it for good luck, a tradition handed down through decades of writers passing through the portals to executive meetings. As she pulled her hand away, Dee did a double-take. She could have sworn the famed writer-director winked at her. Then she realized it was a trick of light caused by the sun briefly going behind a cloud.

The assistant led Dee into Ashley's office. To her surprise, Julie Epstein, the network's Current Programming executive on the show, was there as well. Both women stood up and took turns hugging her.

Ashley motioned for Dee to take a seat across from where they were parked on the room's sleek new sofa. "Julie and I wanted to thank you together for what you did. It was incredibly brave of you to out Marc as a horrible human being. Wow."

"Can you imagine if all this came out *after* we hired him?" Julie said. She mimed wiping sweat from her pristine brow. "We really dodged a bullet."

"Julie and I agreed we had to find just the right way to acknowledge your actions," Ashley said. "And I think we have."

Dee sat up straighter. Her heartbeat picked up speed. Maybe it wouldn't take a deal with the devil that was Marc to make a credit leap—if not the stratospheric bump from story editor to co-executive producer than at least to co-producer or even producer.

Ashley bent down and picked up a large box at her feet. She handed it to Dee. Perplexed, Dee opened the box. She pulled out a large, fluffy lap blanket decorated with the show's logo—a grinning toilet bowl.

"It's the Christmas gift we gave to supervising producers and above," Ashley said. "Something to snuggle up under when you're sneaking a nap during a late rewrite."

"You're the only lower-level writer who has one," Julie added.

Dee ran her hand over the blanket. "It's very soft."

"Top of the line," Ashley declared with pride.

"I can tell."

Dee carefully refolded the blanket and placed it back in the box. She handed the box back to Ashley.

"I quit."


**TAG**


Dee woke up on her office couch, where she'd collapsed after packing up her belongings. Feeling foggy, she wondered if she'd dreamt the whole thing: Lucy's murder, Sarah's confession, Marc's cocky explanation of how he set her up. The inane lap blanket. Then she saw the black plastic bags stuffed with her stuff that confirmed the last forty-eight hours had been all too real.

She noticed her phone lying on the floor by the couch and reached for it. The screen lit up with a string of interrobangs and profanity, her agent Lexi's response to Dee's text announcing she'd quit the show. *Time for a new agent*, Dee thought to herself. She sighed, knowing it would be a tough search thanks to the cascade of *On the John* scandals. There was also a text from newly minted showrunner Brandon pleading with her not to quit: *I need you.* She texted back *Good luck! I know u can do it.* This was a lie.

She rose and shook off the dust from the decrepit old couch, then plodded over to her computer. She pressed Enter, and her work-in-progress came into view.

"Nice job on the pilot," came a male voice with a slight German accent.

Dee started. She turned to see an elderly man with a round face and round glasses sitting on the couch. She rubbed her eyes. *I'm hallucinating.*

"A couple of places needed more jokes," he said. "But I think you're good now."

Dee bent down and saw the words "Fade Out" on the last page of her script. "Whaaaa…"

She started at the beginning of the document and scrolled down. Places she'd marked "punch up" were punched up. Places where she'd written "joke to come" had jokes. At long last, the script—her ticket to moving on—was done.

"Oh my God," Dee murmured. "Thank you so, so…"

She turned around.

Billy Wilder was gone.

# Bloodsurf

by Tiffany D. Plunkett

He stood on the slick wet boards with the easy balance of a native, hands in the pockets of a long pale coat that whipped around his legs in the dripping, windy weather that meant the summer was almost done. He faced the horizon to the east. I followed his gaze and saw only the white-tipped waves splitting against the pier and the roiling grey clouds battling in the sky.

I'd never seen the man on the dock before. The production had been on set six months. Rabbit Island almost never had visitors before they—I mean *we*—started filming. Then, like a rogue wave, Hollywood crashed onto the shore and filled not just the streets, but our lives. I'd been among the first to be swept away.

My whole life had been on the island. I knew most everybody, and everybody mostly knew me. I didn't know the man on the dock, but somehow he didn't *feel* like a stranger.

I leaned over and breathed on the diner window. Fog appeared on the glass, separating me from the strange-but-not-stranger figure being absorbed by the rain. He was wet and cold. I was comfortable and dry in my usual seat at the café. I was protected not just by walls that had endured centuries of hurricanes without complaint, but by the sweet scent of the strawberry-rhubarb hand-pies Arabel was pulling from the formidable oven behind me. Her face was flushed with heat. Flaps of freckled fat swung from her upper arms as she hefted the sheet of fruit-stuffed pastries to the counter, then slipped the steaming desserts one by one onto the cooling rack.

I looked away, too familiar with the process. My fingers traced the man's silhouette. The glass was as cold and hard as the plummeting raindrops outside. Just that fraction of warmth from my body melted the thin cloud on the window that separated us.

I was suddenly, painfully lonely. Intensely aware of the length of my booth and the empty seat across from me. Arabel's hand-fired ceramic mug of steaming coffee was a blue dot in the vast sea of solitary gray table.

I took the napkin from my lap and wadded it into a loose ball, then set it like a centerpiece, not quite in the middle. An *off-centerpiece*, I joked to myself.

My sister Lisbeth would've groaned and twirled her long black hair around her finger, if she'd been there to hear. But she was swollen fat with her fourth, and unlikely to waddle in for a piece of pie or slice of gossip, especially when everybody on *Bloodshore* had skipped off-island. Bad weather meant filming was delayed by a week. Maybe two. Nobody here but us chickens now, minding the roost.

I should check my messages again, I mused. Wyc was probably wearing out the carpet back at the location production office, also known as two third-floor hotel suites in the Hoppy Bunny Inn. It's pretty much the best we have to offer around here.

I set my studio-assigned tablet safely back on the diner's faux-leather banquet next to the phone strapped to my right hip. Sixty-three emails, thirty-two texts, and seven tasks checked off today already. I'd Zoomed, Slacked, and Snapped. I'd filed script changes, replied to PR requests, refilled the mini-fridge at the office with Spendthrift fizzy water, and created Bobbi's daily messaging summary. I'd installed the new updates on all the office phones and devices. I'd dusted the custom Lucite box that housed Bobbi's famous red heels. I'd ordered more of the orange tennis balls she insisted on, and as a precaution, safety tape for the court lines. Lucky for me, I know where the petty cash is, and Wyc didn't notice me casually zooming in to capture the lock code my first week on the job.

Before I'd started working for *Bloodshore* and then for Bobbi herself, I'd have thought today was overwhelming. Now I had the sails straight, though. I could recognize today as a slow day for this production, storm or no storm.

Was I proud of myself? You better believe it. I started as a runner. Then one day, as I happened to be standing next to the 1st AD, her walkie crackled, and Bobbi demanded that she go to channel 15. Private isn't good.

One of the PAs had accidentally texted Bobbi a dick pic. I heard the whole story. Mr. Dick Pic was out. I was Jenny-on-the-spot, volunteered, got the job. Three weeks after that, Bobbi's second assistant was fired for repeatedly sending Bobbi to the wrong meeting at the wrong time. Lucky for me again.

When I was promoted, Wyc had warned me that working for a producer like Bobbi Schwartz was a 24/7 effort. I'd only actually managed to speak to Bobbi eleven times in three months, and once was when I accidentally butt-dialed her. No, my work wasn't the glamorous stuff. I got Wyc's overload, his scutwork. But at least with him in place, I wasn't going to be the first hit when Bobbi came in tomorrow like a tropical storm on scarlet high heels.

My phone buzzed next to me. Wyc again. I could just imagine him panicking over the publicity leaks and paparazzi pics that had been popping up with increasing frequency. Script pages, costume pics—even audio of our posh (and lactose-intolerant) actress having a rough time in the honeywagon when somebody switched her almond milk for the real stuff. Bobbi was flying over from the mainland tomorrow to deliver new protocols and probably a cannonload of threats.

I ignored the phone's annoying vibration. Wyc could wait. Instead, I adjusted my off-centerpiece. The table looked slightly less sad for a moment. Then Arabel casually swept my napkin up with one hand and refilled my mug with the other. She nodded toward the man on the dock. He hadn't moved, but the rain was licking at him less. The waves were only nibbling at the old planks, not gnashing them with white-capped teeth.

"Not the usual catch in the lonesome season." Arabel's voice was carved out of cigarettes and salt air.

"Nothing's usual these days," I responded. I looked away.

*In the lonesome season,* an echo whispered to me.

As far as I could figure, my own lonesome season had been going on for seven unlucky years. Seven years of waiting tables, answering phones, tarring rope, tending bar, mowing yards, fixing computers, sluicing boats, and making endless bouquets at the local florist, all the while filming weddings and birthdays and imagining I was some kind of island-trapped female Wes Anderson.

Then Bobbi Schwartz arrived. The precursor to the Hollywood hurricane.

When the location scout came round the first time, he ducked into Arabel's diner. She told him I could show him the island. Afterwards, I took my shot. I flat-out asked him for a gig on the production. Anything. I guess I did a good enough job. Lucky for me, two phone calls later, I was out of my apron and in a headset. The newest hire on a famous producer's comeback movie.

And now what?

I could sense Arabel leaning in to tuck an errant curl behind my ear. She's been doing that all my life. "You can't fool me, Tamsin," she said, lowering her voice, as if anybody else was in the diner except the two of us. "You don't get this quiet 'less you're squirrelin' round with two different thoughts in your head. I'll tell you what I told you when all these folk came round. You need to do what's best for you, girl. Whatever you're fightin' about up *here*—" She poked my forehead with a floured finger. "—you just pick what's most likely to put butter on your biscuit, and you hustle your skinny butt off Rabbit Island. Last thing you want, last thing I want, last thing your mama would've wanted, it's to see you sloshin' coffee to hungover seacaps at three in the morning when you're my age. You do whatever it takes, y'hear?"

She reached to refill my coffee, pulled her arm back when she noted with surprise that the cup was already full. She huffed, straining the buttons on her shirt. "Well, that's my two cents, and what I don't know about anything." She nodded at the front window, where the stranger on the dock was still being pelted by rain. "Now you get out there and offer that man some coffee and something warm for his belly. And if he won't come in, give the dang fool this." She hustled to the counter and filled a Styrofoam cup with coffee, then slipped it inside another cup.

I thought about telling her that I got enough of running coffee to people on set, but then I reckoned her job might not make her that sympathetic.

No sense rasslin' with a mountain. I hunched into my jacket, gathered my things, and headed out. At least the rain was dropping off for now.

My boots splashed in fresh puddles that threw back the reflection of the diner sign and the safety lights dotting the length of the dock.

The man didn't turn around, but I knew he felt me approaching. There was a slight defensive shift of his body as he moved his weight from heel to toe. I stopped. His shoulders tensed, then relaxed. The rain had slowed to a drizzle.

I held out the umbrella I'd snagged from the stand by the diner door. "It's a little late to keep you dry, but there's pie, or a burger, and the blackest coffee on the island if you want it."

The stranger tilted his head toward me. He was old, at least fifty, maybe even fifty-five. Not a cheerful, well-lived-in old walrus like Arabel. Not a lean, tanned, stylish lioness like Bobbi. It looked as if someone had taken him when he was asleep and painstakingly drawn his bones as thin and long as they could be and still cling to the barest minimum of flesh and muscle. The rain had plastered strands of loose gray hair to his skull, and the skin stretched fine across his face was a patchy, pale mask. His eyes were dark and bottomless with grief. I suddenly thought of a forgotten summer, where my sister and I had snuck out at midnight and gone night-swimming in the surf, only to find the ocean a much more frightening place than we'd ever imagined.

The stranger hadn't answered, and I was feeling like a clown at a cotillion just standing there holding two umbrellas. The phone buzzed again at my hip. I ignored it. I raised my voice, just a little, to be sure he heard me this time. "I'm Tamsin. You here for the production? I can show you to the hotel."

He shook his head, then turned back toward the ocean before shrugging and returning his gaze to me. "I don't mind the rain. Production?"

How did he not know? "*Bloodshore*. Sequel to *Bloodsurf*?"

His voice was emotionless. " I know it. From 1993."

"1995." I saw his fist clench. "Year I was born. Yes, sir. That movie's one of the reasons I went to film school. Now I'm with Red Heels." I held out the coffee, invading his personal space. Extra Styrofoam or not, it was hot, and this time I was tired of toting it. If he'd been important, he'd have let me know by now. I was ready to bail when he finally accepted the cup, mumbling a "thank you" half-lost in distant thunder.

"Tamsin," I reminded him, and force-handed the second umbrella into his grip. I'd read in Bobbi's autobiography that repeating your name confidently would make you seem immediately powerful, and thus worth meeting. My first copy of the book was so worn that the binding glue was loose, and the cover felt as soft as an old t-shirt. If you did a CAT scan of my brain, you could probably read the whole thing. So I repeated myself. Confidently. "Tamsin Ballenger. Assistant to Bobbi Schwartz. Red Heels Films."

He seemed surprised. "Bobbi Schwartz? Herself?" His focus was returning, and he'd almost lost that distant stare. "Well. Um." I could tell he had no idea what to say next. "Thank you."

"You can thank Arabel." I gestured behind me. "Her idea. So, the hotel?"

He shook his head. A look of embarrassment was illuminated in a sudden flash of lightning out in the dark waves beyond the white line of surf. "I'm here to…I'm not…making any movies. I guess you could say I'm looking for someone. About someone?"

*In the lonesome season,* Arabel's voice echoed again. Whoever this man was, he had the same hungry gap inside that gnawed at my edges. He didn't want Arabel's mothering care. He needed the rain to wash the pain away. Pressing him wouldn't help.

We waited together, staring at the surf and whatever he saw for himself on the horizon. Me, all I saw *was* the horizon. *Dear God, let me get the hell off this island and find the world behind that line,* I prayed quickly. It wasn't the first time I'd sent that wish up since film school at USC. The same USC Bobbi graduated from. I mean South Carolina, not the famous USC, even though that's not something I call out to most people, not without a direct question. Besides, I couldn't even finish once my loans ran out and Mama got herself hurt. So here I was, snared on muggy old Rabbit Island.

Maybe Arabel's coffee made the man speak. It was no struggle to hear him over the wind this time. "My name is Michael. Michael Weaver, Assistant to Nobody. I quit my job and sold everything I own except that name. And now here I am. Without even my own umbrella. Jacob was the Boy Scout. My brother. Always prepared. Me, I'm just…here." His eyes met mine. "I've where I wanted to be, and now I don't know what to do."

I spoke without thinking. "When Bobbi doesn't like the way something looks, she says try a new angle. Let's walk. It's going to get windy out here again soon."

That startled him. He took a peek at the sky. Yes, those clouds were getting closer.

I shrugged. "What's the worst that can happen?"

We turned our backs on the warmth and safety of the diner. Our steps took us wetly down the dock, then we turned left, and headed around the wide curve of the harbor.

I told Michael about how when I was little, the beach was rocky and dark. Now it gleamed like bone, thanks to tons of sand imported from Charleston and the Gulf. When I was nine and Lisbeth thirteen, I'd pushed her from one of the rocks. Her collarbone broke in three places. It always ached in thunderstorms. I wondered if it ached now. Not that it was my fault. She started it. I was the one who said I wanted to look for starfish. The first one we found should've been mine.

I hadn't thought about that in a long time. I had to wrap up the story, bring us back to the present. Michael's gaze was locked on me as I continued. "That was the night I first had our whole house to myself. Mama was in the hospital. So I watched *Bloodsurf*."

Michael shook his head. "Sisters aren't that different from brothers. Jacob twisted his ankle jumping off the roof when I was eight. We were playing Batman and Robin. I swore Batman would catch Robin. But when he jumped, I got scared and ran off. Definitely did not watch horror movies that night."

"*Bloodsurf* is a thriller, not a horror movie!" I defended. "It's a tense exploration of a woman rebuilding her psyche and facing her fears. The death is just a—"

"Murder," Michael corrected. "She deliberately seduces him, makes him take her out on the boat—"

"*Makes* is a little strong, he could've stayed where he was. He didn't have to—"

He ignored me. "Gets him drunk—"

"—he could've said no—"

"—and then stabs him through the eye with one of her red high heels. She's a monster. It's a horror film."

I don't like being ignored. Besides, just hours ago, I'd just made sure there was no dirt on the box that protected the very same heels that inspired *Bloodsurf.* The heels she wrote about in the autobiography that had been my Bible for the last two months. The heels Bobbi bought in 1993 with her last office-job paycheck, a symbol of her freedom and her new life. There had probably been a dozen dozen identical pairs since then, but good-luck tradition meant the real ones were kept on set for every picture.

We'd made it around the curve of the harbor, up the incline, so that we were now looking over the old stretch of beach. Here, no imported golden sand hid the slick black rocks below. The dock where I'd first seen Michael was a Morse code of lights in the distance.

"Do you know why she picked this island for the sequel?" he asked, suddenly.

I flicked a glance around. Why not here? "Bobbi always has reasons for her choices," I answered. "Why did you pick this island to search for your brother?"

Michael turned away quickly. I stepped back to avoid the wet flap of his coat against me. "It is your brother, right? The one you're searching for?"

"I know where he is." His voice had a wall in it I couldn't see past. "He's buried next to my father and mother in our family plot in Philadelphia. They found his body in 1993. It was caught in the anchor line of his boat. What was left of him." Now he turned to me, a fierceness in his eyes. "The last circle on his map was Rabbit Island. I know my brother. It wasn't an accident. There was a fracture inside his eye socket. His bank accounts were empty but there was no money on the boat. Somebody murdered him. And

I think your boss…I think she wrote the story for *Bloodsurf*"—he almost spat the word —"based on what she did. I think she took his money and made a movie about it."

I looked out at the dock again, trying to read the message in the lights, but there weren't enough of them. I needed a city full of lights, a blinding horizon.

"Goddamn," I said, after a long beat. "I'm so sorry. I wish you didn't think that."

He searched my face, then scoffed. "You don't believe me."

The wind was picking up. Rain pattered down.

I shook my head. "I believe you." I watched his expression change. "She was at USC then. South Carolina not Southern California. A three-hour drive to Charleston. Easy enough to find a rich guy with a boat, get him drunk. Maybe slip him something. Once you're out on the water, anything could happen. Especially if you're committed and determined like Bobbi."

His lips twisted in disgust. "You sound like you admire her." He turned away.

"Of course." It only took one push.

He fell much farther and much harder than Lisbeth had. At the bottom, he looked like a starfish, splayed across the rocks. He didn't move, except where the surf tugged at his legs and arms. It pulled Arabel's double-lined Styrofoam coffee cup out into the tide. Soon, it'd pull him out into the dark waters beyond the horizon.

The ocean has a way of taking what it wants. I admire that, too.

With the wind kicking my coat around my legs, and two umbrellas tucked under my arm, I headed back to the warmth and safety of Arabel's. Tomorrow, Bobbi would be arriving, only to discover evidence that Wyc had been stealing from the petty cash for months. A search of his phone would prove he was also behind the paparazzi leaks. No matter what he'd protest, the evidence would be clear.

Taking over his job would be hard, but I was confident I could do it. And if Bobbi wasn't on board, I was sure I could convince her. After all, I was just following in her footsteps.

# Grand Theft Auto in the Heart of Screenland

by Robert Rotstein

Here in Hollywood,[1] the opportunity to represent celebrity actors, writers, producers, and directors serves as a siren call to the talentless and uncreative who yearn to bask in the reflected light of the talented and creative—and to take a decent percentage of the tens of millions of dollars that the clients earn as compensation for doing their bidding. Not a bad gig, as the entertainment lawyers and talent agents say. Based on my decades of experience as an attorney, I'd estimate that a good fifty percent of young lawyers who take jobs in Los Angeles—whether as associates in firms that specialize in criminal defense, toxic torts, intellectual property, bankruptcy, real estate, domestic relations, international relations, personal injury, impersonal injury—just below the scratchable surface have a smoldering desire to practice entertainment law.

A caveat: the late Julius "Groucho" Marx famously said, "I don't want to belong to any club that will have me as a member."[2] Here's a piece of advice to ambitious young law students who aspire to charge a five-percent contingency fee to near-billionaire A-list screenwriters, directors, producers, actors, and singers while basking in these luminaries' reflected light: *the entertainment bar won't accept anyone who says they want to become a member.*[3] No, the tradecraft of the entertainment lawyer requires serpentine guile and vulpine cunning, such that those gullible, street-dumb wannabes who openly express an interest in the practice area are, by definition, guileless and naïve. The true entertainment lawyer starts out by disclaiming any interest in the club while engaging in every possible underhanded, unctuous, and ruthless move to gain admission to it. I say this without a scintilla of shame.

Take my initial foray into the world of Hollywoodland-ish transactional jurisprudence during the 1970s. I was a fifth-year associate at a prominent Beverly Hills entertainment firm, litigating real estate and construction matters and pretending to love those mind-numbing pursuits, when what I really wanted to do was…well, any kind of legal work for firm clients like Paul Newman, Elizabeth Taylor, and Marlon Brando. Hell, I would've settled for a matter representing TV actors like Jack Klugman or even an aging Kathleen Freeman. No luck.

The closest I got to an entertainment matter was representing Tillie Lipschmann, whose son-in-law was a fairly successful producer of made-for-TV docudramas. One day, the son-in-law called our managing partner, Marvin Sussman, screaming, "I need you to sue my neighbor, because her damn rottweiler puppy bit my mother-in-law in the tuchus!" Marvin chose me to vindicate Mrs. Lipschmann's[4] only slightly injured left buttock.[5] The client wanted $5000 for his mother-in-law's injuries. When I proudly told him I'd gotten $5800, he complained that I'd settled for too little because the insurance company gave in too quickly, at which point he called me a spineless putz and slammed the phone down in my ear.

Hooray for Hollywood.

* * *

The life-changing phone call came on a Thursday morning.

"It's Marvin. Get down to my office now. I've got an urgent new matter for you. It's for Lindy."

I hoped my intimidating boss didn't hear my gasp. *Lindy* was Charles Lindburg, III,[6] president of the motion picture division at Colossal Pictures and, more importantly, the genius who'd greenlighted four movies that had outgrossed the original *Star Wars* and had won multiple Academy Awards. No wonder they called him Lucky Lindy.

Despite my knowledge that enthusiasm was a dangerous thing for a would-be entertainment lawyer to reveal, I hurried down the long hall, earning a wave from Nathalie Kitcheon, a young associate who commanded little respect—not because she lacked intelligence but rather because the powers-that-were noticed her exuberance for life. To this day, good lawyers are *not* supposed to show exuberance for life. Ordinarily, I would've stopped to chat with Nathalie about our shared ill-treatment by the firm, but now I gave a quick wave back and began sprinting.

A bit winded, I reached Marvin's office. The man's craggy face was lowered to his desk as if he was reading, though there was nothing on the desk to read except the grains in the mahogany.[7] The only objects on the table were a souvenir feather pen-and-ink set that Marvin had purportedly received from Clark Gable and a picture of Marvin and Stacey, his third wife, during their disastrous vacation in Tahiti that, according to law firm rumor, threatened to make Stacey his third *ex*-wife. Mostly, I saw his prematurely white hair, which signaled experience and wisdom to the gullible and a genetic mutation to the cognoscenti.

It took a knock on the open door and three throat-clears, the last admittedly a bit too phlegmy, before he looked up.

"Yes, what is it?" he said, appraising me with his avian-predator eyes. Even after he summoned you, Marvin Sussman always seemed mildly irritated that you showed up. Well, that *I* showed up. I didn't know how he reacted to my colleagues' arrivals.

"You called me about a new matter for Charles Lindburg. How can I help?"

"When you clerked for that judge, I assumed you handled criminal cases?"

"Yes, sir, absolutely," I said with unwarranted conviction, because while I'd drafted opinions on heady Fourth and Fifth Amendment issues—my judge was a big deal—I didn't have a clue about the nitty-gritty elements of criminal law. Hell, I couldn't have defended a littering case if the accused were Mother Teresa.

"The police have arrested Babs Spangler for stealing a Maserati." Barbara Spangler was Lucky Lindy's wife, a former starlet known mostly for playing wholesome "girls next door"—which she wasn't in real life.

"Did she hotwire the car or steal it at gunpoint?"

Marvin glared at me.

"Just joking," I said—exactly the wrong response.

Titanium silence from powerful people can reduce an underling's confidence to congealed belly fat more effectively than harsh criticism or even screaming. Marvin Sussman was the master of titanium silence. As my confidence morphed into congealed panniculus, I forced myself not to apologize.

"Do…do you have any more details?" I asked. "I mean, did she really steal a car?"

"I wouldn't put it past her just for the publicity value and attention, especially because her career is down the toilet. When I spoke with her, she was overwrought and on the verge of hysteria. I could make out a bevy of expletives; the words, and I quote, *police brutality*, and the fact that I was her second phone call because Lindy refused to take her first phone call because he was allegedly in a casting meeting, and why won't he cast her in a movie, and after she sues the cops for violating her civil rights, she wants a divorce and half the studio. Get down to the station now and fix it."

Those sweet words—*fix it*. Because there's no more important skill for an entertainment lawyer than to fix problems for the client. This, I knew, was my chance to leave the world of dog-bite cases behind forever and to watch in person as my clients walked the reddest of carpets.

* * *

I didn't go to the station right away. Preparation is everything, right? I hustled back to my office and checked the bookshelf for the California Penal Code. I had the Civil Code, the Code of Civil Procedure, the Commercial Code, the Business & Professions Code, the Labor Code, the Health & Safety Code, the Family Law Code, but no Penal Code. So I headed to the Beverly Hills police station ignorant of the law. This concerned me for a moment until I remembered that you didn't need to know the law to practice entertainment law. Rather, you needed to know the going profit participation figures for A-, B-, and C-level actors;[8] whether your client was powerful enough to command a full-time personal fitness trainer and first-class travel; and how to use their celebrity and net worth as leverage to get them out of trouble and cover up scandals.[9] Relieved, I hurried to the lobby and ran past the elevator bank, down five flights of stairs, and out into the sunny Beverly Hills morning.

The Beverly Hills Police Department was only a half a mile away, and L.A. traffic being L.A. traffic, I determined that I'd reach the jail on foot more quickly than I would by car. Besides, I feared that Babs Spangler (or worse, her spouse, Lucky Lindy), would spy my rusted yellow Volkswagen Rabbit with the dent in the right-front fender and think me unworthy of a prime place in the Hollywood legal community.

Rather than wasting precious time walking south to the traffic light, I headed north up Bedford Drive and started to cross in the middle of the one-way street. Next door to our office building lay the Ginger House Restaurant, owned by two actors, one of whom played the lead character on an iconic, unforgettable, groundbreaking television series that at least three subsequent generations have forgotten. The man who honked the horn at me and skidded to a stop as I crossed in front of him was the less famous, more serious actor-owner. I froze, he got out of his car, and I suspected that he was going to dress me down for jaywalking and almost getting hit by his car, and maybe I could apologize and bring him in as a client, but I never found out or had a chance, because a Beverly Hills cop pulled up, cut his engine, and got out of his patrol car.

"Why were you crossing the road like that?" the Patrol Cop asked.

"To get to the other side, Officer."

"That's not only disrespectful, it's also lame," the actor said with the kind of disgust only a moderately successful Thespian can convey. "There is not an ounce of credit to be gained by comparing yourself to a chicken, even in jest, man." At least someone got one of my jokes that morning.

Hearing the actor's diction, I remembered that he'd started in theatre. "With mirth and laughter let old wrinkles come," I said.

"You're quoting Shakespeare? Now?" This observation came not from the actor, but from the Patrol Cop—this was Beverly Hills in the seventies. Half the police force did Shakespeare-in-the-Park in the summer.[10] Upwards of ninety percent were writing screenplays.

He pulled out his ticket book and began to write slowly.

"Could you write a little faster, please?" I said.

"Somewhere you got to be," the Patrol Cop asked, "besides the other side of the road?"

"Yeah, as a matter of fact…" Then I noticed the leather cover to his ticket book. "Hey, that's a Gucci notebook. Does the city pay for that, or did you buy it out of your own pocket on your paltry salary?"

The actor stood smirking, his arms clasped behind his back. "Are you accusing this police officer of taking bribes?"

"Yeah, are you accusing me of corruption?" the cop said.

"Of course not. I would never. I was bemoaning the injustice that public servants like yourself receive such unconscionably low pay."

"I'm an honest cop. I find your insinuation about Gucci offensive." A beat. "It's Louis Vuitton, I'll have you know."

I checked my watch, thinking how I wished I would've taken my jalopy.

The actor put a hand on my shoulder. "Good luck to you. Proceed more carefully the next time."

I pulled a business card from my inside pocket—though he might've disliked me for jaywalking, never miss the opportunity to tout your entertainment-law wares—but the actor waved a hand and said, "Remember Dick the Butcher's immortal statement: 'The first thing we do, let's kill all the lawyers.'"

"Shakespeare's *Henry VI, Part 2*," the Patrol Cop said. "You know, I played Dick the Butcher two seasons ago."[11]

The actor bowed and walked toward his restaurant.

I checked my watch again.

"Do not rush me," the Patrol Cop said. "The wheels of justice don't work if they're forced to spin out of control."

"I just have to get down to—"

"You should've thought of that before you violated important provisions of the California Vehicle Code and slandered an officer of the law." He returned to filling out the ticket, writing so slowly he might've been chiseling hieroglyphics on granite.

All at once, I became afraid. Afraid that I wouldn't reach the police station in time to help Babs Spangler, that she'd make bail without me, that Marvin Sussman would fire me for incompetence, that I'd be relegated to a career filing lawsuits on behalf of slip-and-fall victims as I labored in a cramped law office located in a strip mall and situated over a dumpster.

I grabbed the ticket book out of the cop's hand, tore the partial jaywalking ticket from the bindings, ripped it to shreds, and tossed the paper in the air as if celebrating New Year's Eve. Two pieces of paper, the tiniest shreds, floated down in the wind and fell on the officer of the law's shoulders. My actions signified neither irrationality nor ill-directed malice. No, I confettied the ticket to get myself to the police station *tout de suite* and thereby free Babs Spangler and save my career.

The ploy worked. I was in the rear seat of the patrol car within sixty seconds.[12]

* * *

The patrol cop brought me in front of the watch commander, who sported a deep tanning salon tan, a shaved head, tinted glasses, and a black moustache—central casting, in other words, not for Shakespeare in the Park but rather for Porn in a Sleazy Theater on Santa Monica Boulevard.[13]

"Book him," the Patrol Cop said in lingo that I'd thought only happened on TV. "Resisting arrest, assault and battery of a police officer, and jaywalking."

"I neither assaulted nor battered you," I said.

The Patrol Cop pointed to a piece of confetti still stuck to his shoulder. "You threw a foreign object at me…assault. The foreign object made contact battery. Do you want to get a photograph, Gil? Call forensics?"

The Watch Commander rolled his eyes. "We're dropping the assault and battery charges."

The Patrol Cop indignantly brushed the sliver of paper off his shoulder. I was tempted to make a joke about violating the city's stringent littering laws, but the watch commander gave me a slight shake of the head. Had my reputation preceded me? The Patrol Cop gave his superior a dirty look and skulked off to harass another honest citizen of the City of Beverly Hills.[14]

"I want to see my client," I said. "I'm an attorney."

"And who's your client?" the Watch Commander asked.

"Barbara Spangler Lindburg," I replied with uncharacteristic pride. I was a humble man, which some might've called a liability for an aspiring entertainment lawyer.

"You're Babbling Babs's attorney?" the Watch Commander asked. "Get out of town."

"I am, and I must say I resent your description of Mrs. Lindburg."

"Ah," he said. "You obviously haven't met your own client."

"What's she in for?"

"Violations of Penal Code section 487(d)(1) or Vehicle Code section 10851."

Inexperienced lawyers think they're supposed to know everything, so I tried to act like I understood what he was talking about.

He gave me a disdainful eyeroll and sighed impatiently. "The Penal Code violation is for grand theft auto, the Vehicle Code violation is for joyriding."

"I want to see my client."

"You forget. You're under arrest yourself." He scratched his bald pate with such panache that for a moment I wondered whether he'd lost out to Telly Savalas for the lead role in *Kojak*.

"I insist on seeing my client!"

"Oh, you'll see her all right."

He guided me through a heavy security door, led me to a holding cell, and deprived me of my freedom.[15] None of this bothered me, because in the cell across the corridor stood Babs Spangler herself, wearing tight spandex workout pants and a leopard-print blouse,[16] and standing still as a petrified statue. With her back to me. Still, I knew from the taut neck skin that seemed about to strangle its owner that I was looking at Spangler—cosmetic surgery, you know.[17]

"Miss Spangler!" I said sotto voce. "Babs!"

My new best client didn't respond.

"Mrs. Lindburg!"

She whirled on her heels, regarded me for a half-second with beautiful hazel eyes sweltering with insult, and shouted, "If you don't leave me the fuck alone, I'm going to call the warden!"

"*Savage Cellmates*," I replied. "I loved that movie. And especially your portrayal of…….Gisela." I told you I did my research.

Babs Spangler melted at my words, and I realized then and there that if you want to be a successful entertainment lawyer, you have to learn how to kiss ass. Before that, I'd believed that the rich and powerful didn't respect brown-nosing, but of course they do—it was *invented* for them. No one kisses the asses of the poor and weak, which maybe we should, because the poor and weak eventually rise up and kick ass.

"You saw that picture?" she asked, forcing a smile through the cosmetic surgery, which made it appear as if she'd just visited a credit dentist who'd double-dosed the Novocain.

"I did. And you were wonderful."

She frowned as best she could. "I only had the one line."

"Sure, but it was groundbreaking."[18]

I thought she would smile again, but the frown persisted. "Who the fuck are you?"

It hit me then that there are nuances to brown-nosing—the rich and powerful only like *subtle* ass kissers. I told her my name. "I'm your lawyer."

"Marvin Sussman is our lawyer." She put her hands on her hips and leaned forward aggressively. "Although he won't be if I'm not out of here in the next fifteen minutes. I'll make sure my husband shit-cans his ass."

"I'm Marvin's associate," I said, trying to sound confident but in fact sounding apologetic. "I'm here to get you out."

She regarded me as if I were a lab rat who'd failed a maze test.

"I'm in jail because of you." I told her the story. I wasn't certain, but I sensed that my disrespect to the Patrol Cop made me rise in her estimation.

"Tell me what happened," I said.

The ethical and evidentiary rules inviolate prevent me from disclosing exactly what Spangler told me, even though she passed away years ago. Like gossip and innuendo, the attorney-client privilege survives death. To summarize what I *can* say, the studio had just finished principal photography on what turned out to be a blockbuster, action-packed, dystopian thriller. The producers made an early product-placement deal with Maserati, the make of the car that the hero drove in the picture.[19] Once principal photography ended, the studio had no use for the car. So, they offered it to Babs Spangler, who'd always wanted a Maserati—then only available for retail in Europe. Like any rational potential buyer of a used car, she wanted to test drive it first. The problem was that she tried to make every traffic light on Santa Monica Boulevard from Rexford Drive to Wilshire Boulevard without stopping—a crowded strip of roadway where there's a traffic light on every block. When a patrol officer stopped her in front of the Beverly Hilton for running two red lights, crossing into the oncoming lane, and speeding, she told them—and these are her words—to "fuck off, don't they know who the hell she is and who her husband is." The cops ran a check of her license plate—which bore the unfortunately personalized *Outlaw1*—and found no record of it. Apparently, the studio had left the dummy plates for the movie on the car. In the moments that followed, my client didn't go gentle into that good jail.

"Did you tell the police about the dummy studio plates?" I asked.

She crossed her arms in unrighteous indignation. "I don't have to explain myself to anybody."

"But..."

She crossed her arms tighter, and I had the sense that she was mentally wrapping them around my neck. "Don't worry," I said. "I'll explain the situation about the dummy studio plates, and you'll be out in no time. They can't incarcerate you for running a red light or speeding."

"*Two* red lights," she said proudly. "And you better get me out of here in the next twelve minutes, or your law firm is fired."

I called for a jailer—in a civil tone the first two times and in a not-so-civil tone the third. And who should respond but the Patrol Cop.

"I need to talk to the Watch Commander about my client," I said.

"He's off his shift."

"Then I need to talk to the officer who's taken his place."

I'd say he puffed out his chest, but his chest was so barrel-ish to begin with that he didn't need to do so to make his point. "That would be me."

I envisioned myself spending the next few months in the Beverly Hills Police Department lockup.  But my own freedom was the least of my concerns. "Look, let me tell you what happened with Miss Spangler, and I'm sure you'll release her. She was—"

"You're a jail inmate, not a lawyer."

"If you'd just listen, I wanted to tell you that my client's car—"

He put his hands over his ears like some kind of Muscle Beach five-year-old.

I took a deep breath. "Okay. If I'm an inmate, I want my one phone call."

He pulled something out of his pockets, and when I realized it was a roll of quarters, I thought he was going to use it in his fist to beat me senseless, but he placed the money in my hands and said, "This is Beverly Hills. We can afford more than just one call. The pay phone is over there. Go to town."

* * *

My next brainstorm proved career-changing. It took only one quarter to call my colleague Nathalie Kitcheon, the exuberant one. Marvin Sussman compared her to a bunny—not a Playboy Bunny (though a definite possibility in the Sexist Seventies), but a literal bunny that hopped. Indeed, Nathalie Kitcheon—a physical education major in college—was always so cheerful that she did appear to bunny hop down the law firm's venerable corridors. She smiled when they failed to give her a well-deserved bonus after she'd completed her first year at the firm.  She smiled when they assigned her to a case involving turn-of-the-century insurance policies and asbestos pollution; she downright giggled when she told the story of how, at one of

75

the factories that used asbestos, she reviewed documents in a warehouse full of rats, which she thought were kind of cute. Nathalie and I had bonded because we both occupied the lower rungs of the associate ladder.

"Nathalie Kitcheon," she bubbled after one ring.

"Hey, it's me. I need your help. I'm in the Beverly Hills Jail."

"Oh, that's awful," she giggled. "What can I do?"

I explained the situation. When she stopped laughing, she repeated, "What can I do?"

"Come down and get me out, and then I can speak on behalf of Babs Spangler and get *her* out."

"You got it. I'm just a hop, skip, and a jump away."

Twenty minutes later, the Patrol Cop returned to the lock-ups, his set of keys at the ready. I thought of giving a fist pump, but this was the 1970s, before the fist pump enjoyed broad popularity, and I didn't want the Patrol Cop to take my gesture the wrong way.

"All cleared up," he said in a frighteningly amiable voice as he inserted the key in the lock—of the cell adjacent to mine.

* * *

I languished in jail another twenty-five hours, winning release only after Donnie, an acquaintance from law school and lawyer in the L.A. City Attorney's Office, used his contact in the Beverly Hills City Attorney's office to get the charges against me dropped.

"Thank you," a bedraggled me said to Donnie when I was out of the station and back on the street.

"You owe me," he said.

I searched for any sign that this statement was friendly banter, but found none. I reached into my pocket. "I have some quarters left over from the money that the cops gave me for my phone call. You were my fifth call, so there's probably $2.50 left."

"That's a start," he said, grabbing the quarters.

* * *

Nathalie Kitcheon retired last year after the *Hollywood Reporter*—for the thirty-first consecutive time—named her one of the top five entertainment-law powerbrokers in the country. Upon her retirement, Babs and Charles Lindburg III's son, Lucky, Jr. [20]—the CEO of the largest media conglomerate in America—told a quaint story about how Nathalie first started representing his parents after a funny incident where his mother had been arrested for driving a car that appeared in a picture, and the studio had forgotten to replace the mocked-up license plates. As a retirement gift, he presented Nathalie with the very Maserati that had appeared in the picture.

"In appreciation for the years of loyalty to my parents, who relied on your wise counsel just as I have—just as so many in this wonderful business we call 'show' have."

Nathalie hopped to the dais, in an exuberant voice thanked Lucky, Jr., and added that the Maserati was the perfect addition to her collection of classic sports cars, accumulated over the years while taking five percent of the vast sums that her A-list producer, director, writer, and actor clients had earned in their careers.

Or so I read in the trades. I wasn't invited to the gala. In fact, I haven't spoken with Nathalie Kitcheon since that call so many decades ago, asking her to spring me from the hoosegow.

When I went into work the following morning after my arrest and incarceration, Marvin Sussman immediately summoned me to his office.

"Your services are no longer necessary," he said.

"I'm fired?"

"We don't fire people at our firm. Sometimes their services simply become unnecessary. To wit, yours."

"Why? I just—"

"Moral turpitude."

"The charge for assaulting a police officer? That was—"

He waved a dismissive hand. "Not that. The jaywalking. We don't do that in Beverly Hills. I'm a resident, you know."

"I do know. I've heard about your backyard tennis court."

"Do you play?"

"I do," I said. "I was number four singles on our high school varsity team."

"We could use a fourth in doubles. A pity that your services are no longer necessary. Moral turpitude."

"Seriously. For jaywalking."

"That and losing the Lindburgs and their studio as clients. That's a major blow to net profits per partner, you know. An existential threat. Existential."

"How can that be, Marvin? I arranged for Babs Spangler to get released from jail. I called Nathalie Kitcheon."

"Who's Kitcheon?"

"You know, the blond associate who works on the asbestos insurance cases?"

"The hoppy girl. Why didn't you say so? Lindburg and Spangler think the hoppy girl got Babs released from jail. The hoppy girl gave notice yesterday, and she now has Spangler and Lindburg and his whole goddamn studio on retainer. She accomplished it in the space of a day. I offered to make her a partner, even to put her name on the door, but she told me to take a hike. Smiled when she said it, though, and quite a winning smile at that." He raised his eyes to the ceiling and gave a whistle in admiration. "I knew that girl had charisma and presence."[21]

So, I took my services elsewhere, eventually hanging my own shingle as a solo practitioner in the Heart of Screenland. You never know where expertise will come from. Let's just say that I managed to put my kids through college with minimal help from student loans by specializing in dog-bite cases, particularly those involving injuries to a part of the anatomy that lies south of the scalp and opposite the pelvic region. I finally got used to my office in the strip mall, especially after the Mexican restaurant took over from the sushi bar, and the aroma from the dumpster became less aromatic.

That's not to say that I haven't had some entertainment-industry cases. I defended a producer of a legal-thriller/zombie/straight-to-video picture in a lawsuit against his neighbor when the producer's retaining wall failed during the floods of 1992. I handled a personal injury case for the sister of a famous actor after she'd been rear-ended in a crosswalk in Santa Monica Canyon.[22]

I have asked Nathalie to lunch many times over the years for old times' sake. I hold no grudges. To become a successful entertainment lawyer, you do what have to do, even if it means stepping on the heads of your friends. In response to my invitations, she ghosted me, and good for her, because forgetting those who knew you before you became rich and powerful is essential to a successful career as an entertainment lawyer.

Sometimes I envy her lifelong accomplishments, the adulation, the vast wealth, the car collection. All of which she accumulated while basking in the reflected light of the truly creative luminaries she represented. In those moments, I remind myself of a case I handled pro bono for a civil liberties association, where I convinced a trial judge and an appellate court that the cops have no right to hold arrestees in jail longer than twenty-four hours without a hearing in front of a judge. True, the result is but a small pinpoint of light in the star-speckled sky of jurisprudence, but at least I generated the pinpoint all on my own.

## FOOTNOTES

[1] By Hollywood, I mean Culver City, California, where the underrated Desi Arnaz invented television syndication; where actors playing the Munchkins mercilessly harassed and tormented Judy Garland during the filming of *The Wizard of Oz* at nearby Metro-Goldwyn-Mayer; where Sony Pictures and Amazon creative have gentrified a once working-class neighborhood.

[2] Over his illustrious career, Marx retained several entertainment lawyers, one of whom was ever so briefly one of my mentors.

[3] (Emphasis added.)

[4] Because these events occurred in the less enlightened 1970s, I use the dated, sexist honorifics even though the term "Ms." was beginning to gain traction.

[5] The dog had received all necessary vaccinations, and Mrs. Lipschmann

didn't need stitches. I had to rely on the theory of severe infliction of emotional distress in pressing her claim with the predatory insurance company—more predatory than the puppy, which arguably had only "playfully nipped," as the adjuster claimed.

[6] No relation to aviator Charles Lindbergh, which is not to say that studio-mogul Lindburg didn't use the striking similarity in names to his advantage—the fact that studio-mogul Lindburg's fear of flying was an open secret in the industry to the contrary notwithstanding. He also suffered from violent seasickness. No transatlantic flights to the Cannes film festival for studio-mogul Lindy.

[7] In contrast, my desk accommodated so many treatises, case books, yellow legal pads, pleadings, pens, pencils, office memos, legal briefs, client documents, and souvenir baseballs and bobbleheads that I hadn't seen its Formica surface for two years.

[8] D-level actors worked full time as bartenders. F-level actors bussed tables.

[9] Law schools were notoriously derelict in teaching these important skills.

[10] As actors, not security detail.

[11] Much later, I learned that the cop had received solid reviews from the *Beverly Hills Courier*, the city's local throwaway. The *L.A. Free Press* panned his "ham-ish" performance.

[12] To this day, I believe the handcuffs were unnecessary.

[13] I drew no inference about what the watch commander did during his summers.

[14] Technically, I wasn't myself a Beverly Hills resident. I lived in an apartment building adjacent to an alley on the corner of Pico and Sepulveda.

[15] U.S. Constitution, Fifth and Fourteenth Amendments.

[16] As for the tight slacks in public, Babs Spangler broke ground in 1970s Beverly Hills fashion.

[17] This was the late seventies, and cosmetic surgery wasn't what it is today.

[18] As to this statement, I wasn't exaggerating. The line received significant

publicity from many quarters of the media and government for being one of the first uses of the f-word in a mainstream film.

[19] I wish I could say "heroine," but in the 1970s the guys, never the woman, drove the cool cars. You didn't see Jacqueline Bisset drive the Mustang in the famous car chase in the movie *Bullitt*.  No, that was Steve McQueen. What I wouldn't have given back then to represent one of those actors.  Hell, I would've settled for the stunt double.

[20] Lucky, Jr. is his legal name.

[21] I didn't feel it was a propitious time to tell Sussman that "charisma" and "presence" were redundant. In hindsight, I wish I had.

[22] Rear-ended by an automobile, not a canine, in this particular case. It was nice to step out of my comfort zone.

# Killer in the Woods

by Adam Meyer

**KILLER IN THE WOODS**
SEASON 1/EPISODE 10

Written by Lucas Noyes

COLD OPEN

EXT. WOODS - DAY

HOLLY MCGUINN—a fresh-faced teenager—runs frantically through the woods, breathing heavily, leaves tangled in her blond hair. She glances behind her, sees nothing, keeps going.

NARRATOR V.O.
Eighteen-year-old Holly McGuinn had it all.
She was an honors student, class president and a beauty queen.
Everyone who knew her loved her.

CLOSEUP DIRTY BOOTS smashing the dirt, hurrying through the woods in pursuit of HOLLY.

NARRATOR V.O.

Well, almost everyone.

Holly stumbles on a rock and goes down. She scrambles to her knees, tries to get up, but someone grabs her by the hair. Flings her back to the ground.

TIGHT ON HOLLY'S EYES as she looks up in terror.

A HAND swings a rock at her.

HOLLY'S MOUTH opens in a scream.

CUT TO:

*KILLER IN THE WOODS* OPENING SEQUENCE/THEME MUSIC

* * *

Lucas parked at the end of the long driveway. Although Kristen McGuinn had tried to keep a low profile, he had no trouble finding her. She had stayed in the same house where Holly had grown up and her address was in all the old police reports.

The clapboard walls had peeling paint and a porch that sagged off to the side, a worn sedan slumbering beside it. Not very photogenic. That didn't matter, though. For the reenactment, they would use a stand-in for this house back in L.A.

Lucas took the uneven concrete path to the front door and looked back across the road. A dense wall of woods rose against the gray sky. Ten years ago, Holly McGuinn would've headed through there on her way to school. Later that day, as the sun was going down, she'd started out on the return trip but had never made it home

When Lucas pressed the doorbell, it didn't make a sound.

He pressed it again.

After a few seconds, the door opened.

A woman peered out. She looked nothing like the pretty thirty-something woman he'd seen in old news clips. Her hair had gone from blond to white and lay thinly across her scalp. She studied him with the skittishness of a wounded dog.

"Can I help you?" she asked, eyes narrowing. "Do I know you?"

Lucas answered the second question first. "We spoke on the phone a few times, and I sent you an email saying I'd stop by today. My name is Lucas Noyes. I'm the creator and executive producer of a true-crime series that's doing a story about your daughter's case."

He deliberately didn't mention the name of the show, *Killer in the Woods*, or the third-rate streamer where it would air. He also didn't tell her that he had already written a reenactment script about the last days of her daughter's life and her death.

Kristen McGuinn shook her head. "Like I told you before, I'm not interested."

"And I respect your decision. But I wanted to see if we could sit down and talk, just for a few minutes."

"Please, go away."

Her voice was soft, barely any force behind it. But her eyes seemed to plead.

Over the years, Holly McGuinn's story had been told on true-crime shows more than two dozen times, everywhere from *Dateline* to *Your Worst Nightmare*. Back in the day, her murder had even earned a two-page spread in *People* magazine. Holly's biography—president of her senior class, off to Virginia Tech that fall, beloved by classmates—had made for a good story, and the photos of her wearing a swimsuit as the first runner-up of the Miss Amherst County beauty pageant hadn't hurt, either.

The streamer wanted to do Holly McGuinn's case again for *Killer in the Woods,* but they needed something "fresh" before they'd greenlight it. That was why Lucas had flown to Virginia a day early for tomorrow's shoot in Richmond—for another episode, about a teenage boy who'd murdered his parents—and driven three hours out of his way here to Heflin tonight. He was hoping to please his bosses and find something their online ads could tout as "exclusive."

The prospects were slim. All the cops on the case had been interviewed *ad nauseam*, the prosecutors too. The parents of Perry Schindler, Holly's killer, had both died a few years after their son's conviction. Holly's best friend, a girl named Anna Philips, had moved away years ago and gone into hiding. A handful of Holly's classmates had been willing to talk, but by now they'd told the same stories again and again.

That left only one real get in the case, which was Holly's mom, Kristen.

"This won't take more than a few minutes," Lucas said. He kept his voice low to match hers. A strategy he'd learned years ago for trying to connect with the families of crime victims. "I've come a long way and—"

"This isn't a good time."

He looked past Kristen at the framed photographs on the wall. Sun-bleached images of Holly as a little girl, leaning forward on her tricycle, and then about twelve, mortarboard hat balanced on her blond hair for middle school graduation. Another shot of her as a teenager, wearing a long black sweater, smiling at the camera as if she could see right through it. No high school graduation photo. Holly had been killed a couple weeks before senior prom.

"Please, go," Kristen said. But she didn't close the door.

Faintly, he heard what sounded like a kid's voice in the background. He frowned. Holly had been an only child, and so had her mother.

"You always told reporters you wouldn't talk about what happened until Perry Schindler was gone." He tried to meet Kristen's skittish gaze. "This is your chance."

Perry Schindler had been on death row for a decade, his attorneys bringing appeal after appeal to keep him alive. Last spring, just six months before he was finally scheduled to be put to death by lethal injection, he committed suicide. Hung himself with a bedsheet while the guards looked the other way.

"I changed my mind. I don't want to talk about this *ever*." Kristen glanced back at the wall of Holly photos. "Perry's gone and…I've made the choice to forgive him and move on."

"I know you never liked him. How come?"

All he knew was what he'd read over the years: that Kristen had told Holly to stay away from him, that she thought he was trouble, and had turned out to be more right than she could've imagined. In the final weeks of their senior years, with Holly thinking about breaking up with him, Perry had lashed out and killed her.

"What's it matter?" Kristen sighed heavily. "It was just some stupid teenage romance no one even remembers."

"But you do. Because if Holly hadn't dated Perry against your wishes, she'd probably still be alive. Right?"

Something flashed in Kristen's eyes. Anger, but also another emotion— hurt? Regret? Lucas couldn't pinpoint it. But he saw that he'd done the opposite of what he wanted, pushing Kristen away. He tried another tack.

"Some people in your situation have told me that it can be healing to talk to a stranger. After all these years, you might even find closure in it."

"I'm not looking for…."

Kristen trailed off as a little girl moved in, grabbing her leg.

She had dark hair and splotches of paint on the front of her T-shirt. "Aunt Kristen, who is it?"

"Hi there." Lucas smiled at the girl. She looked to be about the same age as his younger daughter. "You painting a picture?"

The girl said nothing. She looked up at Kristen, who moved in front of her.

"Don't come back here," Kristen said.

Faintly, from deeper in the house, Lucas heard the sound of a baby crying. Kristen glanced away and then back at Lucas, seeming more weary now than upset.

"What's done is done, and that's all I have to say."

He felt a slight breeze as the door crashed into the frame.

* * *

INT. HOLLY'S HOUSE - NIGHT

Holly lies sprawled on her bed, doing her homework. A TAPPING SOUND from outside.  She looks up, frowning.  Then another TAP. She sits up, nervous, and goes to the window. Pulls back the curtains.

ON THE WINDOW

PERRY SCHINDLER (18, dark-haired, good-looking in a rough way) peers in through the window, standing on a small outcropping of roof.

Holly looks both exasperated and exhilarated.

                    HOLLY
          What're you....

She yanks open the window to let him in.

                    PERRY
          So what're you doing?

                    HOLLY
          What's it look like? Homework.

                    PERRY
          Homework's boring. Besides, it's senior year.

He pulls her close, starts to kiss her.

                    HOLLY
          Yeah, but I gotta keep my grades up if I want to be valedictorian.

PERRY

Who cares about that?

HOLLY

I do....

She peels his hands off of her, picks up her textbook. Perry gives her a look as if to say, *Really?*

Holly sighs, sets the book aside. Perry smiles. He's won. Then, faintly, from off-camera:

KRISTEN (O.S.)

Holly? What's going on up there?

Holly looks at Perry, freaking out.

HOLLY
(whispers)

You gotta get out of here!

She gestures at the window. Perry starts to climb through

A knock at the door. Holly pulls the curtains on Perry.

KRISTEN MCGUINN (late-30s, pretty, blond, an older version of her daughter) opens the door to the room.

KRISTEN

How's the studying going?

HOLLY

Great.

KRISTEN

You know I found this really cute prom dress. I think you might like it.

HOLLY

Mom, I told you—I want to pick my own dress.

KRISTEN

Sure, of course. You're not still thinking of going with Perry, are you?

HOLLY

I like him.

KRISTEN

He's not right for you, Holly. And I don't want him coming around here anymore.

HOLLY

I told you, he won't. All right?

Kristen touches Holly's cheek.

KRISTEN

Don't stay up too late, okay?

Kristen heads out of the room, closes the door behind her. Satisfied that she's gone, Holly rushes to the open window. Looks out.

Perry is gone.

* * *

After leaving the McGuinn house, Lucas drove back into the nearby town of Heflin, Virginia. Not that there was much to see in the sparse downtown. He ran out of road on the main drag within minutes, and another half mile along he found the town's only motel.

Inside, the clerk slumped on a stool behind the counter, his attention divided between his phone and desktop computer. He took a few seconds to notice Lucas.

"Help you?"

The clerk wore a Nirvana T-shirt with a nametag pinned above the graphic image of a naked baby. The white letters spelled GRAYSON.

"I'd like to check in."

Grayson did a double-take when he saw Lucas's driver's license. "You're from California?"

"Los Angeles."

"Long way from home." Grayson studied the driver's license a moment. "What brings you here? Wait, don't tell me, Holly McGuinn. Am I right?"

Lucas sighed. "I'm the executive producer of a true-crime TV series, *Killer in the Woods.*"

"Yeah, I've seen that show. It's on Netflix, right?"

Lucas named the third-tier streamer where the show was going to air. Grayson's enthusiasm was undimmed.

"Wow, man, that's cool. A real-life TV producer. We used to get a lot of you guys, but it's been a minute, you know."

Lucas nodded.

"You doing a show on Holly?" Grayson asked, looking past Lucas. "Usually there's a whole crew."

"I'm just here for research. I was hoping to talk to Kristen McGuinn but…" He paused, thinking about how interconnected small towns like this could be. "Do you know her?"

"Not really. See her around town sometimes. She doesn't really talk to nobody."

Lucas nodded wearily and put his license away. "So, about my room…."

Grayson started tapping at the keyboard, only half-glancing at the screen.

"You know, I'd be happy to talk about Holly for you. I didn't know her too well, but I'm great on camera. Me and my friends make YouTube videos, we got like a couple hundred thousand subscribers, and we think we could really go Hollywood with it. Maybe you could take a look?"

Lucas had seen plenty of amateur junk, and this was likely more of the same. Besides, being a producer on a true-crime show like *Killer in the Woods* didn't give him the clout that Grayson thought it did. But he didn't want to say so.

"Sure, send me a link."

Lucas pushed his business card across the counter. It had his cell phone number and email. Grayson snatched it up.

"Thanks, man, that's awesome."

Grayson tapped the keys some more, printed a form, told Lucas where to sign.

"You know, Perry Schindler, that guy was so whack."

"Did you know him?"

"A little. He was older, but he'd play ball with me and my friends sometimes. Man, that guy could throw." Grayson mimed hurling a baseball. "I remember how shocked everybody was when they found out he was the killer."

Lucas knew the story well: for the first few days, detectives had looked at several suspects, including the high school janitor, until they found a cap with the initials PS scrawled inside the brim. It was hidden in some bushes in the woods, near where Holly's body was found. When traces of skin under Holly's fingernails matched Perry's DNA, he was arrested.

In his interrogation, he claimed he was innocent. Said his skin must've gotten under her nails when they had sex, which he claimed they had the night before. But he swore he didn't know how his baseball cap ended up in the woods.

Eighteen months later, he was on death row.

Lucas wondered what it must've been like, going from dating the most popular girl in school to being a convicted killer. But Perry didn't talk to the media much. In his last interview before he committed suicide, he'd said only, "I hope to find peace in the next life."

Now Grayson pointed at Lucas as if he'd had a great idea. "You know, maybe you want to talk to my big sister."

"Your sister?"

"Her name's Chelsea. She knows Kristen McGuinn. Used to babysit for Holly all the time. Kristen likes her a lot."

"Really?"

Now the wheels in Lucas's head were turning. If he got in good with the sister, and she had some sway with Kristen, then maybe….

"Chelsea works the evening shift over at the Sunnyside Diner. It's right in town, if you want to talk to her." Grayson held up Lucas's business card. "And I'll send you those videos later, okay? I think you're gonna like them."

After dropping his laptop and luggage at his room, Lucas followed Grayson's directions and drove over to the Sunnyside Diner on Main Street. As he entered, he felt a pang of homesickness. His girls would've liked this quaint little diner. He pulled out his phone, wondering what they were up to. Maybe he could FaceTime them. Then he realized it was only four p.m. back in LA. The girls would still be in daycare and Emily at the office.

"Can I help you?" a waitress asked. She looked to be about forty or so, her dark hair dyed black, a red mouth webbed with lines. "Oh, you're the TV producer. I'm Chelsea. Grayson texted me about you."

Chelsea brought him to a booth and handed him a menu. She leaned in conspiratorially. "He says you're doing a show about Holly."

"We're thinking about it." He put the menu aside. "Grayson said you used to babysit her."

"A few times. I wasn't the regular sitter or anything." She looked almost apologetic. "Grayson exaggerates sometimes."

"So you're not tight with Holly's mom?"

"Me and Kristen? No, I've barely talked to her the last few years. She kind of became a hermit after…well, after everything."

He thought about the little girl he'd met at Kristen's door. "Do you know if she does any babysitting herself?"

"Babysitting?" A cell phone buzzed in the pocket of Chelsea's apron. She ignored it. "Not that I know of. Like I said, she barely ever talks to anyone, and she doesn't come into town all that much either."

Lucas could see he was getting nowhere and changed his approach. "So what was Holly like as a kid?"

"She was sweet and smart, maybe a little spoiled. Of course, Kristen…she was a single mom and she could be kind of protective, you'd even say a little *over*protective. Left a list with like three different numbers to call when she went out, and told me exactly what time to put Holly to bed. Not that Holly listened…she always wanted to stay up late, and I'll be honest, I let her." Chelsea frowned. "Maybe that's why Kristen never asked me to babysit much."

Another buzz from Chelsea's cell phone. She glanced at it this time.

"You know, my dumb brother texted a whole bunch of people about how you're here…and now everybody wants to know when you're going to start shooting this movie."

"It's not a movie, it's a TV show."

Chelsea frowned, as if unsure what the difference was or why it mattered. "Grayson's really hoping maybe you can give him a part or something, or help get the word out about his YouTube show. He and his buddies, they do this stuff…it's pretty funny, you know."

Lucas didn't tell her that there were probably ten thousand twenty-something guys doing internet shows and hoping to get rich quick. In his experience, making TV was more of a middle-class gig, and often not even that.

"I'll check out his show," Lucas said.

"Excuse me?" A man across the room waved an empty plastic up. "Can I get some service here?"

"Hold on, Frank." Chelsea looked back at Lucas. "You know what you want to order? We got all-day breakfast, it's pretty good."

He ordered pancakes, eggs, and bacon, the full heart attack special as he liked to joke during family brunches at Mel's Drive-In. Chelsea's nylon skirt swished as she walked away. His phone pinged, and he picked it up.

A message from Emily.

HOW'D IT GO WITH THE GIRL'S MOTHER?

He hesitated, then typed.

SHE TOLD ME TO SCREW OFF.

Emily didn't reply right away. Within minutes, Chelsea brought over his heart-attack special, which looked surprisingly tasty. The eggs a bright yellow, the pancakes golden brown, the bacon crisp but not burnt. His phone pinged.

TOO BAD. YOU GOING TO DITCH THE STORY?

He took a bite of the bacon. It was even better than it looked.

PROBABLY. NETWORK CALL, NOT MINE.

He dug into the eggs, which melted in his mouth. He'd promised Emily he would stay on his diet, especially after his last blood test. When he wondered why his numbers were so high, even though he took medication, the doctor said, "That depends, is your job high-stress?"

Lucas had laughed. Was there anyone working in TV whose job wasn't?

He chewed on the bacon, feeling a pang of guilt when his phone pinged again, as if Emily could sense what he was eating.

When he picked up his cell, however, he saw the message wasn't from her. The sender was UNKNOWN. He studied the words on the screen.

WANT TO KNOW MORE ABOUT HOLLY?

Had the message come from Kristen McGuinn? She'd been pretty clear that she didn't want to talk. Maybe she'd changed her mind? But then why hadn't her number showed up?

He started to work his thumbs.

WHO IS THIS?

No reply.

He chewed absently on another piece of bacon. It tasted like ash. This was probably just a prank. Lucas's cell number had been on the card he left Grayson. Maybe the motel clerk and his friends were trying to get some material for a new episode of their YouTube show. Or else someone had heard about him being here in Heflin and gotten his number from Grayson to mess with him.

His phone pinged again.

MEET ME WHERE HOLLY'S BODY WAS FOUND — 9PM

Lucas stared at the screen.  Holly's body had been found in the woods between the high school and Holly's house. Images of crime scene photos flashed in his head.

Lucas's hands were sticky with sweat and syrup as he fumbled with his phone.

WHO ARE YOU???

He stared down until the reply came.

DON'T TELL ANYONE WE ARE MEETING OR ELSE!

This was a prank. Had to be. But he read the message again and pushed the plate away, most of his pancakes and half a slice of bacon untouched.

"Everything okay?" Chelsea asked, frowning.

It took him a moment to realize she was asking about the food.

"Great." He picked up his phone again but saw no new messages. "Can I get the check?"

* * *

EXT. HIGH SCHOOL BLEACHERS - DAY

Holly sits on the highest level of the bleachers with ANNA PHILIPS (17), her best friend. She stares off into the distant woods.

HOLLY

I just don't know…my Mom really wants me to break up with Perry.

ANNA

Since when do you do everything your mom wants?

HOLLY

I don't, it's just…

Holly looks away.

ANNA

You're thinking about breaking up with him anyway, aren't you?


HOLLY

I like him. But…I'm going away to college in the fall. He's staying here. It's not going to last anyway.


ANNA

So? You're just having fun until then. Right? What's the big deal?


Holly stares off into the distance, looking pensive. Anna watches her closely, looking like she's about to say more when—


PERRY

Hey, what's up?


Perry moves in, beaming at Holly. He barely seems to notice Anna.


PERRY

You want to hang out later?


HOLLY
(glancing at Anna)
Can't. I got to stay late, we've got a yearbook committee meeting. Then I've gotta study… Mr. Leonard is giving us a science test tomorrow.


He plops down on the bleacher in the slight gap between the girls. Anna slides out of the way. Holly glances at her watch, gets up.


HOLLY

Look, I gotta run. See you guys.

Holly heads off, running a hand through her long blond hair. Perry stares after her longingly.

* * *

Just after seven-thirty, Lucas left the diner and headed for the high school.

He considered telling someone that he was going out there to meet a stranger about the Holly McGuinn case, but he didn't. Whoever had texted him had warned him not to. Then again, how would they know?

Besides, what did he have to worry about?

Holly's killer had died in prison two months ago. The person who'd invited him out here was no murderer, just someone who liked a little drama. Maybe they had watched too many true-crime shows, the kind he himself had written.

If he was smart, he would've ignored the text and gone back to his motel room. But the streamer really wanted an exclusive angle on Holly's story, and if he got it…well, the chances of a *Killer in the Woods* season two would go way up. Maybe he'd even get a decent raise. That was money he and Emily could put toward house repairs and the girls' college funds and that trip to Hawaii they'd been talking about for years, just the two of them.

The spot where Holly had been killed was about half a mile from the high school.

He parked his rental in the lot and looked up at the shabby brick building. The long rows of windows glinting in the setting sun reminded him of a prison. Heading past the baseball field and a set of metal bleachers, Lucas angled toward the woods. He wondered what Holly had thought as she'd followed this same path on the last day of her life. Was she eager to get home and study? Worried about her impending breakup with Perry?

The sound of rustling carried from the woods ahead.

An animal, most likely.

He stopped and listened and waited, but all he heard now was the buzz of a car from the distant road. He kept going.

Into the woods.

Leaves crunched underfoot. Branches clacked on either side of him. He kept going, following a path through the brambles. He didn't know exactly where Holly had met her fate, but he had a general idea from the maps he'd seen and the crime scene photos.

He checked his phone and thought of calling Emily to tell her what was going on. But he had no signal.

Still ten minutes before his appointed meeting time.

He turned on the recorder app on his phone. Luckily, he didn't need a signal for that. The recording would go right into the phone's memory.

A branch cracked in the dark woods ahead. Lucas's skin prickled with fear.

He whirled.

A figure stepped from the shadows.

A woman.

For one surreal moment, he thought it was Holly. She had long hair framing a thin face, her eyes cast at the ground.

As she drew closer, he could see that she was older and wearier than Holly had been, purplish bags under her eyes, her dirty blond hair limp against her shoulders. Her loose black sweater hung loosely around her hips.

"You're Anna," he said.

Holly's best friend. He had seen interviews with her from the time of Holly's murder. She had been heavier then, face fuller, hair a washed-out brown color. She must've dyed it.

"How'd you know I was here in Heflin?" he asked. Was she on Grayson's group text chain? If so, why hadn't he mentioned it?

"You can't keep secrets in a town this small."

Lucas took a step toward her. She seemed to flinch. He stopped, not wanting to scare her off. Then again, maybe he was the one who ought to be scared.

"I tried to find you," he said. "No one seems to know where you went after you moved away."

She shrugged. "I got married and changed my name years ago. That made it harder to track me down, which was good. After I left Heflin, I didn't want to be found."

"But here you are."

Ignoring the question, she went on. "I took off about a year after high school graduation and thought I'd never come back. Too many bad memories. Of course, I never really wanted to leave, not like Holly. Always thought I'd stay forever. Marry a local guy, have a bunch of kids, join the PTA like my mother did. It didn't work out that way."

It rarely did, as Lucas knew.

"I thought Holly loved it here," he said.

"Holly? She hated this town. Always thought she was too good for it."

He frowned, realizing her description of Holly didn't align with the one he had in his head. Anna seemed to read his mind, or maybe just his face.

"Surprised? Well, you can't believe everything you read in the papers…or see on TV." Anna's smile didn't touch her eyes. "Holly wasn't the happy-go-lucky princess everyone made her out to be. She was nice, but she had…sharp edges, too."

"You two were close," he said, hoping to keep her talking. "When did you meet?

"Third grade. That's when we moved here. Holly was the first kid to talk to me on my first day of school. We had lunch together every day after that, and from then on, I just sort of followed her around. I mean, why not? She was way more popular than me, and as long as I was with her people didn't seem to mind having me around."

"You two were good friends," he said. It was almost a question, but not quite.

"Most of the time. I mean, for a while I wanted to be just like her, and I acted like her, dressed like her…." Holly hesitated. "Like I said, she could be prickly. Sometimes she'd turn on me, want to know why I was following her around like a pathetic little puppy. But then she'd say she was sorry, she didn't mean it, and things went back to normal."

"How did you get along with her boyfriend, Perry?"

"Perry and I were friends before they started dating; that's how Holly got to know him in the first place. He was a jock but not a mean one, and me and him used to hang out a lot." Her face darkened. "Before he and Holly got together, I mean."

"So you and Perry were…?"

"No" Anna pulled her long black sweater around her as if she felt a chill. "I wasn't pretty and popular like Holly. I knew I could never compete."

Lucas studied the long sweater. There was something familiar about it.

"How did you feel when she and Perry started dating?" he asked.

"How do you think I felt?" The bitterness in her voice was unmistakable. "He became obsessed with her, the way boys always did. I hardly saw him anymore, and when I did, all he wanted to talk about was her. My whole life, I'd been in her shadow, and there I was again."

"So you were hurt."

"I couldn't believe she took him from me," Anna said, one foot pawing at the dirt like a bull in an arena. "She could have any boy she wanted. Why'd she have to take mine?"

Lucas had a lump in his throat. He tried to clear it, but it felt like swallowing glass.

"What happened the night she died?" he asked.

Anna looked away. "It wasn't supposed to happen the way it did. But I wanted to talk to her about Perry, so I waited for her after school. And I followed her out here."

Lucas thought of the way Perry had looked in the courtroom footage of his trial. Haunted, his face gaunt, eyes so sunken they might go all the way into his skull. He'd always claimed he was innocent, right until the end.

"You wanted to talk to her about Perry," he said.

"I *did* talk to her. She'd been saying she was going to break up with him, and I begged her to do it before the prom. She didn't like him that much, anyway! But she said she couldn't, going to the prom without a date, how would *that* look? I told her any guy in our class would be thrilled to go with her, but no, she wanted Perry." Her voice got quieter. "Or maybe she just didn't want me to have him."

"What did you do then?"

He had to ask. It was the TV producer in him. He moved a step closer so that his voice recorder app would be sure to catch whatever she said next.

"She was standing right about there, where you are now. I didn't plan it, I just felt this rage moving through me, so strong I could barely see straight. And I picked up this rock and…"

Lucas could see it in his head, just like in the reenactment he'd scripted for *Killer in the Woods*. Only, instead of Perry, it was a teenage Anna who snatched the rock as Holly turned away. Then cut to Anna moving in with purpose, bringing the stone down against her scalp, hard, even as Holly whirled, stunned and disbelieving.

"You killed her." Lucas knew this was true, though he still couldn't quite believe it. "And then you framed Perry. How come? I thought you liked him."

"Turned out I liked the old Perry." She shook her head. "After Holly died, all he wanted to do was talk about her, how much he missed her. And then the cops started asking me questions, and I got scared and…well, I had a baseball cap Perry had left at my house a couple months before. I left it here in the woods. The cops did the rest."

Lucas took it all in. The attack. The double betrayal. The deception.

In his mind, he could see flashes of the story unfolding on screen. Maybe he could get Anna to go on camera, but even without that, he'd have something more than just another episode of *Killer in the Woods*. It could be a standalone special, for which he'd easily get ten times the usual budget, and maybe even a celebrity to do the voiceover.

"I'm sorry about what I did." Anna took another step toward him, her hand reaching into the pocket of her long black sweater. "But you can't tell anyone about this."

Anna pulled a gun from her pocket. It looked like a .38, but Lucas wasn't sure. The only guns he'd ever handled were props for the reenactments. She pointed it at the center of his chest.

"Come on, you didn't bring me all the way out here just to kill me."

His voice was tight and sounded far away.

"I came out her for closure." She aimed the gun at his chest. "You said it could be healing. And I think you might've been right."

His mind was racing. Closure. Had Kristen McGuinn told her what he'd said earlier? But that didn't make any sense. Everyone agreed that Kristen was a hermit, barely talked to anyone. But he took another look at the black sweater and realized where he'd seen it. In a photo of Holly on her mother's wall.

"I don't understand. You and Kristen McGuinn...?"

"We've become close the last few months, since I came back here." She glanced down at the gun and then at him. "My father had a stroke a few years ago and never really recovered. My mother died last spring. I don't have any other family except..."

She trailed off, but Lucas could fill in the rest. She had no other family except her kids, who Kristen had been babysitting earlier that day. But why had Anna come back to Heflin in the first place? Then again, it was obvious. To return to a place that felt like home.

"You don't have to do this," he said, nodding at the gun. "I won't tell anyone about this. I promise."

"Your promise doesn't mean anything."

His mouth felt dry. He wanted to assure her it did, but how could he? As a producer, he often made promises to interview subjects that he ultimately knew he couldn't or wouldn't keep. Anything to get them to go on camera.

"If you think killing me is going to make things better...."

"I don't want to hurt you," Anna said, taking a step toward him. "Now show me your cell phone."

"But why—"

"Just do it!"

He held out his cell phone, trying to swallow the huge lump in his throat. Anna took it and flung it down on the ground. Stomped on it until the glass and plastic shell shattered.

Then she aimed the gun at him again.

"I won't shoot you," she said, taking a step back. "I've...done enough. But I've got my kids to think about. I can't let this get out there."

She turned away and started to run. He took a couple of steps after her and stopped, all too aware of his racing heart, his jagged breathing, the slight thrum in his head. He had gotten a confession, just like the ones recorded by police that he sometimes used in the last act of the show. Only now he had nothing, and it was his word against hers.

He picked up one of the shattered pieces of his phone.

If Anna wouldn't admit what she'd done, he had no story.

He could feel it all slipping away. The special episode, the second season of the show, the extra money for house repairs and the college fund and that long-delayed trip to Hawaii.

Looking ahead through the dark woods, he thought: *Hold on.*

Maybe there was still a way to get this story after all.

* * *

INT. HOLLY'S HOUSE - NIGHT

A small group of people dressed all in black. Off to the side, Holly's friend Anna confides in Perry.

ANNA

I still can't believe she's gone.

PERRY

Me either.

ANNA

Do you think they'll ever catch the killer?

PERRY

I hope so.

Anna sees Holly's mother, Kristen, standing alone, distraught, clutching a glass of wine.

ANNA
Mrs. McGuinn, are you all right?

KRISTEN
I guess I don't know. Does that sound strange?

ANNA
Not to me.

Perry comes over, nods at Kristen.

PERRY
You know, I'm so sorry about all this, Mrs. McGuinn.

KRISTEN
Thanks.

Kristen looks away from him, fighting back her grief. Then she notices something.

THROUGH THE FRONT WINDOW

A police car pulls up.

KRISTEN
Is that the Sheriff?

Perry looks over, concerned. CLOSE ON Anna as she looks back out the window.

ANNA
Maybe they've finally figured out who killed Holly.

* * *

He was breathing heavily by the time he knocked on the front door of the McGuinn house. Kristen came to the door right away. He could see the photos of Holly through the doorway again. Big hair, big smile. They'd never be able to cast someone with a smile quite like that for the show, but he would try.

"What do you want?" she asked, acid in her voice. The house was silent this time.

"Did Anna call you?" he asked, still trying to catch his breath. "She must have, or you wouldn't have opened the door for me."

When Kristen said nothing, he knew he was right.

"She told me some things about the night Holly died...but I'm guessing you already know."

"What do you want?" she asked. She didn't sound angry anymore, just tired.

"I could go back to LA and pitch a show based on the true story about what happened to your daughter—how Anna killed her, and you let her get away with it." This was a bluff, of course, given all the legal hurdles. But after all his years in Hollywood, he knew better than to let the truth stand in the way of a good pitch. "But I don't think you want that. And I'd like to know why."

Kristen said nothing at first. But she didn't close the door.

"What do you want to know?" she asked.

"The truth."

She stepped back to let him in and closed the door behind him. The air smelled of lemon spray and baby powder. She circled around to the couch and sat. He took an armchair to the side, waiting for her to go on.

"I knew this day would come," she said. "From the minute Anna told me the truth."

"When was that?" he asked.

"A couple months ago," she said. "I always thought it was Perry."

"You didn't like him."

Kristen shook her head. "I didn't think he was good enough for Holly, that's all. He wasn't a bad kid. Even after the police told me he was the killer…I didn't really hate him. I mostly felt sorry for him."

"So all these years, even though he said he hadn't hurt Holly, Perry sat in prison."

"You think I don't feel awful about it?" She blinked, tears in her eyes. "But I'm not the one who put him there. If I had known…."

She let the thought trail off. Yes, she hadn't known, but someone else had. Anna.

"She let an innocent man go to prison," Lucas said. "It ruined his life. Like Holly, all his hopes and dreams were cut short before he even graduated high school."

Kristen studied the photos on the wall. "Anna used to hang out here all the time back when she and Holly were little. Sometimes she'd even stop by just to say hi, when Holly wasn't around. She didn't have much of a home life, and I was always happy to sit around and talk to her over a couple of cookies or a plate of spaghetti."

Lucas could picture it as though it were a scene he was going to write for *Killer in the Woods*. Kristen at the stove; Anna waiting at the kitchen table. "She left after Holly's murder," Lucas said.

"Yes, and we lost touch. I thought she was just so torn apart over what happened…like I said, I didn't know the truth."

Lucas studied her. Had she somehow suspected what Holly had done? He didn't know. And he didn't suppose it mattered, not anymore.

"A few months ago, Anna came back. She'd been married and divorced, had a couple of kids, needed someone to watch them while she worked. I said I'd do it." Kristen smiled. "They're the sweetest…" Her smile froze. "…of course, you saw them earlier."

Lucas nodded.

"Holly always wanted two kids," she said, looking at the photos again. "A boy and a girl. She said being an only child was too lonely sometimes."

Lucas had been an only child himself and had insisted to Emily that he wanted two kids. He started to mention this to Kristen but stopped himself.

Better to wait and listen.

"I'd been watching Anna's kids for a couple of months when Anna said we needed to talk. She told me everything."

Kristen stared at Lucas's feet. When he looked down, he saw a small pink shoe poking out.

"You told her you wouldn't go to the police. Why not?"

For a long moment, Kristen didn't answer. Then she said, "What happened between Anna and Holly…Anna made a mistake. Do you let a young woman spend the rest of her life paying for one mistake she made a long time ago? Or let her live?"

Lucas didn't have an answer.

"I'll never be a grandmother," she said at last. "This is the closest I'll ever get."

She stood and waited for him to do the same.

"That's all I have to say."

Lucas started for the front door, turning back to Kristen. Her face still looked pale, but there was a brightness in her eyes that hadn't been there before. It reminded him of the sparkle he'd seen in old photos of Holly.

"Good night, Mrs. McGuinn."

"Will I hear from you again?"

He shook his head. "No, I don't think so."

Heading down the front path for the second time that day, Lucas trailed along the side of the road, going the same way he had earlier, toward the motel. No way was he walking back through the woods to the high school parking lot to get his car.

He'd have to call the execs at the streamer and let them know the Holly McGuinn story hadn't worked out, and they'd have to find another crime to take its place. But that could wait until tomorrow. Tonight, he just wanted a good night's sleep. First, he'd get on his laptop and FaceTime with Emily and the girls.

He couldn't wait to see them.

* * *

EXT. CEMETERY - DAY

Kristen stands solemnly over a gravesite. She looks down at THE HEAD-STONE. It reads:

HOLLY MCGUINN, BELOVED DAUGHTER

Kristen sets a flower on the stone.

> NARRATOR V.O.
> Months after her daughter was murdered, as Kristen McGuinn waited for her killer's trial to begin,she searched desperately for a way forward. And she prayed that justice would be done and that she could find some peace at last.

Kristen turns from the grave and sees Holly's friend, Anna.  She crosses to Anna and puts an arm around her. Together, they walk into the bright sunlight.

# Confessions of a Background Artist

by Stacy Woodson

I settle into the chair. The shirt I'm wearing is scratchy. But I'm not in charge of Wardrobe. And I live with it. Just like I live with the choices I've made that brought me here.

"You really expect me to say this?" I hold up the script so the producer can see it. I think her name is Wendy. But as far as I'm concerned, she's just another Krystal.

"It's true, isn't it?"

"The tone isn't. I'm supposed to tell my story, not your version of it."

"It's for the teaser. Framing is everything."

*New Hollywood.*

Framing is how I ended up here—and a walkie I swung like a billy club.

I read the script again, still hate it. But don't push back. The Union Awards start soon, and I won't be late. Not this year.

I tell the producer I'm ready, look at the camera, and clear my throat.

"It started with a union voucher and three generations of resentment. My name is Elizabeth Wilson. In the nepo-verse, I am the nepo baby of background actors—an underrepresented, disrespected and yet necessary group in Hollywood. We aren't human props. We breathe life into a scene and create energy for actors. Few people in this industry are willing to dim their lights so others can shine. For three generations, my family has made a living juggling one to two-day gigs in the name of motion pictures.

"This is my story."

* * *

## Six Months Earlier

I cut the hospital band from my grandfather's wrist and ease him into the recliner in the family room.

"I think I should stay, Pops."

"And do what? Watch me sleep. Don't be ridiculous. You don't turn down jobs, Lizzie. Not in this business. Especially this job."

Exhausted from the late-night trip to the emergency room, I blow out a breath and can't muster the energy to argue with him again.

"Call Martin if you need me, okay?" I make sure he sees the cell phone on the table next to him. Then, I grab a bottle of water, the remote, and put those next to him, too.

I turn to leave when he grabs my hand.

"Bring it to me, would you?" He nods toward the fireplace at the photographs along the mantel, images from Old Hollywood, an era when making great films was the priority, an era when people gave more to the industry than they took from it.

I know the one he wants and hand him the three-picture frame.

He smiles—not at me—at the photographs.

Pops with his union card. My dad, the day his card arrived in the mail. And a placeholder for me. Inside the empty frame, where a photograph should be, Pops wrote: *Coming Soon.*

"Three generations, Lizzie. It's something, isn't it? I'm glad I'll be here to see it."

"Me too, Pops." I swallow hard.

I go to my bedroom, change my clothes, grab my bag. Then, check on Pops before I leave for the lot. He's asleep in the recliner, the photographs still in his hand.

* * *

I am late—not because of traffic or the all-nighter with Pops. My call time changed. And I missed the midnight email. I missed the background shuttle, too. It pulls away just as my Maverick rattles into the Warren Brothers parking lot.

I watch the shuttle disappear. Wish I could follow it through the gate. But privately owned vehicles aren't allowed on the lot unless you're above-the-line talent. So, I'm forced to find a parking spot.

I send a text to Martin, grab my messenger bag, rush through the parking lot, past the visitor's center, and rows of golf carts. When I finally reach the security checkpoint, I can barely breathe, and sweat pools along my forehead. Fran sits in the guard booth at a makeshift desk, shuffling papers. The door is shut, but the sliding window is open.

She looks up, sees me, bangs her fist against a stapler.

"Early is on time in this business, Lizzie."

"I know," I tell her, the words coming out in two short bursts. I drag in a breath, exhale, inhale again while I fish out my driver's license and hand it to her—at least I try.

But she ignores me.

I groan.

More mumbling. More shuffling.

Another bang.

"You know how important the union is to your grandfather. Breaks for Background actors—a featured role, an opportunity to join the union—don't come around often."

Fran's right.

Background actors need three union vouchers to join. Vouchers are usually allocated for featured roles, roles filled by union members. On rare occasions, they're vacant, and non-union actors may fill them, a decision made by the casting agency or a production assistant.

After years of chasing jobs and a lot of luck, I'm one voucher away from making my grandfather's dream come true—and mine.

I hope.

"I can still make my call time if I hurry." I hold out my license again, wave it this time. "Please, Frannie."

"Don't Frannie me." She eyes me over her readers—the same way she did when I got suspended from school for smacking Felix Pinkerton in the head with a lunch tray.

Fran and Pops met at a grief group after my parents died, when they both found themselves alone, raising two children. Pops with me. Fran with Martin. And they've helped each other raise the two of us ever since.

She keeps me in purgatory for another second or two before she finally yanks the license from my hand.

While Fran types on the computer, I glance at my watch, estimate the time to walk from the gate to the parade field, and send Martin another text.

"She's here, you know."

My stomach tightens. "When?"

"Rode through on that shuttle you missed. New Hollywood, they're going to be the death of us." Fran hands me my temp badge and a key. "Take one of the golf carts."

"What about Walter?"

"If Walter gets crabby, I'll buy him a case of beer. Now go before that woman gets another notch on her vlog."

* * *

I reach the parade field, park the cart, look for Holding. I walk past rows of trailers: writers, wardrobe, hair and makeup. And I know I'm close.

But I can't find a sign pointing me there.

Desperate, I look for a walkie-wielder. In this business, walkie-wielders have authority or access to someone who does. And I find one—a grumpy guy from props. He points me to a building across the street from the parade field.

Holding is a repurposed screening room with stadium seating, theater-style chairs, and worn red carpet. In front of the yellowing movie screen is the check-in table. Martin works behind it—cellphone, walkie, calls sheets, and a stack of union vouchers in front of him.

*She's* in front of him, too.

Krystal with a "K" Carrington. She's what industry old timers call New Hollywood—internet influencers, You-Tube-It personalities, reality TV stars—people who want to Kardashian their way to the top. And despite what her vlog, *Confessions of a Background Artist,* suggests, there's nothing "background" about her. All acrylic nails and highlights, she has no desire to blend into a scene. She wants to be the center of it. I didn't know who she was until I became content fodder for her recent three-part series, *How to Voucher Your Way to the Top.*

I rush down the stairs, but today is a cattle call. The theater is packed, and I don't get far.

*Come on, Martin.* I wave, hope he sees me.

He doesn't.

He's focused on *her.* "Number?"

"Oh, Martin, you know who I am," she gushes.

Thanks to the acoustics in the theater, I can hear their voices. Part of me wishes I couldn't because I know what comes next—the ask. It's how I lost my last voucher. After the twenty-four hours I've had, I'm not sure I can handle watching it happen again.

"You know this is a number-driven business," Martin tells her and sighs. "We're shooting a graduation scene, nearly two hundred extras. I don't have time to look for your name. When you're ready, let me know." His radio squawks, he adjusts the volume, calls for the next person in line.

But *she* doesn't move. She stays there, blocking the line, stilettos rooted to the floor, while she digs through a Gucci bag the size of a weekender.

I reach for my phone, fingers flying, and text Martin, again.

But the message doesn't send.

Turns out the theater is a dead zone for cell phones, and the text messages I sent Martin earlier weren't delivered either. I swear under my breath, look up again.

Martin is on his walkie.

She's still digging.

And I still have a chance.

I decide to jump the line.

But the theater is small, and the seats are filled. People, garment bags, duffels, backpacks all spill from the chairs, and there's no sliding by anyone. The shuttle must have made another run because people are behind me, too.

Desperate, I cup my mouth and yell, "Martin."

People look.

Not Martin.

The side door bangs open, a walkie-wielder appears, a senior production assistant, one I haven't met.

"Wardrobe is ready," he yells into the theater, holding the door, while people pushing rolling racks with caps and gowns slide past him. "Where we at, Martin?"

The production assistant walks over to the table, glances toward me and the line that runs to the top of the theater, and his eyes go wide. "Christ, Martin. Where's Alex? He's supposed to be helping you."

"10-2."

"Christ. How long?"

"I don't know, Spencer. Thirty minutes, maybe. I think he ate the sushi."

"Great. That makes three in the bathroom. It's going to be a long day. Give me half your call sheets." He pulls up a chair. "Numbers fifty through seventy-five form a line on me."

People shift.

The good news, I'm closer to the table. The bad news, Krystal shifts, too, right in front of Spencer.

"Good morning," she flashes a prom queen smile. "Krystal. With a K. Lucky number seven."

"Of course it is." Spencer smiles back at her. "You're checked in. Take a seat, and wardrobe will be with you shortly."

But Krystal doesn't take a seat.

She steps closer to the table and touches his arm. "I just wanted to check and see if there were any union roles for background still available?"

Spencer winks. "I'm sure we can find something."

He picks up the vouchers on the table, and that's when Martin finally sees me. "I told you to get here early, Lizzie."

* * *

Krystal is the Headmaster's Assistant—the featured background role that was supposed to be mine. She sits with a principal actor and background actors an assistant director used to fill seats on the stage. I'm stuck watching her hand out diplomas from the parade field, along with two hundred other fellow "graduates." Wide shots, closeups, drone—we stand, we sit, we stand some more. We do this for one scene. And we do this through the morning into early afternoon.

When we break for lunch, I'm exhausted and hot. Costumes collects our gowns. Craft services sets up a buffet lunch under tents with tables and chairs next to the parade field. Union members are called first to get in line.

I don't care.

My mind is on Pops. I want to call and check on him. But there's a no-phone rule for background on set, and I left mine in Holding.

Krystal didn't.

Her pink phone sticks out of the back pocket of her jeans. I see it when she walks past me to get in line for lunch. Hair and makeup did a good job softening her look for the scene we shot today, but could do nothing about her perfume, which I can smell several feet away.

I don't have the energy to eat or think about Krystal anymore. And I collapse in a chair in front of a sea of empty tables.

* * *

"Hey."

I blink. Martin stands in front of me. The tables behind him are nearly full. And I wonder how long I've slept with my eyes open.

"Brought you some coffee. You look like you need it." He puts it in front

115

of me. "Sorry about earlier. Once Spencer got involved—"

"I was late. It's not your fault."

"Are you okay?"

"Just tired."

He lingers. "You have that look. You were at the hospital again, weren't you?"

I stare.

"It's bad, isn't it?"

"Please don't tell Fran."

He unclips his walkie, pulls out a chair, and joins me at the table.

I tell him what the doctor said, how the tumor is progressing, how Pops made me promise not to tell anyone.

"When does he plan on telling Aunt Fran?" Martin asks.

"After the Union Awards."

"That's six months away, Lizzie."

"You know how much he loves our awards party. He doesn't want his health overshadowing it."

"Pizza and beer. The four of us staring at a flatscreen."

"You know it's more than that for Pops. He loves union members pick the winners, that each vote counts. That his vote matters." My voice turns gravely. "He's had this dream one day I'd join the union and vote with him, something he never got to do with my dad. I thought I'd make it. Then, Krystal happened. I hate disappointing him."

I flick a tear away.

Then, another.

Martin doesn't say anything. He just leans his shoulder against mine, the same way he did when we were kids after my parents died.

* * *

"Mind if I join you, Lizzie?" Bridgette stands next to me with her lunch.

A background newbie, Bridgette and I sat on the parade field together during the graduation scene, and she's been asking me questions ever since.

116

"Take my chair." Martin pushes to his feet, grabs his walkie, lingers near the table again. "Waiting is a mistake, Lizzie," he says before he walks away.

"What's a mistake?" Bridgette asks, sliding her tray onto the table.

"Waiting for the bathroom," I lie.

"Right?" She glances toward the portlets. "The line is awful. I went before food."

"Smart move for a newbie."

She rearranges her food—salad, apple, water—scoots closer to the table, and frowns at me. "Not eating?"

I hold up my coffee.

"I respect that." She grabs her fork, stabs her salad, leans forward to take a bite, and the tassel on her cap flops in front of her face. She pushes it aside and tries again with the same result. "This cap is driving me nuts. I'd take it off, but after what Hair and Makeup said—"

"It's not worth it." I pat my shellacked head, find a hairpin, fight the hairspray, manage to free it from my hair. "Lean toward me."

She leans, and I pin the tassel to her cap. Then, she takes a bite and grins. "Nice!"

"You do this enough; you pick up a few things."

"How long have you been doing this?"

"You know what? I'm not sure." I shrug. "It's the family business."

She returns to her salad. I finish my coffee. Krystal walks past us with an empty lunch tray, sees me, smirks.

"Perfume, much?" Bridgette wrinkles her nose. "What's up with her anyway?"

"New Hollywood." I tell her what it means, about Krystal, how she's chasing union vouchers, and how I was fodder for her drama-laden vlog.

Bridgette shakes her head. "I'm glad I don't want to be an actor."

"Why are you here?"

"Film student. Professor Middleton told me to apply. I'm glad he did. I've always loved movies. But never understood what went into making them. So many talented people, only a fraction we see on the screen. Just like apples."

I frown. "Apples?"

"Apples," she echoes the word. She grabs the apple on her tray and holds it in front of me. "You go to the grocery store. Buy an apple. You bring it home, wash it—maybe you cook with it. You don't think about the farmer who grew it, the workers who harvested and boxed it, the team of drivers who transported the apple to the store, or the grocer who shelved it. Dozens of people, different talents and vocations, make that apple happen, but the consumer never sees it. The consumer just sees the apple."

"Wow. I never thought about it that way."

"Farmer's daughter. I grew up in the Midwest." She smiles. "Take mine. You need to eat something."

* * *

It's dark when we wrap. It's even darker when I pull up to the security booth with the golf cart. Fran takes off her readers and lets them dangle from the chain. "Your eyes look like two piss-holes in the snow."

"Thanks, Fran."

"You know I see no point in sugarcoating things." She takes my badge. "How did it go?"

"Let's just say, Krystal has more content for her vlog."

"New Hollywood," she mumbles. "They're going to be the death of us."

I don't want to think about the union or vouchers or Krystal. All I want to do is go home, check on Pops. Then, climb into bed and pretend this day never happened.

"Thanks for the golf cart." I hand her the key, reach for my bag, swear under my breath.

"What did you forget?" Fran asks.

I sigh. "My bag. I left it in the theater. My phone and keys are with it. I need to go back."

"I'll take you."

"Really, Fran. I'm fine."

"Two piss-holes in the snow, remember? Don't bother arguing with me."

She grabs a walkie from the guard shack, a ring of keys, and slides the door closed. "Background shuttle made the last run a while ago. Door to the theater may be locked. You'll need my key. Now scoot." She waves her walkie at me.

I slide into the passenger seat.

"I hate this clown car." She drops her walkie into a cup holder in the cart with a huff and works her way behind the wheel, the cart shifting under her weight. "I'm not getting out of this cart unless you need me to unlock something, or Chuck Norris is on that lot signing autographs. You hear me?" She puts her hands on the steering wheel and catches her breath. "Ready?"

* * *

We are close to the theater when I smell her perfume. We are in front of the theater when I see the ring light on her cell phone. She stands on the sidewalk, back toward us, bathed in light.

"What the hell is she still doing here?" Fran asks.

"Vlogging."

"Not on my lot."

"Let it go, Fran. She's live. Interrupt her now, she'll love it. It will only increase her followers."

"You're telling me not to feed the animals."

"Something like that."

Fran leans back in the cart. "What do you think she's saying, anyway?"

I shrug. "Do you care?"

"Not really."

I leave the cart. My plan is to go to the theater, get my bag, and leave with Fran. But I don't get far. Because the truth is, I do care. And I stop when I hear her.

* * *

"Greetings, backgrounders from the lot. Another gig, another voucher for me. Can I get a high-five? A little tip, my fellow backgrounders, leave your personal shit at home. Okay? There was a girl crying at lunch today—same one I told you about last time. Tissue, please! And a little makeup. The bags under her eyes. Oh, my God. I managed to sneak-a-snap. Check out the show notes. You're welcome. Seriously, people, hair and makeup are good, but they're not miracle workers. You need to do your part."

Krystal is still talking when I reach for Fran's walkie.

She took my voucher. She took my dignity. She took Pops's dream.

But looking back now, I don't think this is the reason I reached for it—at least not the only one. Because when I walk toward her and pull back my hand, it's not her face I see. It's the takers who came before her.

The drunk driver who killed my parents.

The tumor that's killing my grandfather.

Felix Pinkerton and that stupid piece of chocolate cake.

And I was tired of feeling powerless.

"Let go, Lizzie." When I hear Fran's voice, I see Krystal on the ground, bleeding. When I feel Fran's hands on mine, I realize I'm holding the walkie. When Fran turns off the cell phone and I see the smirk on Krystal's face, I realize I just gave her the thing she's always wanted.

"Not sure I can buy enough beer to fix this, Lizzie."

* * *

Turns out Fran found beer—the kind Krystal liked.

Fran's been working security on the back lot for nearly forty years. Fran is part of Old Hollywood. She knows people. And she fixed it. Just like she fixed it with Felix Pinkerton's parents when I smacked him with that lunch tray.

Krystal agreed not to press charges if Fran arranged a meeting with a Warren Brother executive to pitch a reality TV show inspired by her vlog. Which they liked. And I had to agree to be interviewed for the show, the interview I'm suffering through now.

"Well?" The producer looks at me expectantly.

I blink. "I'm sorry. I missed the question."

"Did you think that night with Krystal on the lot would lead to something like this?"

"No," I lie.

"What do you think about the accusations that what happened between you and Krystal wasn't real, that it was scripted?"

I think about the teaser, the script Wendy made me read, and fight the urge to laugh. "I think people are going to believe what they want."

"And…cut," Wendy says. "Great job, Lizzie." She waves at a cluster of people standing next to pizza boxes and beer in our kitchen. "Makeup, before we move to the living room for the awards party, can we get some touch-up under her eyes? Lizzie, we are going to open with you holding the union picture, okay?"

I walk through the family room to the mantel to retrieve the three-picture frame. But it's not there. Pops still has it. He smiles at the photographs inside. Pops with his union card. My dad, the day his card arrived in the mail.

And a picture of me holding mine.

Turns out reality TV shows have union vouchers, and that night in the lot with Krystal gave us both what we needed.

"I'm sorry the awards party isn't what you planned, Pops."

"Are you kidding? The camera, the lights. It's even better, kiddo. I never thought I'd be on a set again. I'm glad I'm here to see it."

"Me too, Pops." He hands me the picture. And Wendy starts again.

"Lizzie, I want you sitting on the couch between Martin and Fran, is it? And I need a bowl of apples. I want them on the table in front of Lizzie. Hurry up, people, the awards are going to start."

"New Hollywood," Fran mutters, shaking her head. "They're going to be the death of us."

# What Ned Said

by Gary Phillips

"We had a great time then, didn't we?"

"We sure did." Alex Clayton creaked back and forth in the rocking chair. Seemingly floating in the air before him was a red button.

Ned "Never Late" Gaines whistled. "Still can't get over the size of that bass you reeled in. Sure was something," he enthused, staring off into the near distance. Over the years, the two, sometimes with a group, had gone on many fly-fishing excursions.

On the porch near the foot of Clayton's rocker was a half-empty bottle of beer. It was a brand Gaines had introduced him to almost twenty years ago. But next to his rocker was a mug of green tea. The cup was misshappen, a rescued mistake fired in a kiln and glazed.

The older Gaines turned his head to look at the younger Clayton. "You should start fishing again, Alex. It's been long enough."

Clayton was nonplussed. "How did you know I hadn't been fishing since you died? I hadn't mentioned it to—" He waved his hand but didn't continue.

"How long we know each other, kid? Like forever, right?"

"Like forever." Clayton was in his forties.

Gaines hunched a shoulder. "If it was reversed, I'd be the same way. Truly."

Clayton's eyes got wet. Gaines, the porch, and the residential street beyond shimmered, the images becoming pixelated and unglued. The red button remained solid. He wiped away the tears, and the depictions before him stabilized once again. "It wouldn't be the same without you, man."

Now it was Gaines who waved a hand. "Gotta move forward, Alex. It's fine to look back, to remember the good times, but you have a lot of living yet. There are more good times to be had."

"Maybe, sure," he said.

"No maybes to it. Work, home, eat…repeat, that ain't living, buddy. That there is just existing." A buzzer sounded.

"Already?" Clayton gripped the arms of the rocker, veins prominent on the backs of his hands.

"See you next time, Alex." Gaines stood and stuck out his hand.

Now also on his feet, Clayton reached for the hand, knowing he would feel nothing, but he still pumped his hand up and down as if gripping Gaines's.

"Remember what I say about going forward, getting on with things. 'Cause next time we'll talk about how I died. How it wasn't what it appeared to be."

"What?" Clayton said.

Gaines, the rocking chairs, all of it faded away. Clayton stood in the room lined with thousands of tiny white dots and removed the virtual goggles. A tech in a white lab coat entered. She was tall, her hair pulled back from an alert face.

"How was your session, Mr. Clayton?"

"It was…not sure I have the words."

The tech lightly touched his arm, misunderstanding what he was referring to. "The experience can be both unsettling yet comforting," she said.

"Did you hear what Ned said right before the end?"

With an empathetic look on her face, she answered. "Oh no, sir, our code of conduct prevents us from eavesdropping on or in any way recording these intimate conversations. It's simply not done. That's why the red button is always present, should you wish to cease the visit at any time for whatever reason."

"Right, of course," he said, a sheepish smile on his face. At the front desk, Clayton made a new appointment. "That's the earliest I can get?" he said when he was informed of the next available time.

"Sorry, but since our founder was on TV, we've been inundated. There's talk of opening another branch or at least expanding this one." The young man behind the desk smiled reassuringly. He had orange hair and a practiced manner to set customers at ease.

"Okay, fine," Clayton said curtly, trying not to sound too disappointed.

"See you soon," Orange Hair said.

Clayton walked out of the two-story building into bright sunshine. He'd parked his hybrid on the street at a meter a block or so away from Ethereal Essence. While the name suggested a mortuary, the company was among several in the now burgeoning business of grief tech. The more you were able to provide the generative AI, the better the responses from the simulations of a lost loved one.

Never Late Gaines wasn't a relative of Clayton's, not even an uncle through marriage. They had both been sound mixers and members of the same union local. Over time, they'd become close friends. There were plenty of text messages, phone videos of them goofing with each other, and numerous captures of them at picnics and ball games that Clayton had supplied Ethereal Essence to inform its generative AI. He'd been there for Never Late when his wife had died unexpectedly of an aneurysm. And when Clayton had a health scare involving cancer, the older man had his back, got him through the rough patch.

Today had been his first interaction with so-called grief tech. Clayton had few notions of what it would be like before he'd gone in. There were, naturally, testimonials on the Ethereal Essence site he'd watched and rewatched beforehand. He'd also viewed other videos and read several articles about people's experiences with grief tech. How some found the phrasings and mannerisms of ghostbots, sentiment originating in chips and operating systems, more beneficial than what was offered by human counselors.

Where, though, had this claim of "my death was not what it seemed" uttered by the cyber representation of his friend come from? None of what he'd sent to the programmers at the facility had suggested such. Was it a con, a come-on perpetrated by the business? A way to sucker you into buying more sessions as if there was a big, juicy secret the departed had to tell you?

He left Santa Monica, heading back to a shoot where he was dropping off a secondary mixing console. This shoot for the next few days was taking place at a practical in the West Adams area of Los Angeles. Driving along, Clayton recalled a streaming show he'd worked on a couple of years ago, *The Raven Files.*

The show had been set in the Gilded Age along the East Coast. Edgar Allan Poe and transplanted gunfighter Cherokee Bill, with Teddy Roosevelt as the head of a secretive intelligence agency, solved crimes of earthly and supernatural natures. A sub-plot of one of the episodes involved a grifter using the séance bit to bilk the rich and gullible. Was the computer-generated Gaines plying a variation of the spiritualist hustle?

On Clayton traveled, not sure what to make of all this. He was already itching to return to Ethereal Essence, so maybe he was already hooked. He arrived at the Wilfandel Club House and parked. It was a large home built more than a hundred years ago in the Italian Renaissance Revival style, and it was ideal for receptions and the like with its expanse of manicured grounds. Clayton shifted into work mode as he approached some of the tech crew preparing for the shoot.

"Els, first we're going to get this wild track done, then there's some pick-ups with Ricardo and Tess to get redone," said Wesley Smith, Director of Photography.

"No problem, Wes," sound mixer Elsworth McNally said. The two stood off to the side as the named actors and extras assembled on the lawn for the party scene. McNally went over to a few of those gathered to check the wireless body mics and coordinate with the other sound recordists handling boom mics.

"Right here I'm thinking, get a nice bounce off that low wall," McNally said to the boom operator as they determined where best to station him to record two of the principals later today. The boom operator was holding a modified shotgun mic. When McNally finished with him, he came over to greet Clayton. The two bumped fists.

"Thanks for bringing this, Alex," McNally said, picking up the padded case housing the back-up mixer.

"No worries. Just take care of my baby," he added, pointing at the case.

"For sure," McNally said, clapping him on the shoulder. Then as he turned to walk away, "Buy you a beer later at the hangout?"

"Not tonight, Els. Got some homework to do."

"Your loss, hot stuff."

"Okay, people, we're running behind on our delays, chop, chop," Smith said, clapping his hands, earning a round of good-natured groans from crew and actors.

Below the line guys like Clayton and McNally frequented several bars around town. As it wasn't too far from here, some of the crew on this production would be heading to the Blow Out on Vine.

After the shoot, Clayton went back to his apartment to review the press and his memory regarding the death of Ned Gaines. His best friend had been working on a low-budget psychological horror film, but, as always, had brought his A game to the job. More, as it turned out. Gaines had done the sound design, capturing and repurposing everything from saxophone riffs to real-life sounds into a haunting track, elevating every scene in the film.

"Not too shabby," Clayton had joked with his mentor. He'd come out to set and listened to samplings from the soundscape.

Smiling Gaines had said, "Yeah, I'm really jazzed with how it's turned out. This is my best damn work, Alex."

Two days later, Gaines died with his headphones on. In his head, Clayton recreated those last minutes from what he'd been told by those present. Ned'd been on set, sitting in a director's chair, fine-tuning a section of his moody soundscape. His favorite deformed cup was nearby. A broad smile was on his face as he made a tweak on his digital mixer, the board Clayton had dropped off. The machine had been modified over time by the two of them. Ned took a sip and closed his eyes as he listened through his headphones. But soon his chin was on his chest, mouth open. Cause of death was listed as a heart attack. The film was released, dedicated to Ned Gaines. It became a hit. Posthumously, he was nominated for an Oscar in the sound category and won.

Sitting at his kitchen table, Clayton looked from the printouts of articles about Gaines's demise and his open laptop to the Oscar statuette on his bookshelf. He'd given the teary acceptance speech at the ceremony. He wanted to install the Oscar at their union local, but it was determined he ought to safeguard the award. He started tearing up. Less than two weeks later, he was back at Ethereal Essence, where Gaines followed up on the promise he'd made to explain how his death wasn't what it seemed to be.

"You're shitting me," Clayton said to Gaines. This time they were in their fly-fishing gear standing in a stream, a waterfall in the near distance.

"Nope," Gaines replied, casting his line with the flick of his wrist coupled with a *tik* sound like he'd done in life. The action wasn't lost on Clayton. He was sure he hadn't told them here about this particular habit of his. "Ol' Els did me in. Poison it was. He learned about it on a murder-mystery shoot a while back."

"Why?"

"It is the green-eyed monster which doth mock the meat it feeds on."

"Jealousy?"

The digital simulacrum hunched a shoulder. "I'd beat him out for the soundscape gig. He heard what I was mixing together, and we both knew it was good…very good, to not humblebrag on my damn departed self."

"How do you know this, Ned? I mean, you didn't then, otherwise you wouldn't have drunk the tea he gave you that day."

More Shakespeare. "But, soft: behold. Lo where it comes again. I'll cross it, though it blast me. Stay, illusion. If thou hast any sound, or use a voice, speak to me."

"You're a ghost?"

"Am I not?"

"You're a construct of millions of pixels."

"Then how do I know you're going to have a date with Reese? Which, by the by, I'm happy you are. You need to get out of your self-imposed exile."

Reese Windsor was a former stuntwoman turned stunt coordinator. A handful of years ago, when Clayton had last seen her, she was married. Now she wasn't. But how did Ned know any of this? He hadn't used a dating site to connect with her. And as he recalled, they hadn't texted each other or talked over the phone since then. A computer couldn't have hacked their communications. They'd only talked at the Blow Out last week, and she was heading out of town the next day. Old-fashioned and romantic, they'd exchanged phone numbers written on cocktail napkins. They were scheduled to call each other when she was back.

So was this Ned Gaines more than just a computer construct?

Wanting to do right by his friend, he asked, "Can I find proof of what Els did?"

"I hope you can, buddy boy. Thereby, I can rest as justice will be done."

"I'm not sure what to do."

Ned Gaines smiled in that reassuring way of his. "Pretty sure Els held onto the stuff he used. It's got a long name, but what it does is paralyze muscle functioning, shutting down breathing, among other things. And this poison metabolizes in the body, making it harder to trace. Not that it would've shown up on the routine tox screen the M.E. did on my corpse."

"You figure he kept the bottle to use again?"

"Worked the first time, didn't it? He's number one on the show you're working on now, isn't he?" A pause then, "His pad in Burbank is probably where it's hid."

"Yeah?" Clayton said.

"When we'd been over there for cookouts, I remember there's a window to the bathroom off the kitchen. It's on the lee side of his house, looking out on a tall wooden fence."

"Sure, okay."

"He doesn't keep the window locked." The line spooling from Clayton's fishing rod twitched. He reeled in a bass on the hook. Ned watched it flapping about mightily, thinking about what came next.

* * *

As Ned had told him, the window wasn't locked. It was high up enough that

Clayton had to use the step ladder Ned had suggested bringing along. He removed the window screen using a blade screwdriver without damaging it. This afternoon, he knew Els was busy working on re-recordings.

Ned got inside, wearing gloves as any sensible burglar should. His search of the house produced nothing. But the design of this post-war of the last century abode had an inside door leading into the attached garage. In here was Els' workshop. Eventually removing a tray in a toolbox, he found an unmarked tincture of a clear liquid wrapped in a soft square of cloth.

He held it before his eyes, regarding the solution. Clayton couldn't very well send a sample to a lab to be identified. Too many questions could be raised. He hated to do what he was contemplating, but he had to confirm this was the poison.

At a park, he walked along, having put a dollop of the liquid on a piece of pumpernickel bread. Wearing gloves again, unsure if the poison could be absorbed through the skin, he let the bread drop by a park bench. He walked on, stopping a few yards away to look back. Three pigeons landed to peck at the dark bread, the morsel easily seen against the light gray cement pad the bench resided upon. One of the birds took a few wobbly steps after eating and keeled over. The other two took flight. One of them then nosedived into the park's lake, sinking below the surface. The last one landed on a tree limb and soon fell dead on the grass.

A cart vendor grilling oversized hot dogs amid sizzling onions and peppers saw the dying birds. He glared at the pigeon on its side near the bench. He shook his head, mumbling in disbelief.

Walking along, hands in his pockets, Clayton had the poison. But how could he make the authorities understand that Els used it to kill Ned? He'd obtained the vial illegally, so even if the matter reached a court, the poison was inadmissible. Els would go unpunished, getting work that should have gone to guys like Ned Gaines.

What the hell was he supposed to do now? He wasn't scheduled for another session until next week, as the grief tech enterprise was so popular. In his car, he sat and stared through the windshield, not turning the vehicle on. Unsure of how to proceed, he finally engaged the ignition and prepared to dive off.

"That was a tricky one," a familiar voice said over his car's speakers. It was a dupe of one of the CDs he made for Ethereal Essence. This was an interview with Gaines from the Tin Ear podcast. Its hosts worked in sound, and they had sound mixers, handling production and post-production, sound designers, boom operators, and the like on as guests. Clayton didn't recall having the CD with him in the car—let alone putting it in the deck—before he'd driven to the park. He let the interview play as he drove, happy to hear his deceased friend's voice. At one point, Gaines was describing a shoot where dialogue was recorded live over the sounds of animals at a zoo.

"Yeah," he was saying, "we tried several ways in rehearsal to mic the scene between the two principals, a man and woman. They had to be walking and talking and set to stop before this jungle enclosure with chimps. Who, for some dang reason, would react excitedly at the woman lead. But the director wanted to keep that in for symbolic reasons regarding her character."

"A massive headache in terms of syncing," one of the hosts lamented.

"Such is the business," Gaines said good-naturedly.

"Oh yes," the other host commiserated.

On they conversed. Then Gaines said, "Without even looking at the actors, I could hear the emotion in her voice when she said the line, 'There are times when you have to hold the guilty accountable.' Man, we'd nailed it."

Clayton replayed the line several times. He understood what to do next.

That first evening when he went to the Blow Out, McNally wasn't there. He came back two nights later, and McNally was around. On one wall of the place was a large, framed print from the '70s movie *The Conversation*. The image was of Gene Hackman as the character Harry Caul. He held a headphone speaker to one ear and a word balloon led from his mouth. "Shhh" was his visual line of dialogue.

The old RCA Victor logo of a cute dog sitting before an old-timey phonograph was the bar's logo. It was reproduced in pulsing green and purple neon. More than one of the neon signs was installed inside and outside the bar. Clayton and McNally stood before one of them, over the rack of liquor behind the curved bar top. Clayton had bought the other man several rounds of Jameson on the rocks.

"What?" McNally said, holding up a finger. He took out his phone, tapped on it, and adjusted something on the screen.

"Hearing aid?" Clayton said. "Hadn't noticed."

"Yeah, these modern versions are great," McNally declared. He turned his head, cocking it upward to give the other man a better look into his ear cavity. "It sits in there, and I can adjust for background din on the app."

"Huh." Clayton was still nursing his first beer. The brand Ned had turned him onto.

"Anyway, what were you saying?"

"I *know*."

"Know?"

He showed him the tincture. He returned the small bottle to his pocket and the sock around it. "I've already sent a sample to a lab to be identified," he lied.

"So what?"

"I have Ned's things, including that ugly cup of his. Hadn't been washed." It had been, thoroughly. "That went to the lab, too. I bet they find residue. And I bet when the cops dig into your connections, they'll find a cousin or some damn body with a medical supply hookup."

"Keep dreaming, Alex." Calmly, he finished his whiskey. "You've got nothing."

"In this age of podcasts, you know how many have led to cases being reopened, getting new sets of eyes looking into supposed normal deaths?" He had no idea, but McNally probably didn't either.

McNally stared at the bottles.

"Your hearing loss is progressive, isn't it?"

McNally side-eyed him.

His guess had been a desperate swing, but damned if he hadn't got a hit. "That's why the panic. You were royally pissed Ned had gotten the soundscape job over you. And looks like time isn't on your side. Eliminate your competition. Why you held onto the damn poison."

"You're grasping at needles in the haystack, kid."

"Could be." Clayton got off the stool. "We'll see." His goal had been to rattle McNally, and he'd accomplished that. Now, dammit, he probably was going to have to send the poison to the lab.

Outside the Blow Out, two younger women stood near the curb. "It's almost here," one said to the other as she regarded her phone's screen.

Her tatted and pierced friend nodded.

"Hey, wait a minute, Alex." McNally came up from behind, a hand on Clayton's arm.

Pulling away, he said, "Too late for that. Your ass is going to prison."

"I said, wait a minute, asshole." McNally lunged for him, striking his pocket with his fist, hoping to break the vial.

"Moved it from my pocket, numb nuts, just in case you tried some shit like this."

"You motherfucker." Jameson-flavored spittle erupted from his mouth. They tussled, grabbing and tearing at each other, grunting and swearing. They spilled into the roadway.

"Watch out," the tatted woman yelled.

The low-pitched whine of the electric vehicle went unheard, drowned out by their swearing and fighting. The driverless taxi screeched its brakes, but not before striking McNally. He rolled up onto the hood, cracking the windshield, then rolled off onto the street, lying unmoving on his stomach. People already had their phones out, videoing away. Clayton ran off.

When it was morning, looking haggard and unshaven, he walked up to the Ethereal Essence entrance. It was a little past ten, and he'd been moving about all night into the early morning. He'd come to cajole and bribe the staff to have another session with Ned Gaines right now. Get his advice on what to do. Tugging on the door, he was surprised it didn't give.

"The hell they're not open." He put his eyes close to the glass, hand over his forehead to see inside. No one was at the front desk. He stepped back and noticed the sign on the outer wall about the business being closed for renovations. Dejected and about to turn away, he heard a thump, then another from inside. He pounded on the glass door with the bottom of his fist. A man in plaster-spattered pants exited a hallway, scowling at Clayton.

Both gestured at each other. Upturning his palms, the worker came over and unlatched the door.

"Didn't you see the sign?" he began.

"I have to talk to Ned." He barreled past him.

"The computer wizards aren't here, man. You gotta leave and let us do our work."

"No," Clayton said like an obstinate child. The elevator doors dinged open behind him, and another worker stepped out, engrossed in some paperwork. He pulled him out of the way, and up he rode.

When the four police officers arrived, already on the lookout for Clayton after what had gone down last night, they found him upstairs leaning back in an ergonomic chair, headphones with a built-in mic on. A thin cable led from these to a large console with an array of blinking lights and incongruously, old-fashioned toggle switches. He was laughing and carrying on.

"Can't wait for us to take that trip to the Yellowstone River Basin in Montana. It's gonna be wonderful, Ned." He listened, grinning and nodding.

The cops hollered instructions, which he ignored. They yanked him out of the chair and proned him out. One of the cops put his ear to one of the cushioned speakers.

"It's just fuzz," he said, frowning.

Off they hauled Clayton, a beatific sheen to his features.

# Craft and Consequences

by Shawn Reilly Simmons

"The set designers won't have too much work to do in this dump," Danny said, peering through the dusty windshield. "It's already a horror show."

Head chef and craft services coordinator Margo Reeves thought the same thing as she pulled the catering truck around back of the crumbling Victorian-era sanatorium. She wondered, not for the first time, if her standards had fallen as far as her reputation. The corroded structure sprouted at the base of the Catskill Mountains like a wild mushroom, all broken windows and suspicious stains. It was the perfect place to shoot a low-budget slasher flick. Or dispose of a dead body.

"This place makes the Overlook Hotel look like the Four Seasons," Danny, her sous chef, said, climbing out of the passenger seat and immediately lighting a cigarette. He was three months sober, but anxiety brought out his oral fixation like onions brought out tears.

Margo popped the truck's rear doors. "Do me a favor and don't just drop that anywhere. I don't need you starting a tumbleweed fire on our first day." She eyed the dried-out vines climbing the brick wall near the rear entrance.

Sylvia, the production manager, a rail-thin woman who treated budgets like biblical commandments, appeared in the doorway. "Ms. Reeves. Finally."

Margo glanced at her watch, which showed a few minutes past nine.

"There was traffic on the highway."

Sylvia raised a hand to halt any further explanation for their tardiness. "Your kitchen is in the basement. Through the rear entrance, down the stairs. Just follow the smell of mold."

"Basement?" Margo hoisted a case of knives with the care most people reserved for newborns. "I specified ground floor minimum. Natural light, proper ventilation—"

"And I specified a budget that doesn't include your prima donna requirements." Sylvia's smile could have curdled cream. "Take it or leave it."

Margo considered leaving it. Then she remembered her rent was due on Tuesday, and her checking account had about as much volume as a soufflé made with under-whipped eggs.

"Fine. But if anyone gets food poisoning from cooking in a dungeon, that's on you."

"I don't think so," Sylvia said, turning on her sensible heel.

The basement kitchen was exactly as advertised: dank, dim, and smelling of decades of institutional despair. It was the kind of place where hope went to die, slowly, from sepsis.

"Well," said Kevin, her film school prep cook, adjusting his Brooklynite hipster glasses, "at least the aesthetic matches the film's milieu."

Margo shot him a barbed look that could have filleted a salmon. "The aesthetic I'm going for is not killing anyone with botulism."

"Yo, speak English," Danny said, scratching his forearm. "Just say vibe." A tattoo of a fork with spaghetti swirled around it reddened beneath his nails. "Start cleaning." He tossed a shop towel at Kevin and gestured at the dingy metal tables lining the room.

* * *

Three hours later, the three of them had the kitchen in functional shape, clean enough to pass a visit from the health inspector, but only just. Forty-seven cast and crew members were expecting dinner at six. The menu was simple: roasted chicken, garlic mashed potatoes, seasonal vegetables, and fresh-baked bread. Food that showed competence, and that she understood how to work on a budget. Margo's first meal in a new kitchen was always a no-brainer, something she'd made thousands of times.

She was trussing chicken legs when she heard shouting from the stairwell.

"—I told you the main room needs more blue in the lighting—"

"—don't care what it needs, we're already three days behind—"

"—typical Harvey, changing everything at the last minute—"

Harvey Winters, the director. Margo had researched him before taking the job. He was once a promising young visionary, then abruptly shunned, now desperate enough to direct a hand-me-down horror movie in a condemned building with a cast of hasbeens and neverweres. He was the kind of man who screamed at the crew because he lacked the power to scream at the suits.

Dinner service went smoothly until Harvey appeared in her kitchen at seven-thirty, red-faced, radiating manic energy.

"The chicken is dry," he announced, dropping his plate on the counter and stabbing the breast dramatically with his fork.

Margo looked at the chicken. Perfectly seasoned and cooked, juicy and flavored with carefully chosen herbs. "That chicken is perfect."

"This is my production. I say it's dry."

"And this is my kitchen. I say that chicken is much juicier than all the stories I've read about you on Page Six."

Danny and Kevin stayed focused on their tasks but slowed a bit as they eavesdropped.

Harvey's face went from red to purple. "Do you know who I am?"

"A man with failing taste buds and anger management issues?"

He leaned across the counter, close enough that she could smell the rage beneath his cologne. "I can make sure you never work in this business again."

Margo smiled, her expression sharp enough to julienne a carrot. "I've already been thrown out of this business. That's why I'm here, cooking in your basement from Hell for people who think craft services means a bag of stale donuts."

He stormed out, muttering threats that would have been more impressive if his voice hadn't cracked on the word "blacklist."

"Charming fellow," Danny observed, appearing at her shoulder.

"A real peach. The kind that's rotten from the inside out."

* * *

Margo woke the next morning to a message from Harvey requesting her signature bisque, the one that had once earned a mention in *Food & Wine.* That was before her very public, very viral meltdown turned her from rising star to industry pariah. In a shift from their last conversation, the message was bright and cheerful, which made Margo wonder about Harvey's mental stability.

"Bisque requires shellfish," Margo told Sylvia. "Shellfish requires money. Money requires—"

"Here." Sylvia slapped a purchase order on the counter. "But this is your last budget increase. Make it work."

Margo spent the morning crafting the bisque like she was painting the Sistine Chapel, only leaving the kitchen for brief visits to the pantry and restroom. Lobster shells were roasted to perfection, aromatics sweated until they surrendered their essence, cream enriched with just enough sherry to make the flavors sing *La bohème.*

At noon, she ladled the bisque into a bowl and set it down in front of Harvey. She headed back toward the kitchen stairs but then turned back to watch. Harvey took one spoonful, nodded approval, then took another. And another.

By the fourth spoonful, he was face-down in the bowl, as dead as last week's leftovers.

* * *

Detective Ronnie Walsh looked like central casting's idea of a small-town cop: rumpled suit, suspicious eyes, and a mustache that had enjoyed better decades. He studied Harvey's body with the enthusiasm of a man who'd rather be napping.

"You made the soup?" he asked Margo, leaning against the counter in the basement.

"Bisque. And, yes."

"You argued with the deceased yesterday?"

"I corrected his uninformed opinion about poultry."

"Witnesses say you threatened him."

"I did no such thing. He threatened my employment and future employment. I did not threaten him."

Walsh consulted his notebook with theatrical precision. "Someone from the crew heard you threaten, quote: 'If he does it again, I'll gut him like a fish.' End quote."

Margo sighed. "That was said to my prep chef, about my sous chef's… enthusiasm for cocktails. I told the both of them—drinking on the job is automatic termination. Context matters, Detective."

"Does it? Because right now, context says you're a disgraced chef with anger issues who poisoned a man."

The words hit like a cleaver to her chest, precise and brutal. Margo straightened, drawing on every lesson she'd learned about surviving in professional kitchens where weakness meant exile.

"Right now, Detective, context says you're a small-town cop who couldn't investigate his way out of a paper bag. But I'm willing to give you the benefit of the doubt if you'll do the same."

Walsh's mustache twitched. Amusement or annoyance—with men like him, the line was always thin.

"Nobody leaves the property," he announced as he headed up the stairs. "This is now a crime scene."

Which meant Margo was trapped in a crumbling sanatorium with a dead director and forty-six still-living people who thought she was a murderer. At least she had enough canned goods to feed everyone if the investigation dragged on for a long time.

She'd had worse catering gigs.

* * *

That evening, she served beef stew and biscuits in the main hall, a cavernous room that had probably housed tuberculosis patients back when fresh air was considered medicine. The cast and crew ate in small clusters, shooting glances at her like she might have seasoned their food with arsenic.

Marcus Webb, the film's producer, picked at his plate with the distracted air of someone whose mind was elsewhere. He was probably calculating how much this delay was costing him, Margo thought. Producers were always counting money, even at crime scenes.

"Rough day?" Dean Chapman slid into the seat across from her. Once a sought-after leading man, he was now puffy around the edges and radiated a desperate charm that came from too many ex-wives and callback rejections.

"I've had worse."

"Have you? Because murder accusations usually top most people's bad day lists."

Margo studied him over her coffee cup. He was still handsome in the way that worked well on camera, but that felt hollow in person. "What do you want, Dean?"

"Just making conversation. We're all stuck here together. Might as well be friendly."

"I'm not here to make friends. I'm here to cook."

His smile widened. "So...did you do it? You know, off Harvey? It's not like he was the most likable guy in the industry. You might get a fan club."

Margo set her lips in a line and stared at him.

"Come on, Margo. You're obviously talented, obviously attractive. We could help each other out."

"Help each other how?"

"I have connections. Influence. A word from me could open doors."

"I've been through all the doors already."

"Come on, you know you want back in the big leagues. We can talk about it in more detail in my room."

Margo set down her coffee with surgical precision. "Dean, let me explain something. I've worked in kitchens since I was sixteen. I've dealt with every kind of asshole the industry produces—drunk chefs, grabby customers, critics who think destroying careers is sport. You want to know what they all have in common?"

Dean's smile faltered.

"They all think they're offering something I need more than my self-respect. They're always wrong."

Dean's smile turned nasty. "Self-respect? Is that what you call dumping soup on food critics?"

The words hit like ice water. Margo went very still. "Excuse me?"

"Come on, everyone's seen the video. Margo Reeves, the chef who lost her shit and destroyed her own career over a bad review. You're not exactly in a position to be picky."

"You want to know what happened that night, Dean?" Margo's voice dropped to a whisper that somehow felt more dangerous than shouting. "I'd been working seventy-hour weeks trying to save a restaurant while the head chef was in rehab. The critic who sent back my bouillabaisse had already written his review before he even tasted the food—I saw him typing on his laptop between courses."

Dean leaned back in his chair.

"So yes, I snapped. I took that perfect bowl of bouillabaisse that I'd spent six hours preparing, and I dumped it right in that snide critic's lap. Then I told him exactly what I thought about parasites who destroy people's livelihoods for clicks." She stood up slowly. "The difference between you and me, Dean, is that when I lost everything, it was because I had principles. When you lose everything, it'll be because you don't."

* * *

The next morning brought Kevin to her kitchen door, glasses askew and hands shaking like he'd mainlined espresso.

"Margo, I found something."

He led her to the prop storage room, a cluttered space that smelled of dust and dashed theatrical dreams. In the corner, tucked behind fake tombstones and rubber skulls, sat an old-fashioned medical bag. It was black leather, the kind of thing a country doctor might have carried.

"This wasn't here yesterday," Kevin said. "I was in here looking for extra tables."

Margo opened the bag carefully. Inside was antique medical instruments, a few empty vials, and one small bottle labeled "Digitalis Extract."

"Heart medication," she murmured.

"Or poison, in the right dose."

"Kevin, you watch too much true crime."

"Maybe. But Harvey died of a heart attack, right? That's what the EMTs said. And digitalis can cause—"

"Cardiac arrest. Yes, I know." Margo closed the bag, mind racing. "We need to tell Detective Walsh."

"Do we? Guess whose fingerprints are now all over it?"

Smart kid. Too smart for his own good, just like she'd thought.

They were interrupted by shouting from the main hall. Margo rushed toward the sound, Kevin close behind, and found the cinematographer, Carl Hendricks, backing away from the lead actress, Victoria Sterling.

"—sick of your accusations!" Carl shouted, his usually precise diction slurred with rage.

"You've been sabotaging this film from day one!" Victoria's voice carried the trained projection of someone who'd learned to be heard in the back row. "Harvey knew it, and now he's dead!"

"Harvey was a bastard who destroyed my career! You think I'd waste poison on him when public humiliation worked so much better?"

Detective Walsh appeared, drawn by the commotion. "What's going on here?"

"Carl's been tampering with equipment," Victoria said. "The lighting was wrong yesterday, the camera angle was off during my close-up—"

"The equipment is older than dirt," Carl shot back. "I'm working miracles with garbage, and she's complaining about her close-ups like this is *Sunset Boulevard*."

Walsh looked between them with the weary expression of a referee at a boxing match between drunk toddlers. "Anyone else have accusations they'd like to make while I'm here?"

Silence, thick as hollandaise.

"Right. Back to your business, all of you."

The crowd dispersed, but not before Margo caught the look that passed between Sylvia and the producer, Marcus Webb. Quick, significant, the kind of glance that carried more information than a page of dialogue.

* * *

Later that evening, Margo found Carl in the prop room, methodically cleaning camera lenses with obsessive precision.

"Stress cleaning?" she asked.

Carl looked up, his eyes red-rimmed. "Something like that." He gestured to the ancient equipment. "This stuff is older than my career. Which, considering my career lasted exactly three years over a decade ago, is saying something."

"What happened?"

Carl set down a lens and rubbed his face. "Harvey happened. I was the hot young cinematographer, fresh out of NYU. Harvey hired me for his first real film—*Midnight in Manhattan*. Eight-figure budget, A-list cast, my big break."

"I remember that film. The cinematography was beautiful."

"Was it? Because, according to Harvey's publicity campaign, he shot most of it himself. Called me a 'collaborative assistant' in the credits." Carl's hands tightened on the cleaning cloth. "But that wasn't the worst part."

"What was?"

"I'd developed a new lighting technique—something I'd been working on since film school. Revolutionary stuff, really. Harvey filed for the patent himself, claimed it was his innovation. When I tried to dispute it, he blacklisted me. Said I was a disgruntled employee trying to steal credit."

Margo winced. In the culinary world, stealing recipes was bad enough, but stealing techniques was career suicide.

"Every job I applied for after that, they'd already heard Harvey's version. That I was unstable, ungrateful, a credit-stealer." Carl resumed polishing the lens with vicious precision. "My wife left me when the work dried up. Said she didn't sign up to be married to a has-been."

"Is that why you took this job?"

"Harvey called personally. Said he wanted to make amends, that this would be a chance to showcase my real talent." Carl laughed bitterly. "I should have known it would be just another big disappointment."

"Maybe someone else decided Harvey had had enough chances to make amends."

* * *

That afternoon, she served turkey sandwiches and noticed things. How Sylvia pecked at her food suspiciously, as if expecting to be poisoned. How Marcus kept checking his phone, despite the poor reception. How Victoria pushed her food around her plate without eating, and how Carl drank steadily from a flask he thought he was hiding.

Most telling of all was how everyone seemed to know more about Harvey's business than they were admitting. She watched Marcus nervously rotate his platinum wedding ring with his thumb as he ate, the thick band catching the dim light each time he turned it. Margo wondered briefly if he was getting a divorce. Movie set hours were much like those in a restaurant. Not conducive to romantic or family life with civilians working nine-to-five.

"You're doing it again," Danny said, appearing at her elbow later as she cleaned the kitchen.

"Doing what?"

"That thing where you watch people like they're ingredients you're trying to figure out how to use."

Margo considered this. "People are like ingredients. You have to understand their essential nature before you know what to do with them."

"And what was Harvey's essential nature?"

"Bitter. The kind of bitter that ruins everything it touches."

"Someone decided to remove him from the recipe?"

"Something like that."

* * *

That evening, while cleaning the main hall, Margo found Victoria sitting alone in the corner booth, staring at an old Polaroid photo.

"Mind if I sit?" Margo gestured to the opposite bench.

Victoria looked up, startled, then quickly tucked the photo away. "Of course."

"You barely touched your sandwich today. Everything okay?"

Victoria laughed, but it sounded more like a sob. "Define okay. I'm trapped on a horror movie set, which isn't even a real set. The director is dead. I'm suspected of murder. I'm living my private life out in front of cameras." She paused. "Actually, that last part isn't new."

"What do you mean?"

Victoria pulled out the photo again—a red carpet shot of her from what looked like decades ago, radiant and confident. "This was the premiere of *Second Chances*. My comeback film after rehab. Harvey was a junior publicist then. He promised my recovery wouldn't be exploited."

Margo studied the photo. Young Victoria looked genuinely happy, not just camera-ready. "What happened?"

"Someone leaked behind-the-scenes footage of a bad day...a breakdown during filming at a weak moment...to a tabloid show. Called it 'artistic documentation of the creative process.' " Victoria's voice turned bitter. "I didn't know my therapy sessions with the on-set counselor were being recorded until I heard them on TV."

"Jesus."

"That footage followed me everywhere. Every audition, every meeting— they'd seen me at my most vulnerable. It was entertainment." Victoria wiped her eyes with a napkin.

"Did you find out who leaked this?" Margo asked, resisting the urge to touch the woman's hand across the table.

"I suspected Harvey at first, but he swore he'd never. When he called about this project, all these years later, said he wanted to give me a real second chance, I thought…I thought maybe I could trust him. I do think it was Harvey all along, I just couldn't prove it. When he offered me this role, I figured it was to make up for things he'd done back then."

Margo felt a familiar burn in her chest—the same rage she'd felt when her own meltdown went viral. "Some people don't change, Victoria. They just get better at hiding what they really are."

"You think he was planning to exploit me again?"

"I think Harvey Winters never met a vulnerability he couldn't monetize."

* * *

That evening, she found Marcus Webb in Harvey's office, going through papers with the methodical precision of someone who knew exactly what they were looking for.

"Find anything interesting?" she asked from the doorway.

Marcus jumped, scattering papers. "Jesus, Margo. You scared the hell out of me."

"Sorry. Occupational hazard. Chefs learn to move quietly."

"I was just…Harvey left some production notes. Thought they might help us figure out how to finish the film." He gestured to a specific filing cabinet without looking. "Harvey was always organized about his paperwork."

Margo noted how Marcus had gone straight to the right filing cabinet, knew exactly where Harvey kept things. For someone just looking for random production notes, he seemed remarkably familiar with the office layout. She entered the office, eyeing the stack of files marked with cast and crew names. "That's thoughtful. Mind if I ask what kind of notes?"

Marcus shifted uncomfortably, twisting his platinum wedding ring around his finger. "Background research. Harvey was thorough about the people he hired."

"Background research." Margo picked up a file marked "Chapman, Dean."

Flipping it open, she saw police reports, tabloid clippings, and bankruptcy documents. "This looks more like blackmail material."

"Harvey was paranoid. He researched everyone."

"Did he research you?"

Marcus's laugh sounded forced. "What would he find? I'm a small-time producer from Jersey. My biggest scandal is owing back taxes."

Margo opened another file. Victoria Sterling: drunk driving arrest, rehab stint, breach of contract lawsuit. Carl Hendricks: plagiarism accusations, industry blacklisting, a restraining order from his ex-wife.

"He really did hire the unemployable," she murmured.

"We all needed work. Harvey needed people who'd work cheap."

"Or people who couldn't refuse him."

Marcus snatched the files away. "I think you should focus on clearing your own name instead of making accusations."

"Is that a threat?"

"It's advice. From someone who's seen what happens when Harvey's business gets too much attention."

* * *

Two hours before dawn, Margo slipped upstairs to Harvey's private room. The hallway creaked like old bones, but years of moving quietly through sleeping restaurants had taught her patience.

Harvey's door was unlocked—death had a way of making security seem pointless. Inside, the room looked like a tornado had hit an electronics store. Monitors, cables, and hard drives were scattered across every surface.

She moved carefully, using her phone's flashlight to avoid the mess. On the desk, she found Harvey's laptop, still open to what looked like a video editing program. The screen showed multiple camera feeds—the kitchen, the main hall, even the crew quarters.

"Son of a bitch," she whispered. The timestamp showed the cameras were still recording.

She clicked through folders labeled with cast names. Victoria's folder contained hours of footage—eating alone, crying in her room, practicing lines in the mirror. Carl's showed him drinking from his flask when he thought no one was watching. Dean's captured him trying to make increasingly desperate phone calls to his agent.

Her own folder made her stomach turn. Hours of kitchen footage, including her argument with Harvey, her private conversations with Danny and Kevin, even her changing clothes in what she'd thought was the privacy of her quarters.

Margo clicked on another folder and photographed the screen with shaking hands. When she heard footsteps in the hallway, she quickly closed the laptop and slipped out through the connecting bathroom, into the adjoining room, her heart hammering like a tenderizing mallet.

* * *

That night, Margo lay in her narrow cot in the makeshift crew quarters and thought about essential natures. Harvey: bitter, controlling, vindictive. The kind of man who collected leverage like other people collected stamps.

Marcus: nervous, defensive, hiding something bigger than back taxes.

Victoria: desperate for relevance, willing to work for scale in a condemned building.

Carl: talented but blacklisted, nurturing grudges like an herb gardener, a secret drinker.

Dean: predatory, entitled, still believing his charm was currency.

Sylvia: rigid, controlling, protective of budgets and secrets in equal measure.

And herself: fallen from grace, angry at the world, with means, motive, and opportunity to kill the man who'd humiliated her in front of his entire crew.

Someone was trying very hard to make sure she looked guilty. The question was who, and why.

* * *

The answer came at breakfast. Detective Walsh appeared in her kitchen doorway like a bad omen. "Ms. Reeves, we need to talk."

He led her to Harvey's office, where the medical bag sat on the desk like evidence in a courtroom drama.

"Kevin Marsh brought this to my attention," Walsh said. "Says you found it together."

"We did."

"Your fingerprints are on it."

"Because I opened it. Like any reasonable person would."

"Along with a bottle of digitalis that matches the poison found in Harvey Winters' system."

Margo felt the world shift slightly, like a soufflé beginning to fall. "You got the toxicology results back?"

"Preliminary results. Enough to know he was poisoned, and enough to know this probably held the poison."

"Then you know I didn't kill him."

Walsh raised an eyebrow. "How's that?"

"Because if I'd poisoned Harvey, I sure as hell wouldn't have left the evidence where anyone could find it. I'd have disposed of it."

"Maybe you're not as smart as you think."

"Detective, I've run kitchens in Manhattan. I know how to make problems disappear without a trace. If I wanted Harvey dead, he'd be dead, and you'd never prove it was me."

Walsh stared at her for a long moment. "That's either the stupidest thing you could have said, or the smartest."

"It's the truth. And the truth is, someone is working very hard to frame me for murder."

"Any idea who?"

Margo thought about the files full of secrets, nervous producers, and desperate actors. "Someone who benefits from Harvey being dead and me being blamed for it."

"That's not very specific."

"Give me time. I'll get specific. I have something else to show you."

* * *

She was cleaning up when Kevin burst into the kitchen, blood streaming from a gash above his left eye and his hipster glasses hanging askew.

"Someone attacked me," he gasped, collapsing against the prep counter and leaving a bloody handprint on the steel surface.

"Where? Who?" Margo grabbed a clean towel, pressing it to his wound while scanning him for other injuries.

"The prop room. I went back to look for more evidence." He winced as she applied pressure. "Someone was waiting for me."

"Did you see who?"

"No, they hit me from behind. But they said something weird before they knocked me out."

"What?"

"They said, 'Some secrets are worth killing for.' Then everything went black."

Kevin pulled a crumpled paper from his jacket pocket with trembling hands. "But I found this first. Hidden inside one of the fake tombstones."

It was a contract, signed by Harvey Winters and Marcus Webb, for something called *Hollywood Purgatory: A Reality Experiment*.

Margo scanned the document, her blood turning to ice water. "Kevin, this isn't a contract for a film."

"What is it?"

"It's a contract for a reality show. Harvey was secretly filming everyone here. The whole movie was a cover." She read further, her rage building with each line. "'Document the psychological breakdown of unemployable industry professionals under extreme stress.' They were torturing us for ratings."

"The bastards."

"It gets worse." She pointed to a clause near the bottom. "Listen to this: 'In the event of actual criminal activity, including but not limited to assault, theft, or murder, Producer agrees such events will enhance rather than terminate production.'"

Kevin stared at her, blood still seeping through the towel. "They planned for someone to get killed?"

"They hoped for it. Murder makes better television than just watching people cry."

The implications hit her like a punch to the solar plexus. Hidden cameras throughout the building, recording every breakdown, every desperate moment, every humiliation. A cast of industry washouts, hired precisely because their desperation would make compelling television.

"Oh, that bastard," she whispered.

"Harvey?"

"Harvey and Marcus. They weren't making a movie. They were making a snuff film."

* * *

The next evening, Margo announced a farewell dinner. With filming indefinitely suspended and the investigation ongoing, everyone would be leaving soon. She wanted to send them off properly.

"Like a last meal?" Victoria asked nervously.

"Like a celebration," Margo corrected. "Of survival."

She spent the day preparing her most elaborate menu yet: herb-crusted rack of lamb, roasted vegetables, potatoes gratin, and for dessert, individual chocolate soufflés that required precise timing and perfect temperature control.

As the cast and crew gathered in the main hall, she studied their faces. Nervous anticipation from Victoria. Suspicious calculation from Dean. Barely contained panic from Marcus. Professional curiosity from Detective Walsh, who'd decided to observe the proceedings.

"Before we eat," Margo announced, standing before the assembled group, "I want to share something I learned about Harvey Winters."

She held up the reality show contract but kept her other hand behind her back. "Harvey wasn't making a psychological thriller. He was making a reality show called *Hollywood Purgatory.*"

The silence that followed was profound as a held breath.

"Every conversation, every breakdown, every desperate moment has been recorded by hidden cameras throughout this building." She gestured around the room. "They're still recording now."

Victoria made a sound like a wounded animal. Carl cursed creatively. Dean's face cycled through several expressions before settling on rage.

"But here's what I find interesting," Margo continued, pulling out her phone to show the screenshots she'd taken from Harvey's laptop. "Someone sent Harvey an email just hours before he died. It said, 'This has gone too far. We need to talk.'"

She watched Marcus's face carefully. "The beautiful thing about being a chef is that you learn to read people's reactions to surprises. Like when someone isn't surprised at all by information they're hearing for the first time."

Marcus shifted in his seat but said nothing.

"You see, most people would be shocked to learn they're on a reality show. But Marcus here? He's checking his phone every five minutes in a building with no cell service. Unless, of course, he's monitoring something. Like camera feeds."

"This is ridiculous," Marcus said, but his voice cracked.

"Is it? Because I also found Harvey's laptop. Fascinating browsing history. Lots of research on digitalis poisoning. Except the searches were made after Harvey died. From someone who knew his password."

Margo smiled, sharp as her best knife. "Care to explain how a dead man researched his own murder method, Marcus?"

Marcus stared, his mouth open.

"Actually, I can," Margo continued. "Because you made one mistake, Marcus. When you poisoned Harvey's bisque, you used your platinum wedding ring to stir in the digitalis. Platinum reacts with digitalis compounds in a very specific way, creating trace elements that show up under laboratory analysis."

She gestured to Detective Walsh. "The toxicology report will show those trace elements. And your ring will show the residue."

Marcus looked down at his hand, at the platinum band he'd been unconsciously twisting throughout their conversation. "That's impossible."

"Is it? Because Harvey wasn't giving second chances out of kindness. He was creating the ultimate reality show—desperate Hollywood hasbeens clawing for relevance. But you wanted control of what would have been a ratings goldmine. So you killed your partner and tried to frame the chef."

Marcus's composure cracked like a dropped platter. "You don't understand. I never wanted anyone to get hurt."

"Really? Because that contract says otherwise."

"That was Harvey's idea! All of it!" Marcus's voice rose to near hysteria. "I thought we were just documenting a comeback story. Washed-up Hollywood types getting one last shot. Inspirational television."

"With hidden cameras and psychological manipulation?"

"Harvey said it would be like *Big Brother* meets *Project Runway*. Competition, drama, but ultimately uplifting." Marcus ran his hands through his hair. "But then he started talking about pushing people to their breaking points. Making them crack for the cameras."

"So you killed him to stop it?"

"I killed him because he threatened to release the footage, whether I agreed or not. He had hours of Victoria's private moments, Carl's drinking, Dean's desperate phone calls. He was going to destroy these people all over again."

Marcus looked around the room at the assembled cast and crew. "When Harvey showed me the footage of Victoria crying in her room, talking about ending it all...I couldn't let him broadcast that."

"So this was about protecting us?" Margo's voice dripped skepticism.

"It started that way. But then I realized—if Harvey was gone, I could edit the footage into something beautiful. Something that showed your resilience instead of your pain. I could make millions and actually help people at the same time."

"By framing me for murder."

Marcus's shoulders sagged. "That part...that part wasn't noble. Harvey had already painted you as the most likely suspect. I just...pushed the narrative along."

"You tried to destroy my life to cover up destroying everyone else's. And make money."

"I thought if I could just finish the show my way, make it inspiring instead of exploitative, then maybe Harvey's death would mean something. Maybe some good could come out of all this mess."

Detective Walsh stepped forward, handcuffs ready. "Marcus Webb, you're under arrest for the murder of Harvey Winters."

* * *

Three months later, Margo stood in the kitchen of her new restaurant, a small place in the Hudson Valley where she served the kind of food that made people remember why they loved eating. Danny worked beside her, clean for six months and counting. Kevin had deferred his senior year to work as her chef de partie, claiming he was learning more about human nature in her kitchen than he ever had in any classroom.

The film had been completed. Victoria had found her confidence again and delivered a performance that reminded people why she'd been famous in the first place. Carl's cinematography was being talked about by critics who used words like "redemptive" and "haunting." Dean had surprised everyone by turning in his best work in years.

It would never be a blockbuster, but it was honest. And sometimes honest was enough.

Detective Walsh stopped by on a Tuesday evening, off-duty and looking for a good meal. Margo served him her signature seafood bisque, made with the same care she'd put into Harvey's last meal but seasoned with redemption instead of revenge.

"This is excellent," he said, finishing the bowl.

"Thank you."

"You know, I've been thinking about what you said. About context mattering."

"And?"

"I think maybe I should give people the benefit of the doubt. As long as they extend the same courtesy."

Margo smiled, the expression warm instead of sharp. "That sounds like a recipe for a better world, Detective."

"Think it'll work?"

"Most good recipes do, if you follow them carefully."

Outside, the Hudson Valley stretched green and forgiving under an autumn sky. Inside, the kitchen hummed with the quiet satisfaction of work done well and justice served at the proper temperature. Margo Reeves had found her way back from purgatory, one perfectly prepared meal at a time.

# A Role to Kill For

by Stuart Orloff and Alan Orloff

*Steve*

"You don't see views like this very often." I gazed out at the seemingly endless blue Pacific. Reese Roman and I were running lines on the oversized pool deck of his mansion, and the view was spectacular.

"Maybe *you* don't." Reese Roman smiled, two rows of perfect movie star teeth. "I wake up to it every day. One of the main perks of living in the Hill Section of Manhattan Beach."

With anyone else, I might have sniped back. Reese's Hollywood big-shot attitude rubbed some people the wrong way—me included, at times—but I appreciated his honesty. Most stars tried to pretend they weren't vapid, egotistical narcissists. At least Reese owned it.

"Let's do it again," Reese said. "I can feel it this time."

"You got this," I said, pretty sure he didn't. I sat back on the designer chaise, ready to run the scene again. We'd just landed roles in a big film, *The Last Best Man*. Reese was the star—the Last Best Man himself—but my name would be much farther down the credits. It was a great script, and I'd come very close to landing the lead after seven extensive rounds of callbacks. At the end, the decision was between only me and Reese, and he'd beaten me out.

His role as the main character, Martin Jacks, was a meaty one. Needed to be played by someone with real range and craft. Which is why I made it to the final two. I still wasn't happy how the whole thing had transpired. I mean, Reese was out of town for the earlier rounds, then showed up late. And, despite his wooden acting, he got the role.

Reese launched into his part. "You all know me as Mr. Jacks, the guy who wears the best custom-made suits and drives the nicest cars, but-but-but-FUCK!" Reese yelled. "It's always this part that gets me."

That was the sixth time he'd forgotten his line. After the fourth flub, he told me to stop cueing him, so it would force him to remember. That hadn't worked.

He took off his hat and flung it into the pool. "What is wrong with me?"

Besides he couldn't act? I handed him the script. "You'll get it."

He snatched it from me and read his line. "*The nicest cars, but you never knew me when I was just Marty.*' Gah, why do I keep forgetting the Marty part? Fuck it, let's take a break. I need to recharge my brain. Wanna beer?"

After an hour and a half of running lines with Reese? I needed twelve. "Sure."

"Follow me to the saloon," Reese said, as if that was a perfectly normal thing to say.

I followed him inside the house, then down a fancy spiral staircase, like something out of *Gone With the Wind*. He had everything else in this gorgeous mansion, two pools—indoor and outdoor, a theater, a gym, a sauna. I guessed a saloon wasn't that far-fetched. We got to the bottom of the stairs, and there it was.

An old-west saloon!

Complete with two swingy doors and all wood flooring and furniture, like we'd stepped back into the 1880s. To the right, a signed poster of John Wayne hung over an old piano. Straight ahead, a fully stocked bar beckoned, with beer on tap and an assortment of whiskey bottles lined up along a mirrored shelf. Reese grabbed a glass and worked the tap. "This is an IPA, but I also have Guinness and Coors. Feel free to help yourself."

I grabbed a glass and was pouring myself some Coors when I noticed a revolver on a shelf under the bar. "What's with the gun?"

"Oh, that's my whiskey gun."

Of course it was. "What the hell is a whiskey gun?"

Reese scooped up the gun, slipped it into his mouth, and pulled the trigger. Then he swallowed. "It's a prop gun I had modified to shoot whiskey. The handle is actually a flask. Pretty sick, right?"

*Sick* was certainly an apt description. "Where'd you get it?"

"I collect John Wayne stuff. This is a prop gun from *The Man Who Shot Liberty Valance.* I have another one in my bedroom, from *Angel and the Badman*, and it's the exact same type of gun. That one actually *works*, though."

A guy like Reese with a firearm didn't seem like a great idea. "Why do you need a working gun?"

"Dude, this is Hollywood. Full of crazies. What if some homicidal stalker comes around, just like in our movie? You have to protect yourself. You should get one. I'll give you my guy's name. Tell him I sent you, and he'll set you up good."

"Sure," I said. But with my father's history, there was no way I was getting a gun. I changed the subject. "This saloon is incredible."

"Thanks. I wanted it bigger, but I guess this'll do."

I could tell it was something he'd put a lot of thought and effort into, plus lots of cash. Must have cost a hundred grand for all this stuff. It was a shame he didn't put that much care into his work. If he did, he might be a half-decent actor.

"Ta da!" A female voice rang out, and three seconds later, the saloon doors burst open. In strode uber-influencer-Insta-model Evie LeMay in what seemed to be full hair and makeup, wearing designer jeans and a pristine white Supreme shirt. And plenty of jewelry, all given to her by fashionistas in the hope of getting Evie to promote them, if I had to guess.

She practically vibrated with electricity. *Presence.* I'd never seen her before, in person. Of course, I'd seen almost *all* of Evie LeMay on Instagram. As had millions of others.

Reese lit up when he saw her. "Hey, babe, how was the photoshoot?"

"Great! The makeup artist wasn't a bitch this time," Evie said as her gaze shifted from Reese to me. "And who is this?"

"Babe, this is Steve. From the movie. Steve, this is Evie."

"Steve! It's so good to meet you." Evie came up and hugged me. Air-kissed both my cheeks. She smelled like a combo of licorice and lavender. I'd never been hugged by someone with over two million followers before. "How did your rehearsal go?" She flashed her pearly-white influencer smile.

"Great, great," Reese said. "Right, Steve?"

"Sure. You were one of the two best actors running lines today," I said.

Evie laughed. "He's handsome, *and* he's funny." Evie blew an exaggerated kiss to Reese. "I'll leave you all to work in peace. Come upstairs when you're done," she said to Reese as she batted her eyes, then swept out of the saloon, setting the swinging doors swinging.

"She's something, huh?" Reese said.

"Yeah. She is." I could definitely see what Reese—and millions of others—saw in her.

Reese gulped down the rest of his beer in two huge swallows and set his mug down on the bar with a thud. "Well, thanks for coming over today. I really appreciate it," he said, clearly trying to hurry me out, eager to get started on something—someone—more enjoyable.

"Oh, uh, yeah, no problem. Thanks for inviting me." I followed Reese up the stairs, and he walked me straight to the front door.

"Later, man. Thanks again. And remember, I'll text you about the hike."

I stepped out, and Reese wasted no time slamming the door behind me. Rude, but I honestly couldn't blame him. I would've done the same thing. I didn't even get halfway through my beer. An abrupt end to a frustrating afternoon.

Running lines with Reese made it even more apparent just how putrid an actor he was. And I had to sit there and help him memorize his part, wincing as he butchered every other line? He didn't deserve this role. I did. But he was a box office draw, and I wasn't. Yet. I just needed to pay my dues, I kept telling myself. I'll work my way up, and then one day I'll have my own mansion by the ocean. With two saloons.

When I was a kid, my mom would always say, "There's no shortcut to success. Hard work wins out." It was her motto, one she strived to live by. My dad, on the other hand, had a different outlook. His motto? If you have an opportunity to get ahead, take it. Don't be afraid to pull the trigger, no matter the consequences. For most of my life, I'd tried to follow in my mom's footsteps, since my dad was an abject shithead.

Every so often, he'd try to contact me, and I'd just ignore him. I figured that would piss him off more than if I just blocked his number. Sometimes—often—I wished he'd have a heart attack and die. How could a father just abandon his young kid like that?

I took a deep, cleansing breath and thought of something else my mother always said: *Enjoy the climb.*

Unfortunately, my climb now consisted of sitting in rush hour traffic all the way back to my hovel in the godforsaken Valley.

* * *

## *Phil*

Phil Gunderson cracked open another Bud, took a long swig, and swiped a dirty sleeve across his mouth. Ever since he'd seen the news recap in *Deadline*, and then the fifteen-second sound bite on some entertainment website after a hurried online search, his mood had been bouncing up and down like a clown on a trampoline. His kid, his actor kid, had landed a part in an upcoming big-budget movie, a stalker movie called *The Last Best Man*.

That was the good news.

The bad? The kid who'd landed the starring role, Reese Roman, was a talentless, two-bit, toe-dragging pretty boy amateur. Right after he'd heard the news, Phil streamed Roman's latest two flicks, and they brought him to the point of puking. The preening hack had somehow managed to drag down everyone else on screen, rendering the films almost unwatchable.

Phil's boy Steve had more talent in his toenail trimmings than Roman possessed in his entire body.

Phil had called Steve when he'd seen the announcement, but it had rolled into voicemail. He'd texted him, too, but no response. Not unusual. Steve never responded to Phil's attempts to communicate with him. Not once, despite his good intentions. All of Phil's attempts to reconcile had fallen flat.

On some level, Phil deserved it. He'd been a shitty father, through and through. Going upstate for nine years hadn't helped, but when he'd gotten out, wanting to erase the slate and start over, it was too late. His ex-wife had poisoned the well. It had been three years since Steve had uttered a word to him. Three excruciating years.

Phil had had enough. He wouldn't accept being a non-factor in his son's life. Even if Steve never spoke to him again, Phil vowed to do whatever he could to help Steve accomplish his dreams.

Whatever it took.

If Steve didn't recognize the effort, that would be okay with Phil. It was never too late to try to make amends.

In his mind, Phil replayed the video clip of the casting announcement. Steve, huge grin on his face, bubbled thanks for getting a part. Happy to be included. What an amazing cast to be a part of, the screenwriter was brilliant, the director was a genius, blah, blah, blah.

Steve seemed appreciative, but Phil thought he detected the darker, underlying truth beneath his son's gushing. Putting a brave face on such injustice. Steve's part was minor. That undeserving jagoff Roman had somehow finagled the plum role. Why couldn't his kid display a little more ambition? Maybe show some outrage? Fight for what rightly belonged to him?

Didn't he know that big breaks didn't just fall into your lap? Sure, you only needed one yes to get a role, but you had to earn that yes. You wanted something, you had to bust your ass going for it. How could Steve ever succeed in cutthroat Hollywood with his accepting, defeatist attitude?

If he'd been around more during his kid's formative years, he woulda taught him right. Steve would be the one in the starring role, and that shitkicker Roman would be out on his privileged ass.

But Phil hadn't been around. He'd failed as a father, and he owed his kid. When Phil wanted something, really wanted something, he usually found a way to make it happen.

The mistakes of the past were in the past. Steve might have been too proud—and, face it, pissed off—to ask his old man for help. But that didn't mean Phil wasn't going to do his damnedest to help his kid become a star.

Phil's father had been a bastard, and Phil had been a bastard too. Now, he had the opportunity to break the chain.

What were fathers for, anyway?

Phil grabbed his phone, started Googling. In five minutes, he had the contact information for Steve's agency. Made a call.

"Hello? This is Dylan Hobart, and I'm calling from the offices of Bigelow Entertainment, with regards to Steve Gunder—er, Steve Gunn. You see, I screwed up and I—"

Click.

It took Phil three more tries, using three more fake names and companies, before he found someone who would even let him get his lies out. "Yes, Steve Gunn. You see, I messed up and forgot to enter the details for an upcoming meeting between Mr. Gunn and my boss. And if I don't get this squared away, I'll get fired, for sure. Can you please help me? Please?"

"Of course. Us lowly assistants have to stick together, right? What is this regarding?"

Phil could almost see the agent's assistant smiling broadly as she helped out a fellow peon. "It is regarding the upcoming shoot for *The Last Best Man*. If I recall, their appointment is sometime soon, locally. He's going to meet Mr. Gunn there, take him out for a meal. I just wish I could remember better. You know how it is, so much pressure all the time. It's a wonder I don't forget more things. My boss is kind of a mentor and acting teacher to Mr. Gunn, and if I blow this, well…" He talked fast, running the words and sentences together, just an overworked lackey trying to save his job.

"Of course," she said with a calming voice. "Just a sec."

Phil waited for what seemed like five minutes before she got back on the phone.

"You're in luck. We don't always have our talents' weekly calendars, but Mr. Gunn has a table read scheduled in two days."

"Yes, yes, that's the one."

"It's at a little studio in NoHo. I'll give you the address, but you can't say you got it from me, okay?" She chuckled as she spelled out the details.

"Got what from who?" Phil said, chuckling back. "Thank you so much for your help. You're the best."

"You're welcome." She paused. "There's a note in Mr. Gunn's file you might want to pass on to your boss."

"Oh?"

"A handwritten note, from a phone call with the film's casting director. Says that Mr. Gunn was just barely edged out for Mr. Roman's role. Evidently, it boiled down to those two actors. Which is quite an accomplishment. I'm sure dozens of actors were considered for that role, and to finish in the top two really says something. I'm sure your boss is very proud of his student."

"He is," Phil said. "He really is."

* * *

*Steve*

After we finally made it to the iconic Hollywood sign on Mount Lee in Griffith Park, I stood there gazing at the L.A. skyline. It looked different from up here. Like it actually *was* the City of Angels. If only that were true.

I knew there was a devil around every corner.

Reese threw his arm around my shoulder. "You have a better view from my place, but this one isn't so bad. Of course, you have to contend with a few ugly-ass buildings like that shithole." He gestured toward Hollywood and the distinctive Capitol Records building.

Did I mention his utter lack of class? I was still plenty torqued that he got the starring role in the film, and I didn't. He had the name. And the jawline. He'd gotten his start as a model, and you could tell. It also helped having a girlfriend who was a mega-deal celebrity.

162

On the other hand, I'd snagged the role because of my craft. The craft I'd done so much to master. And I had finally gotten a part in a blockbuster, even if it was a one-scene gig. My character? Hiker. As in, the hiker who dies in the first scene after saving Jacks during an epic chase down a mountain. That's why Reese suggested we hike together. So we'd be able to incorporate our experience into our roles, in addition to fostering a little on-screen chemistry.

I had to give him some props. Not a terrible idea.

Reese glanced at his phone. "Shit. Time to get going. Come on."

We left the great view behind and headed down. Instead of using the main path, Reese veered off onto a narrower, less-used trail. "This way will cut off some time."

We scuffed up pebbles and dirt as we negotiated our way down the dry-as-bone path. Steep in spots and rockier, this was a little more of a hiking test than the way up. I was in pretty good shape—credit a lot of time in the gym—but I was working up a pretty good sweat.

"Let's pick up the pace, okay? I've got to go grab my girl and get over to FaZe house for a party."

"The FaZe house?" I wasn't surprised he knew those douchebags.

"Yeah. And Evie likes to make a grand entrance at just the precise time." Reese went faster, and I had to hustle to keep up. He pushed a branch out of his way, then let go, and it almost snapped me in the face. "She's got some new deal with FaZe to promote a female-focused gamer brand. Basically, just pink controllers and shit. Anyway, she's gotta appear at their events for the next six months. And since those FaZe guys are major sleazeballs, I gotta go too. Gotta make sure my *assets* are protected, if you know what I mean."

Probably a good idea. I imagined everyone wanted to *manage* Evie's assets. "I catered one of their parties once, and they go all out. No expense spared. Be careful near the pool, though. They think it's hilarious to randomly push people in."

He laughed. "You used to cater? Very...nice. How'd you like it? I feel like caterers have been hella depressed recently. Which really kills the vibes. That's why I stopped having my parties catered. I just rent food trucks. Everyone loves food trucks. In fact, I've hired three for my party on Saturday. You *are* coming, right? Everyone from the movie will be there, plus lots of friends, and other VIPs."

"Wouldn't miss it." I guessed he didn't care about all of us struggling actors looking to pick up a few catering shifts to pay the rent. When you owned a place in the Palisades and got mega-millions for each picture, why would you?

We picked our way down the slope, and Reese broke into a jog whenever he could. Was this some kind of test he was putting me through? See if I could keep up with the star? This was supposed to be a hike, not a race.

He'd gotten so far ahead I could only see snatches of his signature white shirt peeking through the brush.

A few minutes later, I heard Reese yell something I couldn't quite make out. That was followed by a string of *Oh Shits* and *Fucks,* which I definitely could make out.

I rushed to catch up. When I reached him, he was sprawled on the ground, precariously close to the edge of the cliff. His right knee was bleeding, and he had bloody scratches on his hands. "Fucking trail."

"Need a hand?"

"Fuck off." Slowly, he picked himself up and dusted the dirt from his shorts. Gingerly touched his scraped knee and winced. "There should really be a railing here. I mean, someone could die if they fell over." Reese's too-cool-for-school demeanor had cracked, and the ugly face of fear shone through.

"Yeah, definitely there should be railings." I took a tentative step toward the edge of the cliff. We weren't really on a trail anymore, so I doubted the county would be putting up railings. I peered down. A fall of forty or fifty feet, sharp rocks protruding everywhere you looked. Nothing soft to break a fall.

If you went over the side of that cliff, you would almost certainly die. It was a Tuesday in the middle of January, and there wasn't much traffic on the nearby trail, so your body might never be found. Not by humans, anyway. The coyotes and other critters would find you in no time.

In fact, we hadn't seen anyone else since we'd begun our descent. I thought back to when one of my dad's friends died after falling off a boat during a fishing trip. They were the only two people on the lake at the time. Whenever that incident came up, he would always say how unlucky their situation was, and my mom would get very quiet.

Reese sidled up next to me and looked down into the gulch. "Whoa. That was close. I coulda been…fuck."

"You all right?" I asked.

"Fine."

A thought flashed through my mind. This trail was deserted. I was sure bad things happened to hikers up here occasionally. A little carelessness. Going a little too fast. Getting too close to the edge while taking a selfie. Perhaps slipping on some loose rocks or stumbling over a root.

Any number of ways someone might go tripping over the edge to their demise.

I glanced at Reese. Pretty boy, sure, but a terrible actor. It would be a shame if something awful happened to him, right before the shoot began. Why, the director would have to bring someone up to speed quickly. Preferably, someone who was familiar with the lines. Someone who could actually act.

Reese was standing two feet away from me, still staring downward into the barranca.

All it would take was a firm shove.

In my mind, I saw myself posing next to my brand-new star on the Hollywood Walk of Fame. Photographers taking pictures. My hot movie star wife, beaming brightly. Hundreds of fans cheering.

Barking from the nearby trail broke my daydream. A hiker and his dog coming our way. A witness. So much for my wild idea. I laughed to myself. Who was I kidding? Murdering people wasn't hereditary.

"Let's keep going." Reese had regained some of his composure after the tumble, but I could tell he was still a little shaken. "Do you mind going in front, bro? That way, if I trip again, you can break my fall. Diego Montez and the rest of the suits at the studio have a lot of money riding on me, and I don't want to do anything that might mess up my moneymaker." He smiled as he gently patted his face.

"Sure. Can't let the studio down," I said, mirroring his smile with one of my own.

I took another quick glance over the edge. There really should be railings.

* * *

## Phil

Phil sat in his car, keeping an eagle eye on the front door of NoHo Artists, a nondescript acting studio in a rundown building not too far from the In-and-Out Burger on Lankershim. Evidently, they'd picked this out-of-the-way dump to confound the paparazzi. Evidently, it had worked, because there didn't seem to be any crazed camera-wielding stalkers crouching behind parked cars waiting to get their shots for TMZ.

What stuck in Phil's craw was the tidbit the agency assistant had let slip—that Steve had been second choice for Reese Roman's starring role.

So close! And yet…

It was almost one o'clock now, and he'd been there since about nine. If they broke for lunch soon, great. If they had a meal brought in, so be it. Phil could wait as long as he needed to. He'd learned plenty of patience serving his time at Lompoc.

Two hours later, the front door swung open, and people came streaming out. A dozen emerged before Steve. When he saw his son, Phil choked up a bit. He sported a different haircut than when he'd seen him last—different even from the one in the online video clip. And he'd filled out. Hitting the gym regularly.

This wasn't the first time Phil had driven down from Bakersfield to see how his boy was doing in person. But each time, he hadn't had the courage to talk to him, afraid that his son would reject him flat out. Curse him. Tell him he never wanted to see him again. Get a restraining order.

Outside the studio, Steve stopped to chat with someone. His boy looked happy, and that warmed Phil's heart. But he wasn't sure he believed it. His boy was an excellent actor after all.

Phil debated getting out of his car and running over to Steve. Pulling him aside to apologize in person. But if things went sideways, Steve might never forgive him for embarrassing him in front of his castmates.

Phil stayed in the car, watching.

After a few minutes, Steve walked away.

Phil started his car. He would be perfectly happy to follow Steve around all afternoon and evening, seeing what he'd be doing, who he'd be doing it with. A few drinks with the guys? A workout? A rendezvous with a new girlfriend? Just a trip to Albertson's to get some groceries and cleaning supplies?

It didn't really matter. Watching his son from afar didn't—couldn't—make up for all the time lost between them. But it did make Phil feel closer to him.

Maybe another day. He had more pressing matters to attend to.

Steve disappeared from view just as Reese Roman came out of the building, jawing with a couple of guys. They laughed and patted each other on the backs, as if they were best buds. Then, after a final clap on the back from one of his sycophants, Reese strolled over to a red Maserati parked illegally in front of a hydrant, hopped in, and took off.

Phil put the car in gear and followed Roman out of the Valley.

They took the 101 to the 405 to Wilshire. A few surface streets to a trendy restaurant in Santa Monica, The Wiggle Room. Roman left his car with the valet and went inside.

Phil parked in an adjacent Jack in the Box lot and hopped out. Walked next door. Into the restaurant, ignoring the withering glance from one of the hostesses. In his grubby clothes and steel-toed work boots, he looked more like the guy there to fix one of the appliances than a patron.

Phil was used to that.

He spotted Reese Roman in a corner booth, talking to an attractive blonde. Two heavyweight goons hovered nearby. Roman gestured wildly with his hands, and although Phil was too far away to hear the words, he could tell from the tone that Roman was worked up about something.

Phil walked over to the bar and motioned for the bartender. "Got a quick question. Who's Reese Roman talking to?"

The fifty-something bartender gave him a smug smile. "We respect our customers' privacy."

Phil reached into his pocket, pulled out a roll of bills. Peeled off a twenty. Held it up so the bartender could get a look. "This enough respect for you?"

The bartender did a comical glance-around, then plucked the Jackson from Phil's hand. "That's Evie LeMay. Big celebrity."

"What's she famous for?" Phil asked.

"She's famous for being famous. An influencer, I think you'd say." The bartender shook his head. "I miss the good old days when people got famous for doing something notable." One eyebrow arched. "You in the business?"

Phil stared at the guy. Did he look like he was in the business?

"'Cuz if you are, I've got a dynamite screenplay. Very original. Very inventive." His face reflected the desperate hope that Phil recognized all too well.

"Let me guess. It's about a bartender who gets his face bashed in for asking strangers for favors," Phil said, deadpan.

The bartender's hopeful expression vanished. "Have a great day." He drifted down the bar to fill another customer's glass.

Phil turned his attention back to Roman and LeMay and watched for a while as he gathered his thoughts.

A dozen scenarios flitted through Phil's mind. All situations where Roman wouldn't be available to shoot the film, and the director would have to replace him with Steve. Blackmail? Phil didn't have anything on the guy. Serious injury? That could be arranged, but knowing how obsessed actors could be with their roles, Phil guessed that a simple kneecapping might not do the trick. Roman would do everything he could to recover quickly—and delays in shooting schedules happened all the time.

Phil focused on the corner booth. Roman had his arm around her, and she was hand-feeding him a variety of tasty morsels, stopping before every bite to take a picture of them, no doubt to post on social media.

The happy RomaMay couple.

Getting rid of Roman would solve Phil's problem, and it would have the added benefit of showering their project with a shit-ton of publicity. And really, wasn't that what Hollywood was all about? Being popular, no matter how?

Phil had killed a guy once. It wasn't as hard as he thought it was going to be, in the end.

And this time, he'd be doing it for a damn good reason.

** * **

## Steve

I leaned in close to the gorgeous redhead I'd just met, struggling to be heard above the din of Reese's party. "Yeah, I'm working on a movie with Reese. Still getting used to the Hollywood celeb lifestyle. So far so good." She giggled; so far so good indeed. "What about you? How do you know Reese?"

She opened her obviously fake lips to respond, when I felt a firm hand on my shoulder. "Steve! Good to see you!" I turned to see Diego Gonzalez, the producer of our movie. "You're just the man I'm looking for. Come on out to the patio, there's someone I want you to meet."

"Oh, uh, sure," I said to Diego.

"I'll text you," I called over my shoulder to the redhead, as I followed Diego outside, wondering what big shot celeb I was gonna meet now. I had already met more stars tonight than I had in my entire life. When I catered these parties, I couldn't chit-chat with the guests. For the first time, *I* was the guest. I definitely preferred being the guest.

I caught up to Diego, and standing next to him was legendary screenwrite r/director Harold Carpenter. "Harry, this is Steve. Steve meet Harry." I was starstruck. A rare occurrence for me, but Harold Carpenter? *The* Harold Carpenter? He was my favorite screenwriter, as well as a favorite of the academy. A great guy to know.

We shook hands. "So, Steve, Diego showed me your screen test for *The*

*Last Best Man.* Great stuff!"

Harold Carpenter had seen my work? Holy shit! I tried to be cool. "Thanks, man," I replied, but my voice cracked, and I was anything *but* cool. *Keep it together, man!*

Diego continued, "Steve, I'm producing Harry's new script, and it's a masterpiece. About the Bataan Death March. Do you know what that is?"

Good thing I paid attention in history class. "Yeah, in the Philippines in World War II, right?"

Harry smiled. "I'm impressed. Not many people your age know what it is. Reese sure as shit doesn't."

I tried not to laugh. Diego said, "What Harry means is, we think you're perfect for the lead. It needs to be played by someone with a real mastery of craft, and we think you've got what it takes."

I was stunned. This was the break I had been waiting for. Finally, I found my voice. "Wow, that sounds epic."

Diego smiled. "It'll be about an eight-month shoot, in Thailand. Plus, basic training beforehand. I know it's a lot, but we're really going all out for this one."

To a normal person, this sounded insane, but to an actor? Spending eight months in a rainforest across the world making a movie about a famous war crime is a dream. Again, I didn't know what to say.

Harry gave me an earnest look. "Steve, I've heard the buzz about your movie, and I have a feeling you'll be fielding all kinds of offers soon, but we'd like to be the ones to *discover* you. You've got the talent—all you need is the right vehicle. What do you think?"

"Yes," I blurted out. "I would love to. Let's do it!" So much for being cool.

Diego lit up. "Fantastic. I'll call your agent and get the process started."

Oh man, I hadn't even thought about the money yet. I was gonna be rich!

"Well, it was great meeting you, and I look forward to working together." Harry laughed. "Now that we've talked, I can go home and get some sleep. My days of partying are long gone."

Harry went inside, and Diego turned to me. "Exciting, huh?"

"Honestly, it's a dream come true."

Diego nodded. "It's a once-in-a-lifetime opportunity, but don't get ahead of yourself. We've still got *The Last Best Man* to make. If it succeeds, we'll have the cash—and the cachet—to get this one off the ground. But if it bombs at the box office, all bets are off, I'm afraid. So, no pressure!" He laughed, but I detected there was a lot of truth—and worry—behind the warning. "Anyway, it's past my bedtime, too. Later, Steve."

Diego left me standing alone on the patio, overlooking the moonlit Pacific Ocean, tearing up, thinking about the climb to get here. Hard work really does win out.

Now, I prayed that nothing better fuck up the success of this movie and my big chance at stardom.

*Nothing.*

* * *

## *Phil*

Phil entered through the mansion's side door, right on the heels of a woman wearing a *Jocko's Tacos* apron. She told the security guy she needed to use the restroom, and he nodded them both through, not seeming to give even half a shit. Once inside, Phil skipped the bathroom and veered into the main living area where the party was going full-blast.

So many beautiful people. Laughing it up like beautiful people with scads of money did. Phil drifted off into a corner, doing his best to blend in. Luckily, everyone was too self-absorbed—or straining to spot the next A-lister—to notice anonymous Phil.

Instinctively, he located the exits. Found one he'd use when his mission was accomplished. Then he glanced around, searching for his son. And for Reese Roman. The weight of the weapon tucked into his waistband kept him focused on the task at hand.

Take out his target, then disappear in the ensuing commotion. Piece of cake.

A group of large men shifted, and he caught a glimpse of Steve across the room, talking with Reese, Evie, and a couple of other actor-types. They seemed to be having a good time, smiling, drinking, taking selfies, preening.

Phil moved closer, finding a position with a better line of sight. He figured he could pull his gun, aim, and fire in three seconds flat. Then he'd be gone like a puff of smoke. He'd already plotted his escape route. Out the nearest exit, then hoof it to where he parked about half a mile away at the end of a cul-de-sac.

If someone followed him…well, he had more bullets in the gun.

Now, fifteen feet away, he waited for the perfect moment. His pulse quickened, but he tamped it down. He'd done this before. Patience was key. He kept his head partially bowed so Steve wouldn't spot him.

Phil blocked out all the distractions of the party—the noise, the people, the background music. His singular focus remained on Reese Roman.

As he watched, Reese reached into his pocket and pulled out a gun. Pointed it at Steve, who smiled and opened his mouth.

What the hell?

Phil didn't hesitate. He pulled the gun from his waistband, aimed, fired.

Three seconds later, a red stain bloomed in the center of Reese Roman's stylish T-shirt as the pretty boy crumpled to the ground.

Phil turned to flee, but before his legs started moving, he locked eyes—for a split-second—with his son Steve.

Then Phil slipped out as bedlam broke loose.

* * *


*Steve*


"Wouldn't it be better if we went inside and got a drink?" my father asked. "I'm buying."

I'd called him a couple days ago, suggested we meet behind this dive bar in Panorama City. Didn't explain why, but I knew he'd show up. He'd been trying to talk to me for years, and now was his big chance. He would have met me on Hollywood Boulevard in his underwear if I'd asked. "We'll go inside in a few minutes. I wanted to talk to you alone, without any noise or interruption."

"Sure. It's great to see you," my father said. "I've been following your career, you know."

I wasn't here for any pleasantries. "I saw you shoot Reese, and I know you know that."

He didn't say a word.

"Why were you there with a gun? You haven't been in my life for twenty years, and now you reappear and shoot a friend of mine? What kind of sick bastard does that?"

"Wasn't planning to. But then I saw him pull a gun on you."

"It was a goddamn prop gun!"

"I didn't know that. I figured it was him or you."

"That's such bullshit. Why were you even there in the first place, with a gun?" I narrowed my eyes at him. "Were you there to shoot me?"

My father stared into my eyes for the longest time. "How can you even think that? I'd never hurt you."

Now it was my time to stay silent. He'd hurt me his entire life.

He seemed to ponder something. "Okay, here's the truth: I went there to kill Reese."

"You're fucking insane." I'd hated my father for almost my entire life, but I never hated him more than I did at that moment.

He smiled, and I was reminded of a wolf showing its fangs. "I heard you came in second for the role, and I figured if I took Reese out, you'd become the star. A father sometimes has to do some dirty work, but for you, it was all worth it."

"How the hell would you know what a father has to do?"

"Point taken." My father shifted his weight from one foot to the other. "Thanks for not ratting me out."

I was so furious I could barely squeeze the words out. "I didn't tell the cops, not because I wanted to save you, but because I wanted to salvage any remote chance of me having a career. Studios don't hire actors whose fathers kill people. Bad P.R. They've canceled this project—the studio wanted a big name, Reese to be exact—and, thanks to you, the other project I was going to fucking star in got canceled, too. Thanks for all your help, *Pops*."

He'd wrecked my childhood and ruined my big chance at stardom. Would he somehow destroy my future, too? Of course, he would. It was in his genes.

"If it matters, I'm sorry," my father said.

I barely heard him. "Time to go…"

"Inside? Good, I'm parched."

"No," I said. "Just time to go."

I pulled out the gun I'd bought from Reese's guy. Pointed it at my father's forehead. Felt the cold trigger under my finger.

Maybe murder *was* hereditary, after all.

# The Shooting Script

by Kathryn O'Sullivan and Paul Awad

EXT. HOLLYWOOD HILLS – DAY

*A beat-up black BMW ascends a winding drive to the glass and concrete mansion of Hollywood power couple David Murphy and Liz Franklin. The BMW circles the roundabout and stops at the entrance. Twisting topiaries stand sentinel on either side of the imposing mahogany front door. Behind the wheel slumps Billy Murphy, a disheveled fifty-something, one-time Hollywood wunderkind, now a Hollywood...*

Billy struggled to describe himself. *Has-been?* he considered, then deleted the idea. He often thought in screenplay format—writing and rewriting his life. He was a good writer, had enjoyed some early hits, but this was a tough town, and you were only as good as your latest project. His recent films had met with less success. He hoped today's meeting would change that.

He cut the engine. The BMW sputtered into silence. The car had been a gift to himself two wives ago, when he and his older brother, David, were in their thirties and still a writing-directing team. Those were the halcyon days. Now, he only saw his brother once a year at a tony restaurant David and Liz reserved for their annual Christmas party. *Just a little holiday get-together with our closest family and friends,* Liz would say. Every year, Billy wondered if he would still be one of the hundred or so invited guests. He hadn't been welcomed in David's home in years. Not since...he gazed at the second-floor bedroom window. The curtains undulated as someone moved behind and then closed them.

He grabbed the flowers from the passenger seat, exited, climbed the steps, and rang the bell. Chimes sounded inside. When he had called this morning, he heard the wariness in David's voice, knew his brother was bracing for a money ask. But today was different. This time, he had something to offer.

David opened the door and glanced past Billy at the BMW. "I see you hung onto the Beamer. She still sputtering and bleeding oil?"

Billy ignored the jab. "Mind if I come in?"

David allowed Billy entrance and closed the door. "Why don't we talk in the living room?"

Billy followed David from the grand foyer through the library with its floor-to-ceiling bookcases to the great room that could have been featured in *Architectural Digest* with its vaulted ceiling and hard edges. The cement floors were stained brick red and varnished. A slate fountain bubbled in a corner. Persian rugs, curved furniture with cashmere throw pillows, and potted palms added warmth. *Liz's touch*, Billy thought. The fifteen-foot windows faced an enormous koi pond and tiered gardens with native flora.

Billy extended the flowers to his brother. "These are for Liz. She here?"

David's jaw clenched. "No," he said, not reaching for the bouquet. "But I'll tell her you stopped by when she gets home."

Billy felt a pang in his heart. "The life of an A-list star, eh?" he joked.

"Something like that," David said without smiling.

Billy set the flowers on the glass coffee table and sat on the sofa.

David took a chair. "You said on the phone you had something important to tell me."

"You're going to love this," Billy said, brightening. "This morning, I was at the gym and who do you think was working out on the bike next to me? None other than Steph Meyers, you know, from Columbia Pictures."

"I know who Steph Meyers is."

"So, I introduced myself and turns out Steph is a major fan of ours. Even quoted lines from *Lost in Limbo*. It was unreal. Anyway, she asked if we were working on anything, and I pitched *Boulevard Babes*."

David flinched. "You didn't."

"No, no, listen. Steph loved it. Said she'd kill to produce the Murphy brothers."

"We wrote that script in our thirties. The story is completely out of touch with the current zeitgeist and, to be honest, a little…" he said the last word slowly, "…problematic."

"I prefer edgy," Billy said with a wink.

David raised a brow. "Nobody wants edgy. Don't you read the trades?"

"So, we do a rewrite, update a few things. Or we tell Steph it's a period piece and set it in the nineties. Come on, it'll be fun."

"I'm busy with my show."

"*Variety* says you're on hiatus for three months," Billy said. "See, I do read the trades."

"Liz and I are going on vacation as soon as she wraps the Nolan film."

"No problem. We can get the rewrites done in a week. Plenty of time for your vacation." Billy leaned forward. "Think of the payday."

His brother sighed. "It's not about the money."

"Maybe not for you with your Netflix deal and your fancy house and your Oscar-winning wife," Billy snapped.

David rose. "I think you should leave before you say something you regret."

Billy stood, too. "I'm sorry, I'm sorry," he said. "I'm happy for you and Liz. Really, I am. But, David, this is the opportunity I've been waiting for. It will put me back on the map. We made a good team back in the day. Why not give them one last Murphy brothers film?"

David met his brother's eyes and sighed. "Don't make me regret this."

Billy held his fist out, and David half-heartedly bumped it. "This is going to be great. Oh, and there's one other thing."

"What's that?" David asked, on guard again.

"Steph wants Liz to be in it. Said if Liz is attached, it would be a guaranteed green light."

"Absolutely not. There is no way Liz will do *Boulevard Babes*." David crossed to the large windows and stared at the koi pond.

Billy joined his brother. "You know how this town is. Women get to be a certain age, and the roles get, well, predictable—mother, grandmother, heartless CEO. Imagine what this could do for Liz's career. It would be unexpected. It will be like *Lost in Limbo*, the three of us working together again."

His brother gave him the side-eye.

"Please. Just ask her," Billy said, hoping he didn't sound as desperate as he felt.

David rolled his eyes. "Fine. But I'm not making any promises."

"Perfect. Well, I'll get out of your hair." Billy hurried toward the door, eager to leave before David changed his mind. "I'll call tomorrow about a rewrite schedule," he said over his shoulder and let himself out.

* * *

Billy glanced up from his laptop at David, scrutinizing his apartment wall and the colored Post-its that represented the structure of their *Boulevard Babes* script. Billy hadn't felt this alive since they hit it big with their first indie, *Lost in Limbo*. Financed with their grandmother's credit cards, *Limbo* was about two twentysomething brothers working in a record store and searching for love in New York City. Liz played the *femme fatale* who entangled the brothers in a traveler's check forgery ring. The film was a Sundance darling, obtained distribution by 20th Century Fox, and helped them secure an agent and a multi-picture deal. Billy visualized the three of them arm in arm on the red carpet—a happy memory.

"Billy? You okay?" David asked, bringing him back to the present.

"I'm great. Isn't *this* great?"

David surveyed Billy's apartment, littered with Thai food containers and script pages. "It's nice," he said, and sounded like he meant it. He held up eight fingers, each with a Post-it attached. "But we need to cut these scenes."

Billy blanched. "Whoa. What scenes? Why?"

David held up a Post-it finger. "The scene with the homeless fella? We really can't keep that. And the laundromat? I don't know what we were thinking."

Billy groaned. "Okay, we can lose the homeless guy, but what's wrong with the laundromat scene?"

David shot him a look. "If you want Liz to be in this, we cut the laundromat. She is not doing nudity."

"But it's integral to the plot."

"It's gratuitous."

"You're killing me." Billy eyed the remaining Post-its. "What else you got on those fingers? And one had better not be Madame Tussauds. I will fight to the death for that one."

David got a sly smile on his face. "Oh, really?"

Billy grinned. "Are you thinking what I'm thinking?"

"Three out of five?" David said, removing Post-its from one hand.

Billy set his laptop on the table and joined David. "I win, Madame Tussauds stays."

David nodded. The brothers assumed their positions. They repeatedly threw rock, paper, and scissors. Billy came out on top. He cheered, grabbed the contested Post-it, slammed it on the wall, and took a victory lap around the living room.

David shook his head in defeat. "Audiences will never buy the bad guys mistaking the wax statue for Liz."

Billy marched to an overstuffed bookshelf, pushed aside a stack of books, retrieved a 32-caliber revolver, and aimed it at his brother. David's eyes widened. Billy thought he even detected a flash of fear. It made him feel good.

"What the hell?" David said, shaken.

"Now picture this." Billy crept about the living room. "I'm the gangster entering Madame Tussaud's…"

"Hold it," David said, raising his hands for a timeout. "What are you doing?"

"I'm acting out the scene. Like we always do."

David pointed at the gun. "The gun, Billy. What are you doing with a gun?"

Billy glanced at the firearm. "It's a prop."

David inhaled deeply. "Can you, please, not point it at me?"

"Relax. It isn't loaded." Billy opened the chamber for David to see. "Don't know why you're getting so uptight," he said, defensive. "We used it as a prop in *Limbo*."

"Because we were young and stupid," David said, exasperated. "Remember the first day on set when we didn't know it was loaded? We're lucky nobody got hurt." He ripped Post-its from his fingers, tossed them on the coffee table, and grabbed his keys.

"Okay, okay," Billy said, returning the gun to the shelf. "I've put it away. Let's just get back to work."

"It's late." David opened the front door. "I'll see you tomorrow night."

Billy had forgotten how serious his brother could be. He had always worried about every detail on set. While Billy partied with the cast and crew, David watched dailies and adjusted the shooting script. Even when they were growing up, David acted more like his father than his brother, often lecturing Billy while bailing him out of trouble. Moving forward, he would need to handle David better, at least until the script was finished. After that, David could go screw himself.

* * *

For the next five nights, David and Billy reworked the saggy second act, rock-paper-scissored favorite scenes, and plowed toward the climax. With each draft, more buried hostilities surfaced.

"How about this?" Billy said, handing David his seventh attempt at the final scene.

David scanned the scene and dismissed it with a shake of the head. "No way Joey would try to kill Mark."

"Why not?" Billy said with irritation.

David looked up from his laptop. "Because he idolizes Mark. You haven't given Joey a motivation."

Billy felt his cheeks grow hot. He snatched the pages from David's hand.

"This is a comedy about a girl and two brothers," David continued. "Why are you turning it into a crime story? It's not what we do. It's not the Murphy brothers brand." He returned his attention to his laptop screen. "Trust me. What I'm working on is better."

Billy studied his brother as David's fingers danced over the laptop keys. Bile welled in Billy's gut with every click. "Well, I like my ending, and I'm half of the Murphy brothers."

David stared at the laptop screen. "Don't remind me," he muttered under his breath.

Billy sat back on the cushions; his eyes narrowed to slits. "You know who else likes my ending?" He waited until David looked up from his laptop.

David glanced at Billy. "Enlighten me."

"Steph Meyers."

The blood seemed to drain from David's face. "When did you talk to Steph?"

Now he had his brother's attention. "Today. She called to check on our progress."

"What did you tell her?"

"She loved the ending. Said everyone at the studio is excited to be producing the next Liz Franklin movie."

"You told her Liz is in?" David demanded.

"Yeah. So?" Billy said, annoyed. "What's the problem?"

David's eyes flashed with anger. "Liz isn't doing the movie," he growled.

Billy blinked, processing the bomb David had dropped. "Liz isn't doing the movie? Why not?"

"She read the last draft. She thinks the story is juvenile, her character one-dimensional. She's just there to give the brothers something to fight over."

The final scene pages slipped from Billy's hand and fluttered to the floor. He stared at David a moment, dumbstruck. "But the whole reason they guaranteed a greenlight was because Liz was attached. Without Liz..." Billy's gut did flips as he saw his comeback slipping away. "When were you going to tell me?"

"Honestly?" David said. "Never."

The room spun. Billy staggered to his feet. "Then why'd you say you wanted to work on the script?"

"I told you I *didn't* want to work on the script. You practically begged me. I felt sorry for you. I thought if I helped you, you could finally sell a decent script and make some money."

"Are you suggesting I can't write a good script on my own?"

"I saw your last three movies. You keep trying to make a Murphy brothers movie without…"

Billy stepped toward David. "Without you? Is that what you're trying to say?"

David rose to meet Billy. "No, that's what I was trying *not* to say."

The brothers stood inches apart as they had done for their rock-paper-scissors matches. Only this time was no game. Billy wished he had a real rock or scissors in hand. The paper, not so much. Unless it was to write his brother's obituary. David locked eyes with him. They'd had arguments before, but for the first time, Billy saw something sinister in his brother's eyes—unbridled hatred. They had managed to avoid a showdown for years, but Billy had always known it was inevitable. They squared off like matador and bull. Billy didn't care which he was. He planned to leave the ring the victor.

The sound of a melodic ringtone didn't break the tension. It came from the phone in David's pocket. Billy recognized the tune—the love theme from *Match Made in Manhattan*, the rom-com that had catapulted Liz to superstardom. The song played on.

"You should get that. Can't keep the movie star waiting," Billy said with disdain.

David retrieved the phone from his pocket, tapped the screen, and put it to his ear. "Hi, sweetheart," he said, eyeing Billy as he retreated to a corner. "Yes, it's going well."

Billy snorted at David's phoniness.

"What?" David said, glancing at Billy in his peripheral vision. "Yes, I told him."

Billy's mind raced, imagining Liz on the other end. Was she laughing at him? Or worse yet, pitying him, like she had when he had drunkenly cornered her in the second-floor bedroom of her house and declared his love to her? She had patted him on the head like he was a child. Then, to prove his feelings weren't drunken rantings but real, he had kissed her. He didn't know what Liz had shared with David, but until five days ago, that had been the last time he had been to David's house.

"I'll be home soon." David ended the conversation and turned to Billy. "I need to go," he said, calmer now than a few minutes ago. "Liz has a 4 A.M. call tomorrow and wants me to run lines."

David packed his laptop into his messenger bag and walked to the door. He paused and glanced at Billy. "You should consider my ending. I'll send it to you when I get home. Who knows, if you use it, you might have a hit picture again."

And there it was. The condescension that had broken them up. His brother was heading back to his mansion and Liz. What was Billy left with? According to David, a main character who lacked motivation and a script without a compelling ending.

He felt foolish for believing they could put aside their differences and work together. His desperation had clouded his judgement. It seemed this project, like his life, would be stuck in development hell.

Billy spent the next few hours re-reading the script and trying to devise a way to save the project. Then it hit him. It was there in the climax. The answer to his prayers. He had spent days writing and rewriting it. Why had he not seen it? One brother would murder the other and, contrary to David's criticism, his motivation would be clear.

* * *

The drive to his brother's house had always filled Billy with dread and regret, but as he steered his car through the affluent Hills, for the first time in a long time, he felt in charge—the revolver, now loaded, neatly tucked inside his jacket.

Several hours and whiskey sours after his dustup with David, his brother's email had arrived with the subject BOULEVARD BABES – NEW ENDING and an attachment. No message. Billy had no intention of reading David's final scene. Tonight, he would prove that *his* ending was not only possible, but inescapable and organic, the consequence of one brother pushing another too far.

After receiving David's email, he had texted his brother: JUST READ NEW ENDING. LOVE IT! YOU WERE RIGHT. SORRY.

David's reply: DID YOU LIKE THE TWIST?

YES, Billy lied. THE TWIST WAS THE BEST PART. SO EXCITED. WILL STOP BY YOUR HOUSE TO DISCUSS.

David suggested they meet alone after Liz had left for her 4 A.M. call and before the staff arrived. Billy finished the text exchange with a thumbs-up and smile emoji.

Billy rolled down the window and let the early morning air in. The faint smell of jasmine relaxed him. Or was it the whiskey? If all went according to plan, David's death would drive interest in the script, Liz would agree to do the film as a tribute to her husband, the project would be greenlit, the studio PR machine would kick into high gear for the final Murphy brothers movie, audiences would buy tickets or stream it, and Billy would be sitting pretty. Who knew, maybe Liz and he would grow closer as they dealt with their *mutual* grief. Billy snickered as he navigated the Beamer onto the drive to David's house.

As he neared his destination, the denouement of his brother's life played in Billy's head. His brother would invite him in, Billy would play nice, stroke David's ego, and then BANG! —he would shoot David in that big, arrogant brain of his. Later, the staff would discover the body and a crazed fan letter Billy had created from magazine clippings in which the fanatic declares his undying love for the movie star. The police would theorize that once the fan had discovered Liz wasn't at home, he took out his frustration and disappointment on her husband. Nobody would bat an eye at the likelihood of these events, not in Los Angeles. Billy just needed to remember to wipe David's phone of any text exchange once the deed was done.

He arrived, cut the engine, and removed the revolver from his jacket. It felt good in his hand. He tucked the gun into the back waist of his pants and exited. One thing he didn't have to worry about as he approached the house was a security camera. When they had been on better terms, David had confided in Billy that Liz had forbidden cameras after a disgruntled employee leaked footage of Liz in a bikini to TMZ.

As he climbed the front steps, his thoughts morphed into screenplay format...

EXT. DAVID MURPHY HOME – NIGHT

*Billy climbs the steps, reaches for the doorbell, and notices the front door is ajar. Voices waft out on cool, conditioned air. Billy cocks his head, listens, and cautiously enters.*

INT. HOME – NIGHT

*The dim lamps in the foyer throw dramatic shadows up the walls. Billy creeps through the darkened library, following the voices, and enters the great living room where he and David had met only a week ago. One of the fifteen-foot window panels facing the garden and koi pond is open. Billy's eyes dart around the room, concern on his face.*

The scene in Billy's head stopped abruptly, like a mental record scratch. Something wasn't right. This wasn't the scene he had rehearsed in his head. Where was David? Why was the house so dark? Why did the voices sound familiar? It took Billy a couple seconds to recognize the female voice. Liz. What was she doing here?

Billy removed the revolver from his pants waist and inched toward the garden and Liz's voice. He caught his reflection in the glass, gun raised and aimed before him. If David saw him, there would be no doubt about his objective.

He slipped through the window opening, careful not to touch the glass, squinted past the patio lights, and scanned the garden. Suddenly, the voices got louder behind him. Billy whirled around, gun cocked, and started. *Lost in Limbo* played on a large screen television above the outdoor bar. Billy watched Liz on screen as she negotiated with the brothers in the record store. He lowered the gun to his side, entranced. *The camera has always loved her*, he thought.

Suddenly, he felt a hard object press against the small of his back and froze.

"I tried to tell you," David said from behind him. "Your final scene is predictable. I read seven variations of the same ending. You coming here like this was obvious."

He felt David prying the gun from his grip. He wanted to resist, but David pressed his weapon deeper into his back, and he released the gun.

"The key to a good story is not giving away the ending too soon," David said.

Billy's jaw clenched. Even now his brother was giving him notes—about his own murder plot! He whirled around to face David. In one hand, his brother held the revolver, and in the other a television remote control, the "weapon" David had pressed to his back.

David clicked a button on the remote. The screen froze Liz's image, and the garden went quiet. He set the remote down. "I have good news," his brother said with obvious delight. "I talked to the studio. They love the new draft. So does Liz."

Billy's brows furrowed in confusion. "I thought Liz hated the script."

"I was wrong. We had a long talk when I got home. Turns out she doesn't hate the script, she just doesn't want to work with a director who will spend six months mooning over her. And, as her husband, I can't say I blame her after that pathetic stunt you pulled, declaring your love and kissing her. You didn't think I had let you get away with that, did you?"

"Wait a minute," Billy said, trying to process everything. "Liz wants to do the movie?"

"Only if we do my ending," David aimed the gun at his brother.

Billy eyed his brother and the gun with suspicion but said nothing.

David sneered. "You see, in my ending, the younger brother breaks into the older brother's house, no longer able to contain his jealousy over his brother's success or his obsession with his brother's wife." He removed a piece of paper from his pocket. "By the way, you dropped your little 'fan' letter. This will do nicely proving the younger brother's obsession." He returned the note to his pocket. "Anyway, the two brothers struggle, and the older brother, the hero of this story, kills his brother in self-defense. It's already getting buzz. The studio thinks it will be a smash at the box office. They're even upping the budget."

"Are you serious? That's amazing," Billy said. He felt lightheaded with excitement.

"Yeah, the Murphy brothers are back. You're going to have the hit you wanted." David cocked the gun's hammer. "Too bad you won't be around to enjoy it."

BANG!

Billy clutched his gut. Blood pooled between his fingers.

"You really should have read my ending," David said. "I told you there was a twist."

Billy stumbled forward and fell into the koi pond. Morning broke over the Hollywood Hills, bathing the garden in an amber glow. David looked down on him with a sly grin, gun at his side. In the light, Billy thought his brother looked like a certain golden statue. He struggled to stay conscious. Despite his best effort, his head dipped below the waterline. *The studio is making Boulevard Babes...with Liz Franklin...a hit. My comeback will be remembered forever*, he thought with satisfaction, as he felt his life FADE OUT.

# Call "Action, Cut"... And Take the Blame

By John Shepphird

The text exchange went like this:

ANDRE: Regina has been cast to play Luna

MILES: NOT what we talked about

ANDRE: Needed to close the deal today for wardrobe fitting

MILES: No! Regina is NOT RIGHT for the role

ANDRE: Direct her. She'll be great

Miles phoned Andre. It went into voicemail. A moment later, his phone buzzed with a text reply:

ANDRE: In meetings. Let's chat after wrap

Miles thought, *Chat? How about I wring your neck?*

He had been hired to direct *Burning Desire,* a low-budget film. Andre's idea was to bring back the erotic thriller. It was a genre that long since had fallen out of fashion but was wildly popular in the 1980s with titles such as *Fatal Attraction* and *Body Heat.* A femme fatale. Steamy love scenes. All part of the formula.

They were already shooting day two of what would be a grueling twelve-day schedule and yet to cast the starring female role. Miles couldn't understand why Andre had waited so long to fill the part of Dr. Luna Chambers, but now it was obvious. Andre Kramer was the executive producer—he held the purse strings.

Miles was certain Regina was too young for the part. The character, as written, was Dr. Luna Chambers, a criminal psychologist, sexy and smart as a whip. There was *no way* Regina could deliver a convincing performance. Nobody would believe she had a PhD in Forensic Psychology and had published extensively about criminology. And she wasn't even an actress. Regina was an influencer, for God's sake—her fame came from posting insipid vlogs about makeup and outfits. Supposedly, she had a massive following, but Miles suspected most social media metrics were bought and paid for. Trolls. Bots. Bullshit. About as real as Regina's blown-up lips and Botox-ed forehead.

His biggest fear was that Regina would come off laughable. Vapid.

The meager crew, many of them his friends, were shooting on a standing set in Pico Rivera, off East L.A.'s Interstate 5. The script had been written to incorporate the assorted three-walled sets the production space offered. This included a police station, interrogation room, jail cell, psych ward, and hospital room. There were also small rooms for makeup and wardrobe.

Deep down, Miles knew his role was to call "action...cut" and take the blame. Actors and producers can survive a bad movie, but directors are only as good as their last film.

He should have seen this coming. While casting, Andre kept holding out for a name in the role, even though Miles knew that was a long shot. There were a few scenes that required nudity. No respectable agent of any bankable actress would allow their client to take the role, especially considering the low budget.

And from the looks Andre and Regina shared, Miles suspected they had been intimate. That was especially disheartening because Andre was supposedly a happily married man. Miles had met Andre's wife, Diedre, while attending preproduction meetings on the porch of the producer's canyon-side, Mulholland Drive home. She was British, seemed genuine, and had a self-deprecating sense of humor. He liked her. She had brought them iced tea and English cookies before heading off to her league tennis match.

The male lead was Jay DuPont. He had co-starred in a TV series a decade ago, which had been distributed overseas. That meant he still had some name value in foreign markets. Miles had directed Jay in a television pilot that never got picked up, and they became fast friends and drinking buddies. Over martinis at the Musso & Frank Grill, Miles got Jay to agree to take the part of LAPD Homicide Detective Dereck Parsons, who brings in serial killer expert Dr. Luna Chambers to consult on the murder and arson investigation. The scene they were shooting that afternoon was all exposition, sharing notes and compiling evidence with a Los Angeles Fire Department Arson Investigator. Only after Miles had called wrap did he break the bad news to Jay.

"Who?" asked Jay.

"Regina Ray. You read with her."

Jay furrowed his brow. "You're kidding. I thought she was just some chick from casting feeding me lines."

"Apparently not. Andre is making a huge mistake." Miles pulled out his phone. "I figure if we call him together, it's not too late to get a real actress in the part."

"What's she been in?"

"Nothing as far as I know. She's an influencer."

"What about Marina Voss?"

Marina was an actress Jay had worked with before. Her name had come up while casting, and she was a good choice, but it wasn't in the stars. Miles said, "Andre says Marina's people passed, but I'm willing to bet he didn't even make an offer. I think he strung us along so he could wedge Regina in at the last minute."

Jay pondered that for a moment. "Give me a sec," he said before retreating to his trailer parked outside the stage. Miles figured he was calling his agent. He hoped their combined efforts would convince Andre that he'd made a horrible mistake.

Miles was outside the stage, going over the work planned for the next day with Kendra, the no-nonsense first assistant director, to see if it was possible to push Luna's scenes later in the schedule. Jay emerged from his star trailer wearing his usual leather motorcycle apparel. He handed over his suit and tie to the waiting wardrobe team. The prop master took his badge and gun. "I talked to my agent," Jay said to Miles, "but she's useless. She said there's nothing she can do."

Kendra said, "We would need to add another day to the schedule if we're not shooting Luna's scenes tomorrow."

Another day of shooting meant going over budget. Miles knew he couldn't get Andre to agree to that. He called him again, and again it went into voicemail. Then received a text:

ANDRE: Can't talk now. I'll see you on set tomorrow.

*Bastard.*

* * *

On the drive home, Miles came up with the idea. A long shot, but he called Andre's executive assistant, Theo.

"Hey Miles," Theo said, "Andre's gone for the day."

"Yeah…figured as much. Do you know what restaurant? I've got revised pages for tomorrow's scenes."

"I made a reservation at The Ivy on Robertson."

Miles was familiar with the West Hollywood eatery favored by many in the entertainment industry. He thanked Theo, hoping he could get there before Andre left.

Dusk had started to fall by the time Miles pulled up across the street from the restaurant. He had just pulled his credit card out of the parking meter when he saw Andre and Regina emerge from the Ivy. He stood there, wondering if they would spot him, but they didn't. They hung on each other like love birds, further evidence that they were having an affair. This was probably their celebratory dinner now that she'd landed the part. Andre tipped the valet, and they departed in his sleek Range Rover.

Miles knew he'd been beaten, so he walked back to his battered Honda. He hated that he drove such a jalopy. He had hoped to use some of the money from directing this film to put a down payment on a new car. The electrical system was failing, and he feared one of these days the old Honda would betray him horribly.

He looked at the blue-black sky over the palm trees and sighed. His chances of recasting Regina were zero.

Later that night, alone at the kitchen table, he read through the scenes planned for the next day to strategize how he could cut around her.

Back on set early the next morning, Miles was going over the planned coverage with Victor, the director of photography, when assistant director Kendra approached, annoyed. "Regina arrived," she said, checking her watch, "twenty-five minutes late. Blames her driver."

"Thanks, Kendra." Miles needed to play the game, greet Regina, and fake how thrilled he was to be working with her—all the usual bullshit. He wondered if Andre had mentioned that Miles doubted her ability.

Outside the makeup room stood a tall African-American guy dressed in black, arms folded. Miles assumed he was Regina's driver. He gave Miles a steely look before stepping aside, and he and Kendra entered.

From the caustic sneer Regina gave Miles in the mirror, he knew right away that Andre had said something to her about his concerns. Seated in the makeup chair, Regina forced pleasantries, "Good morning, Miles. I'm *so* excited. Thank you for casting me. This is such a great part." Her too-perfect smile didn't reach the suspicion in her eyes.

"Welcome aboard," Miles said. "We've got a great team assembled, both in front of and behind the camera." He informed her the tight production schedule was going to be a challenge and asked that she always be "camera-ready" and "not stray far from set."

Eyes shifting from Miles to her own reflection, Regina nodded vaguely and hummed something Miles assumed was her affirmation. She explained that she'd brought her own wardrobe. *Of course.* There was no actual wardrobe fitting yesterday. That was the excuse Andre had leveraged to cast her without his approval.

"Great," Miles said as enthusiastically as he could muster, and encouraged her to go over the selections with Gabby, the costume designer. Assistant director Kendra got on her radio and summoned Gabby.

Miles excused himself and found Jay coming out of the wardrobe room. "When Regina is ready, let's run lines together."

Jay held up his phone. "Check this out. She's got, like…five million followers."

"Means nothing," Miles said. "If she sucks, this movie is going to be directed by Allan Smithee." Alan Smithee was the pseudonym used by directors who wished to disown a project.

Jay said, "Maybe she'll surprise us."

Miles called Andre again. Wasn't the executive producer supposed to drop by sometime today? Where was he? Maybe his plan was to wait until they shot a few scenes so there was no going back.

Thirty minutes later, the set had been lit and all was ready. But Regina was still fussing behind wardrobe's closed door. Another ten minutes went by, and Miles had had enough. He couldn't charge into the wardrobe room himself because she might be changing, so he asked Kendra to demand that she report to set. He handed her a prop police badge. "Be the bad cop for me?"

"Gladly."

Kendra summoned Regina, who emerged in a snug, sparkly mini dress. The attire was more appropriate for a night out than meeting with a detective. Gabby from wardrobe said to Miles, "It's what she wanted to wear," with a look that said she'd lost the battle.

Miles said to Regina, "Your character is a professional psychiatrist meeting with a homicide detective." To Gabby, he said, "Don't you have something that's more...like, uh...business attire? A skirt and suit jacket or something?"

"But I want to wear this," Regina said.

"What else did you bring?"

"Just this one and..." She pointed to another mini dress Gabby had in her hands, no different than what Regina was wearing. "That's for my other scene."

Gabby said, "We have some stuff for the background extras that might work."

From the look on Regina's face, it was clear she didn't like that idea.

Miles got it. Regina was an influencer. She got paid to feature designer goods. Product-placement. She'd probably promised one of her clients she'd wear this dress in her movie, and her spiked heels, too. What Miles hadn't counted on was the tattoos covering her arms. Chinese characters, line drawings of snakes and flowers, and even a manicured female hand giving the middle finger. When she had auditioned, her arms were covered by long sleeves. Miles felt these moronic tats were not in character, but there was no time to have makeup cover them. That could take another hour.

The scene was the detective meeting Dr. Luna Chambers for the first time in the busy police bullpen. Surrounded by the chaos of uniformed cops and cuffed suspects, he thanks her for her assistance and provides details about the case. Although the dialogue was on the surface, procedural in nature, the subtext suggested a spark of sexual attraction. They started in on rehearsal.

On set, Regina held the printed sides. After running the scene a couple times, it was clear she had not memorized her lines. Miles cut her some slack since she'd only been cast yesterday. To assist, they printed script pages and positioned them just off camera, like cue cards.

They rolled on take one. Miles called, "Action."

Her voice was like nails on a chalkboard. He suggested she try to relax. "Let it flow easy. Don't overthink it." They rolled the camera again. She was no better. He figured if they ran the scene enough times, maybe she'd forget she was "acting" and just react. The problem was Regina kept looking at the camera.

"Cut," Miles said, and explained that she couldn't look at the camera. "That's breaking the fourth wall." She giggled, apologized, and they rolled again. But Regina couldn't help herself. This was her influencer instinct, a forced habit. It took running the scene a half dozen times before Regina finally read all of the scripted lines—plus a few ridiculous improvs—to Jay seated across from her. Then she forced a big smile at the end of the scene, another influencer habit. Miles heard some of the crew stifle laughter.

Jay gave him the *ain't working, bro* look.

*Where's Andre?* Miles thought. *He* needs *to see how bad she is.*

As they reset for Jay's coverage, Miles whispered his plan to Jay and Victor, the director of photography. "As opposed to wider shots that tie them together," Miles said, "only singles. No master shots or over-the-shoulders." Vic and Jay got it. When Regina was recast, they could at least salvage some of Jay's angles.

With the plan to shoot but not use any of Regina's coverage, Miles stopped caring. *Give her enough rope. Let her hang herself.* He even encouraged her snarky delivery and ridiculous improvs. He didn't call "cut" when she looked at the camera. *Wait till Andre sees the dailies.*

Regina was changing her wardrobe, and the crew was lighting a new scene, when Kendra said, "Cops are here."

"We'll work them into the background of the next shot."

"Not extras. Real cops."

Portly LAPD Detective Ajay Singh emerged from behind the bright lights. He introduced himself and asked, "You're the director?"

Miles squinted to see a couple of uniformed cops behind him. "Yeah. Is there a problem?"

"No, no. Just have a few questions," Detective Singh considered Jay with the prop badge and plastic gun on his belt. "What's this movie about?"

"A murder investigation," said Miles.

"I see. And this is the police station?" he said with a smirk, looking around at the battered desks, file cabinets, stained coffee cups, wanted posters, and files of loose paper placed by the set dresser.

"Supposed to be."

Detective Singh asked, "Is there a place we can talk?"

Moments later, near the craft service table, Detective Singh said to Miles, "I regret to inform you that Andre Kramer has been found dead."

That put Miles back on his heels. "What?"

"His body was retrieved from the Hollywood Reservoir this morning. Single bullet wound to the head. I understand Mr. Kramer is the executive producer on this movie."

"That's right."

"When was the last time you saw him?"

"Last night."

"Where?"

"Outside The Ivy on Robertson."

"What time was that?'

"Say 9:30 or so."

With a wave to the camera, Detective Singh said, "Set the scene for me."

Miles told him how he'd gone to the restaurant to try to talk to Andre about replacing Regina.

"Who's Regina?"

He pointed her out. She was on set in her new snug mini dress, holding up her phone as if to record some sort of social media post, unbeknownst to what was going on. In a lowered voice, Miles said, "I saw they were together and figured it would be too awkward to talk about recasting with Regina there, so I didn't talk to him."

"But…aren't you the director?"

"That's right."

"Don't you make the creative decisions?"

"I'm not Scorsese."

"Which means?"

"I was vetoed. My job is to call 'action…cut' and take the blame."

Detective Singh nodded, "I understand," and asked about the relationship Miles had with Andre.

Miles told him how they'd had a few meetings before he was finally hired to direct the movie. He admitted, "We didn't always see eye-to-eye, creatively speaking," and explained he'd only been brought on to direct because he could bring actor Jay DuPont to the table.

"My wife watched his TV show," the detective said. "Do you know of any reason someone would want to harm Mr. Kramer?"

Miles shrugged. "He's a producer."

The detective waited for him to elaborate.

"There's this old Hollywood saying: how do you know when the producer is lying? When his mouth is moving."

"You're saying he wasn't entirely honest."

"Something like that."

Detective Singh asked to speak with Regina separately, one-on-one.

Miles arranged that, and she was summoned into the hair and makeup room, behind closed doors. Meanwhile, her driver stood back in the shadows, observing.  After a moment, Miles heard her burst out with a sob.

Detective Singh emerged and said to Miles, "Since you two were the last to see Andre Kramer alive, I'll need to question each of you further...at the *real* police station."

* * *

Miles was expecting a windowless interrogation room like he'd seen on true crime shows.  Instead, he was directed to a conference room with floor-to-ceiling windows. If there were any hidden cameras, he didn't see them.

He wondered where Regina was being questioned.

His phone had been blowing up with voicemails and texts ever since he'd called wrap for the day. The cast and crew were sent home and told to await further instructions. Some were texting him, needing to know if the movie would be postponed so they could seek other employment. Miles didn't know.

Detective Singh entered the room, accompanied by a tall, attractive woman, whom he introduced as Detective Livingston. She was in her early thirties, professional-looking, and well put-together.  He picked up on a fragrance of some kind. This was how he'd envisioned the character of Dr. Luna Chambers. Too bad she wasn't an actress.

"We're trying to assemble a timeline," Singh said, taking a seat. "Andre's assistant, Theo, said you phoned him last night. Something about dropping off a script?"

"That's right," Miles said. "But once I saw Andre with Regina..."

"After you spied them outside the restaurant," Singh asked, "did you follow them?"

That came as a surprise. "No," Miles said.

"Regina said she saw your car tailing them."

"When? Where?"

"A few blocks from the restaurant."

That was strange. Neither Andre nor Regina had given any indication that they'd seen him across the street. No double-take. Not even a look. "I was there," Miles admitted, "but I didn't follow them."

Singh said, "Regina says Andre saw your car in the rear-view mirror as the two of them were driving back to her place."

"That wasn't me. Like I said, I couldn't talk about replacing Regina in front of her, so I went straight home."

"What time was that?"

"I'd say ten."

"Can anyone corroborate that?"

"I live alone."

Detective Livingston jotted something down before she said, "According to Regina Ray, Andre Kramer left her apartment around midnight."

"I was asleep by then."

Detective Livingston studied him for a moment. "What can you tell us about the funding for your movie?"

"Funding?"

"Where'd the money come from?"

"A limited liability corporation. Desire LLC is on the header of the checks."

"From what bank?"

"City National."

Detective Livingston took more notes. Singh asked, "So, you're not aware of who the investors are?"

"Andre never mentioned them."

"From what we've learned, Andre Kramer owes a lot of money around town. Various complaints filed."

"That sounds about right."

"You knew that?"

"He's got a reputation," Miles said. "Independent film is a gamble…for everyone. And since most of the crew works hourly and fills out timecards, payroll wouldn't come until after the movie had been shot."

"I don't follow."

"Because the payroll company takes two weeks to process a check," Miles said. "And our movie is shot in just two weeks, so…"

"I see. Were you concerned you may not be paid?"

"My terms are half upon commencement of principal photography, and half on delivery of the director's cut," Miles said. "But I'm still waiting on the first payment."

"So…you haven't been paid?"

"I'm supposed to get a wire transfer. Let's see." Miles opened the banking app on his phone to check. "No, I haven't gotten the money yet." He set his phone down. "Andre flaunts his wealth, driving that Land Rover Defender and playing the Hollywood bigshot, but he always has some sort of excuse when people need to get paid."

"And that angers you?"

"Wouldn't it anger you? Working your ass off and getting stiffed? Sorry… it's just…the business is changing these days. It used to be run by filmmakers with real passion for movies. Now tech bros counting clicks hold the reins."

"Speaking of the car," Detective Livingston said, "Mr. Kramer's vehicle was not found anywhere near the Hollywood Reservoir, where his body was discovered, but rather across town in Silverlake." The pair of detectives shared a look before she asked, "Don't you live in Silverlake?"

Miles could see this was not going his way. "Should I get a lawyer?"

Upon mention of counsel, the detectives thanked Miles for his time, stood, and informed him they'd be in touch. He was free to go.

On the drive home, Miles wondered why Regina and Andre thought he was following them. That would explain her cold stare that morning in the makeup room. Not only did she know Miles was hesitant to cast her in the part, but also fearful he was stalking her.

From what Miles remembered, the body language they exhibited coming out of the restaurant was all lovey-dovey, attention focused entirely on each other, not looking around or across the street or anywhere else. He was certain they hadn't seen him.

Maybe Andre's assistant, Theo, had tipped off his boss that Miles was on his way to the restaurant. That must be it. But if that was the case, wouldn't Andre have been on the lookout for him?

One thing was for sure, the shoot was postponed indefinitely.

Miles spent most of the evening calling the cast and crew to bring them up to speed. He knew nothing other than that the film was put on hold until further notice. If another job came up, he encouraged them to take it. More than a few asked if they were going to be paid for the days they'd worked. "I really don't know," was all he could say. "But I'll do everything I can to make sure you do."

Miles poured himself a double Maker's Mark and searched the news on his laptop. One of the local stations had the story about the murder, a live reporter, and b-roll at the Hollywood Reservoir where the body of "Independent film producer Andre Kramer" was found—nothing Miles didn't know already. Their movie *Burning Desire* was not mentioned.

Anxiety paired with bourbon meant he didn't sleep well. His mind raced, worried that the cops thought he had something to do with Andre's murder.

Maybe he did need a lawyer.

The next morning, Miles called his entertainment lawyer to ask her advice. Lynn said she'd seen the news, but "criminal defense" was not her specialty. She recommended an attorney she'd gone to Pepperdine with while in law school. "He's at a firm that handles such matters. Many of his clients are in the entertainment industry."

That afternoon, Miles drove across town and sat across from Douglas Miller, an associate at a mid-Wilshire law office, for the initial consultation. In the lawyer's office, there were photos of Douglas with assorted actors and musicians Miles recognized. There was also a vintage slot machine and a lot of Rat Pack memorabilia.

Miles told the lawyer everything, from the day he'd met Andre to being hired through the turbulent production, and how he'd seen him outside the restaurant but did not approach. "Regina claims I followed them, but that's not true."

Douglas wrote on his legal pad. "If the police reach out to you again, contact me immediately. Until then, do nothing. And don't talk about the case to anyone. Including the press."

"How much will this cost me?"

"A fifteen-thousand-dollar retainer will get us started, but no need to worry about that unless the police reach out to you again. If so, we'll see what we're up against and take it from there."

*Fifteen thousand dollars?* He didn't have that kind of money.

The lawyer handed Miles his business card. "If they contact you, or if you are arrested, I'm your first call."

"They'll throw me in jail?"

"Depends on the circumstances. I can recommend a reasonable bail bondsman, charges less than ten percent. And this firm has a no-interest payment plan."

Miles said, "I don't have a fifteen-thousand-dollar retainer, or any collateral for bail. It's not like I have a job. Now that the film has been postponed, I'm broke and unemployed."

Douglas leaned back in his plush leather chair. "You have the option of a court-appointed attorney, but I advise against that. Consider the retainer the cost of freedom. I'm glad you came to me," he said, standing to offer his hand. "These things tend to take time. Like I said, if the police contact you again, say nothing and call me immediately. Friends don't let friends talk to cops."

The detectives did say they'd be in contact with Miles again, and that had him worried. The question was *when.*

* * *

The next day, Andre's assistant, Theo, called to inform Miles the film was officially cancelled. The executive assistant grew a little emotional, confiding that Andre was his mentor and he'd lost his job too. Miles asked if the cast and crew would be paid for the days they'd worked. Theo didn't know.

"Our people need to be paid," Miles insisted. "Before me."

"The insurance company has stepped in. They may be contacting you."

"I've got a question," Miles asked. "Did you tell Andre I was dropping off the revised pages that night, at The Ivy?"

"No," he said.

"You didn't call him, or text anything about me coming?"

"No."

"Are you sure?"

"Yes. I'd remember. You called me and I told you where he had the dinner reservation. That's it."

If Theo hadn't tipped off Andre, why did he believe Miles was following him? Then it came to him. The guy dressed in black—Regina's driver. Maybe that guy was parked outside the restaurant and saw Miles. Then *he* texted Regina as she and Andre drove to her apartment. They grew paranoid, both imagining Miles was following. That would explain what Regina had told the cops. It would also mean that the guy was not just Regina's driver—he was probably her bodyguard, too.

* * *

Over the next few days, there were social media posts from many people Miles knew, disgruntled crew and vendors from the local film community. Word had gotten around that Miles was at the helm of Andre's latest movie when he was murdered. He was afraid the stigma would rub off on him. Maybe this would be his last movie. Guilt by association.

He wondered if Andre could have stiffed the wrong person. Or was the murder random? A carjacking would explain why his Land Rover was found in Silverlake.

Miles had a feeling Regina's bodyguard knew more details but had no idea who he was or where to find him. Out of curiosity, he started following Regina on various social media platforms to see if she had ever mentioned the guy in one of her posts. Although she had posted videos since the murder, there was no mention of Andre or the movie, just more of the same—shopping, restaurants, lavish hotels, and upcoming music events such as Coachella.

There were clips from months ago of Regina reporting from the back seat of what appeared to be a limo. She'd boast where she was headed, and sometimes called out snarky comments to her unseen chauffeur, "Clive."

Miles found one post from a few weeks earlier when Regina spun her phone to show the driver behind the wheel. It was the same guy from the shoot.

So...Clive was his name.

Miles searched the internet for "Clive" combined with "bodyguard" and came up with a website for Clive Coleman, a Los Angeles-based security consultant. He called to meet him, and Clive agreed.

The office for CC Security was in a Sunset Boulevard high-rise. For visitors, the building offered no self-parking. Miles reluctantly left his Honda with the valet and took the elevator to meet Clive in his office.

Like the law firm he'd visited before, celebrity photos were on the walls. He got right down to business and asked. "You saw me outside The Ivy, right? And let Regina know?"

Clive folded his hands and said, "You could have been a threat. So yes, I messaged my client."

"But that was before you came to set the next day, so how did you know it was me?"

"From her audition."

"You were there?"

"Shadowing my client, yes."

"I don't remember seeing you."

"My specialty is being inconspicuous." Clive studied Miles. "Like that night outside the Ivy. I saw you there, staring at them across the street. I had to run, got an emergency call from another client...but before I left, I gave a full report to Regina. Told her you were there, what you were wearing, what your car looked like."

"You just left her there?"

"I didn't know you were gonna follow them."

"I *didn't* follow them. But it sounds like someone did."

Clive looked away with a frown, aware that he'd left his charge behind with what might have been a killer on her tail. "I asked if she wanted me to stick with her. She said no, Andre could handle it. But she texted me later, saying she thought she saw you behind them on the way home. Said your car was easy to spot because of the broken headlight, but they lost you on the way to Andre's place."

"I don't have a broken headlight."

Clive shrugged his massive shoulders. "She said you did. All I know is, the next morning, I picked up Regina and drove her to the film set. Now…if you don't mind," he said, checking his watch, "I've got a commitment."

"Driving Regina somewhere?"

"I'm not at liberty to say."

Miles suspected it was. He thanked him for his time and said, "By the way, tell Regina that while I may not be her biggest fan, I sure didn't kill her boyfriend."

The next day, Miles saw a segment about the murder on television. A person of interest had been detained for questioning—a homeless guy who had been previously arrested for carjacking. That would explain why Andre's Range Rover was discovered miles away in Silverlake. The news story segued to the recent uptick in crime.

The call from Detective Singh never came.

* * *

To make rent, Miles had taken a job helping a contractor friend install kitchen tile. He was mixing grout when Andre's widow, Diedre, left a voicemail. That came as a surprise. He called her back. She apologized that he hadn't been paid and said, "I've been fielding all these lawsuits and process servers…everyone that is owed money."

"I can only imagine," he said.

"In honor of Andre's memory, I want to do the right thing by paying."

"So, you're paying his delinquent bills?"

"For *Burning Desire* and some of his other movies, yes. It's the right thing to do. I have a check for you, but I need you to sign for it."

That was great news. He'd assumed he would never get paid for the work he'd put into the film, both the weeks of preproduction and the days on set. They planned to meet at the nearby Farmer's Market on Fairfax.

Miles got there first and texted Diedre that he was outside Du-Par's

Restaurant. She replied that she was running late. It was dark by the time Diedre pulled up in her Lexus. Maneuvering into the tight parking spot seemed to frazzle her.

Miles noticed the burned-out headlight and noted that her car was silver, like his Honda. He felt a sudden cramp in his stomach. *Could she have been the one following Andre that night?*

Diedre got out and thanked him for being so patient. She had a ledger and a one-page deal memo for his signature, the check already made out for half of his directing fee. "I believe this is what you are owed," she said, "Is that right?"

"Yes, and thank you," he said. "I saw on the news on TV that they have someone in custody."

Saddened, Diedre said, "It's all been so overwhelming."

"Tragic."

"Andre was complicated," she said, melancholy. "And I apologize for my husband not being a very good businessman. He borrowed a lot of money over the years, much of it from my family…my father and great aunt. I'm just trying to do the right thing for everybody. It's important to me."

Miles asked, "When are you paying the crew?"

"The payroll service will mail checks tomorrow."

He hoped that was true. Thinking of his friend Jay, Miles asked, "What about the cast? Will they be paid, too?"

She nodded, "From bond posted with the Screen Actors Guild."

That made sense to him. Independent films are required to post a bond with the guild to ensure payment. Miles signed the ledger and deal memo on the hood of her Lexus, and she handed over the check. He noted the front of her car could easily be mistaken for his Honda and said, "Looks like you've got a headlight out."

"Yeah," she said. "I've been meaning to take it in."

He asked, "What about Regina?"

"What about her?"

"Will she be paid?"

Diedre clenched her jaw. Her mood changed, fire in her eyes. She took a deep breath before saying, "She'll get hers."

*Could there be double meaning in that?*

Miles said, "It's not like she worked more than a half day…and between you and me, she wasn't very good."

"Trust me," Diedre said, "I'm taking care of everything. Thank you. I'm sorry the film didn't work out for you."

"I'll find another," he said hopefully. He explained the fact that since his cast and crew were paid, that meant the next time he had a film for them they, wouldn't run the other way.

Diedre gave him a light squeeze on his arm, climbed into her Lexus, and waved as she pulled out.

Miles held his hand up for her to stop. He motioned for her to roll down the window, which she did, and he said, "You know, if you turn on your brights, the extra bulb in the lamp compensates for your burnt-out headlight."

"Really?" She tried that and it worked.

"A temporary fix, but you should really take it in. The cops can pull you over for that, you know."

"Thanks for the tip," Diedre said, and drove off into the night.

For a second, he considered tipping off Clive, Regina's bodyguard, to keep an eye out for a silver Lexus—but decided against it.

# Making Your Luck

by Teel James Glenn

*NOW:*

Blood! So much blood and brain matter. It turned the heraldry on his tunic from bright reds and gold to muddy brown and, mixed with the hay of the stall, looked like so much oatmeal. I had trouble keeping my lunch down.

It had to come to this, even though it shouldn't have. The reality in the fantasy. This made me think back to two weeks ago when it all began.

* * *

*THEN:*

"*A Game of Boners?*" I said to my buddy Terry Rhodes. "I don't want to work on that, man. That's the most porny porno title I've ever heard!"

"Like you can afford to be picky, Evan. I know how much money you owe with your ex-wife hounding you. Besides, that is the point of the title," he said. "It's like *Snakes on a Plane*, you know what you're getting." We were sitting in the Residuals Tavern on Ventura Boulevard in Hollywood, where you get a free drink for any residual check under a buck. It was a hangout for a lot of industry folk. "And you're the one who's always saying, 'We make our own luck,' aren't you?"

"Yeah, but *A Game of*—"

"The director convinced the producer to give him the money to add real battle scenes to make the movie a crossover. Totally modular, dude. They can release it in two versions, like they did back in the day with *Flesh Gordon* or *Lord of the G-Strings*. It's shooting on a ranch with a stable where we can house the horses."

I'd known Terry for years back East, but he'd come out to LA three years ahead of me. Back then, he had been the one to jump at the "iffy" jobs—like a couple of horror films I'd worked on with him, one of which was literally canceled while we were in cars on the way to the set. We'd made our union cards in NY, working on the soaps back before the unions merged, and then on low-budget horror flicks to get our Screen Actors Guild cards so we would work on union films. We were lucky enough never to have had to work food service because we both did fairs and acted in a year-round haunted house between soap gigs.

"I've been hired to stage some fight stuff and battle scenes," Terry continued. "Fully clothed."

"Really, man," I said. "That kind of thing can follow you—"

"We're not gonna be on the set with any sex," he assured me.

"Just three days of stunts after they've done the rest of the shooting— we *can* use the footage for reels. And it pays some in advance."

"An advance? Really?"

"I got the lowdown from the director—he's a member of my gym. The deal is he's shooting these three days as a student film," he continued, "and then he's gonna sell the footage to his company and incorporate it."

"So low-end money and no residuals?"

"Yes," he said, "but still money. Good money. I mean, come on, you haven't worked since you did that cruise ship murder mystery in Santa Monica."

It was true. In the eight months I'd been in California, I had gone through all my savings and was in deep debt. I was a month behind on my rent and in danger of being homeless. Thank God my car was paid for.

"Hey, money is money, man," he insisted, pushing hard, "and the lead is six-one, close enough to your size, so I wanna do a bunch of Texas switches with you doubling him."

I'm six foot six, so I usually just played goons. And frankly, most porn actors are not tall in order to make their—uh—assets look bigger on screen.

"Don't you want to get paid to swing swords on a film?"

"All right," I said. It was a childhood dream to be Errol Flynn's Robin Hood. "I guess I'm up for it."

"You brought your period stuff west, right?"

"Yeah, I have about a dozen swords, steel and aluminum, and most of my Ren fair clothes came out with me in the car."

"I thought so." He laughed. He'd done the same; it's hard to let go of the weapons that feel right. "I want to show the producer and director a fight tomorrow—maybe we could revive our chess game fight from New York—you still remember it?"

"Mostly," I said. "Nothing an hour reviewing it can't fix."

"Super," he exclaimed. "I spoke to a couple of guys from the fair here, and we can reuse their routines to save rehearsal time. I've also cleared using two of their horses, Champion and Defender, that are trained to joust. We'll give this SOB a real bang for his buck."

"Really?" I said. "That is your choice of words?" We both laughed.

The next day, we drove out to meet the director and producer at his ranch. It was at the edge of the TMZ, the thirty-mile zone around LA that counted as day work.

"Okay, Evan," Terry said as we pulled up to the Spanish-style main house with two wings. "I've sold you as the fight choreographer with me as the stunt coordinator, but you know I'm thinking of you as a partner on this."

"I appreciate that," I said. "But it's your contact. I'll follow your lead."

The house was two stories and vaguely castle-like with a turret at one end that had been done in a pseudo-stone facing.

I was still skeptical. Everyone I'd met in my time in LA had a delusional view of how important they were, but if I didn't come up with alimony soon, I'd be more than homeless. I needed this job. I grabbed the duffel bag with the swords and followed Terry into the building. We were met at the door by a blonde in high heels, wearing a bikini and holding a martini glass.

Terry and I exchanged a silent look of *Hollywood, eh?* and worked not to snicker.

"Oh, you're the sword guys!" she said with a southern drawl. Then she turned back and yelled, "King Arthur is here, Mort!"

That did get us both snickering.

She led us through the side of a courtyard, then through French doors into the presence of the producing-directing duo.

It was painfully clear which was which at first sight: Mort Devine was in his fifties and might have been sent by central casting. He had a huge cigar jutting out of his mouth below a bushy white mustache. He was bald, about thirty pounds overweight, but fearless about it, with gold chains around his neck and an open Hawaiian shirt that exposed his considerable gut. His skin was a leathery brown that contrasted with his white Bermuda shorts.

He sat behind a Lucite desk covered with papers, and behind him was a wall covered in memorabilia, including a cricket bat, a signed football, and photos of various sports stars, all autographed.

Beside him stood a skinny, dark-haired guy in his twenties, as pale white as this transplanted New Yorker. He wore glasses and dressed in wrinkled khakis that looked like he had slept in them.

"Hi," Glasses said when the blonde ushered us in, "I'm Alan Glick! I'm directing!" He came over and pumped my hand.

"Alan said you guys were gonna show us what you can do," Devine said, with a real show-me attitude.

"Oh, goodie," the blonde said. "A fight!"

"Easy, Candy," Devine said, "we're not gonna see any real blood."

"Not if we do it right, anyway," I said. Terry gave me a death stare.

"We'll need a little room," Terry said, looking around.

"No problem," Devine said. "I think the kids will like the show. Come on." He slipped an arm around the twenty-year-younger Candy's waist and led us out a side door to what turned out to be a patio with a pool.

Around the pool, a dozen people lounged on chairs—most of them women, in little or nothing and sporting more plastic enhancements than a custom model car kit.

"Gather around, kids," Devine announced, "I've brought some entertainment for you!"

I shot Terry a look, and he just shrugged.

"We can work over here," Terry said, pointing to a grassy spot, twenty feet on each side.

I took out two steel swords. Since they rang like bells, they were better than the aluminum for live shows. Then I pulled out gloves. I pushed the circumstances to the back of my mind and focused on the fight.

"This is another fine mess you've gotten me into, Ollie," I whispered.

Terry grinned. "Just another live show. We wow them, and we can get a decent advance."

We went on guard, then assumed our Renaissance Faire personas.

"A pox on you, you slack-jawed, flop-eared knave!" I called.

"Do your worst, villain!" He gave a heroic laugh. I was always the bad guy since he was only five-nine. *Towering goon, will travel* is my career description.

The broadsword fight was only thirty-five moves, with a couple of breathing/acting breaks between. We really sold it, chewing scenery so that the scantily clad audience cheered and laughed.

The fight had a lot of blade exchanges with a really nice twist at the end, where he kicked my sword out of my hand, caught it, and stabbed me. I died with suitable drama.

The audience went wild, clapping with squeals of joy. The women came up to mob us. I felt like a rock star. I tried to forget it had been a while since I'd been that close to any woman—not since my divorce.

Devine and the director loved it, with Glick yelling, "Excellent!"

One of the two who stood out in the crowd was a tall, blond-haired, sculpted guy who introduced himself as Lance. He was the guy I'd be doubling.

The other was a little person, a red-haired, perfectly formed woman who barely reached my hip in height. She came right up to me, smiling. "Hey, big guy," she said in a surprisingly deep voice for her size, "you swing a mean sword!"

"This is the real star of the film," Devine said. He stepped up and beamed down at the woman. "She's our gender-flipped Tyrion, the hottest Adult Video News Magazine star today, Lusty Little Lulu!"

She did a tiny curtsy and giggled, then held out a little hand to me, "My real name's Anna."

"Evan Kent," I said. I felt like Goliath.

"You gonna teach me to sword fight?"

"Uh, yeah, sure," I said, a little off-kilter. "I'm sure there will be time on the set."

"There will be," Devine said. "I want my star sword fighting in the trailers!"

"We are gonna make history," Glick said. He was so excited he was practically dancing.

"Let's head to the office again and talk," Devine said. He turned and called to the others, "Okay, kids, lunch will be in about an hour, and then we meet as planned."

We followed Devine—sans Candy—back into the office with the little redhead waving to me.

Once inside the office, Devine's casual attitude suddenly went all business, and he and Terry hashed out the numbers.

While they negotiated, I found myself fascinated by the sports mementos behind the producer, particularly the cricket bat and a still photo next to it—a black man in uniform with the name Gordon Greenidge signed on it.

"He was great," Devine said when he saw me looking. "Best player from Barbados in the 70s and 80s. I met him when I was ten." He was suddenly reduced to a preteen nerd for getting his hero's autograph, and it helped humanize him for me.

"The kids live in the west wing while I shoot pictures," Devine said when we had agreed on money. "It ensures no one misses a shoot date, and we get more time on site."

"The sex—" I started, but Terry stopped me with a look.

"No worry." Devine caught where I was going. "All that is a closed set."

I must have looked relieved because the producer laughed. "You'll get used to it, pal, but a little bit of advice—don't mess with the talent." The way he said it, and the rumor that he had mob connections, hinted at a dark fate for anyone who didn't heed his warning.

We left with a contract and an advance—enough for me to square my rent. We giggled like two high school girls on prom night.

"Better to be lucky than skilled," Terry said.

"Always," I laughed.

* * *

Three days after our meeting, Terry and I moved into a room in the west wing of what we were now calling Castle Devine. It was very weird. The talent (what the behind-camera folk called "actors" and not always as a compliment) slept on the second floor, while the crew—which we were— slept on the first floor. This counted the camera crew, lighting and sound team, a make-up woman, art department guys, and us four stunt people. It was kind of like a college dorm, but for all of his casual beach dude attitude, Devine ran it like a general. Or a capo.

Devine delighted in making big midday meals for everyone at an outdoor kitchen. He had two coal-burning pizza ovens and crafted gourmet pizzas for us. It turned out Candy (real name Candice) had a degree as a dietician and regulated the meals for the actresses and actors who all wanted to stay trim and fit.

Candy was kind of like the den mother for the other actors who had a strict curfew and, when she was not putting on the airhead act, came off as older than her years.

Terry brought in his jousting partner Joe from the fair and another guy, Ben, and they would coordinate with Glick to figure out the camera angles for the stunts. He also dealt with the horses and set up the stable, which came with the place when Devine bought it.

I had three jobs: helping a carpenter work on a couple of breakaway chairs and a table for the climactic Red Wedding scene, prepping for the fire burn

I was going to do at that same scene, and lastly, training our lead to be believable in a sword fight opposite Lance for the big finale.

Lance, unfortunately, had no physical coordination at all and no memory for moves. I suspect his short-term memory had gone up in smoke at some point.

Anna was another thing.

She had a background with baton twirling and dance, which I worked into her style. I extended the handle on one of the aluminum short swords to allow her to use it two-handed, and I set about teaching her the basics of film sword fighting.

"Okay, Too-tall," she said to me after I explained the basic grip and footwork. "Ready to make me into Xena?" She gave a glottal war cry.

"We'll see about that, Mighty Mite. On Guard!"

I've discovered that students retain more and learn more quickly if they're relaxed, and the best way to relax them is to keep them laughing. While I worked with Anna, we joked back and forth.

It wasn't hard as she had a great sense of humor, apparently no ego about herself, and did learn fast. By the end of our first session, I was pretty sure I could choreograph a good-looking final fight with her, especially if I doubled Lance for most of it. This would give Glick his big finish.

The class with Anna went so well that by the second day, some of the others asked if they could join in. Some had dance backgrounds, so I soon had four Amazons and two guys who were pretty good at sword basics.

I had to get used to the nudity pretty quickly, because the women were not the least bit self-conscious about walking around topless. As long as I viewed them just as students, I could focus.

Over the next couple of days, I worked with Anna and the other actresses whenever they weren't off shooting sex scenes. It was just a bit uncomfortable for me, a very strange concept, knowing that when they were away on set, they were screwing. I had to put those thoughts out of my mind.

Devine took note of me working with the girls, and at lunch on the third day, he pulled me aside.

"I thought I told you not to mess with the assets, kid?"

"What do you mean?"

"I seen you with Anna," he whispered. "And I seen how she looks at you."

"Not to worry, man," I said, the hackles on my neck prickling. "I'm just turning her into the Xena you want her to be. I don't mess with talent, Mr. Devine."

He gave me the hairy eye, and then he was all jovial again. "That's good. Make sure it stays that way." Before I could respond, he was off to cheer on his performers.

I didn't like to be threatened, and I almost quit right there and then, but I needed the money badly. Besides, if I left the production, they'd shoot anyway, and somebody might get hurt.

Glick, the director, came to watch us and, by the end of the fifth day, decided to enlarge a training scene with the women doing simple sword forms. I considered this a testament to my teaching.

Lance never did catch on.

I would have to double Lance for 95% of the fight, which was good because there was no way we could find anyone to double Anna or risk him injuring her. I talked with Glick and suggested that he shoot just POV close-ups of Lance, and he agreed.

I talked to Terry that night to tell him what Devine said.

"We can really get a lot out of this, Evan, if we can hang on," he said. "Just four more days. This could be our lucky break."

He was right, since I'd already made great contacts with the crew. "Okay," I said. "Better lucky and all that."

Still, as I lay there trying to sleep, I had a bad feeling about how things were going.

* * *

Doing stunts is a paradox. On the one hand, it's all about control—set your own pressure in the jumper box, make sure the airbags are inflated correctly. Check the piston on the ratchets to make sure when you get yanked back, it's with just the right amount of pull. If it's too much, it snaps your spine, but too little pressure doesn't look good for the camera.

Yet you also have to give up control.

You can't control what angle they shoot it from. Or the guy who's supposed to put you out for that fire burn is asleep at the switch, and the heat through that gel fries your skin like hotcakes on a griddle.

Yeah, things go wrong, so sometimes it is better to be lucky than skilled.

The day finally came for us to shoot stunts. The art department set up colorful banners around the courtyard for the training sequence, which really upscaled the place. Some dialogue was shot with training in the background that would be integrated into different parts of the film.

We also shot some isolated pieces of Joe and Terry riding back and forth quickly, leaping on or off their horses, and delivering messages to different cast members. Defender, who was the finicky horse when allowed to get bored, behaved himself and only tried to buck Terry off once.

Glick shot with three cameras for most setups to speed production.

It was like we were making a real movie!

Devine was around for most of it, wearing a medieval tabard in case the camera caught him, wandering around the set with Candy hovering near him, making sure things moved. He acted like he was pleased but kept casting side-eye my way.

Lance blew his lines a couple of times—which was not a surprise to me—but Anna nailed her dialogue each time, though I could see her getting frustrated with him.

I noticed Devine watching her and felt a weird sense of annoyance.

Then we did the training yard sequence where all of Devine's so-called kids who had learned sword with me—plus Ben, Joe, and Terry in the deep background—went through simple forms on repeat.

Glick shot long shots.

Then, the cameras moved in for individual close-ups of some barely dressed ladies. Anna did simple drills with two of the other women, and they looked great. I felt like a proud papa.

Glick couldn't control himself. He was giggling the whole time and murmuring "production value."

Then we broke for lunch. I found myself sitting near Anna.

"Did my sword stuff look okay?" she asked.

"You did great, Mighty Mite."

"You're not just saying that?"

"No, I'm not just saying that. You look really good with a sword, like a regular Maureen O'Hara. You really seem to love it."

"Yeah, I do," she said, her expression pensive. "I'll tell you something in confidence." She lowered her voice. "I've been thinking about getting out."

"What do you mean?" I wasn't sure I was comfortable where this was going. Devine was already not happy about my interactions with Anna, and if he suspected he might lose his star, he would blame me.

"Well," she said. "I've been doing this about a year now—which is actually a lotta pictures the way they shoot them. I had a ton of student loans and a bad breakup to recover from. Mort's been great to me and built me up like a star, but really, I don't feel good about it."

Wow, last thing I expected. I looked around at Devine, who was over by the ovens, ladling out more food. When I looked back, Anna's very blue eyes were sincere.

"I've always been physically gifted, you know, sports and stuff," she said. "It's all I've been good at, really, but people judge me. I'm not big enough to be an athlete in the conventional sense. I was sort of drifting when my ex got me into this business. Maybe it's silly, but somehow, when I picked up the sword, it made me think about, well…"

"You can always take classes," I offered. "Believe me, I know what it's like—the first time I held a sword, it was almost a religious feeling." She got a curious look when I said that, so I added, "There are other good sword teachers out here, Speaker and Delongis come to mind. They're amazing."

"Not with you?" she said. "I hoped…"

"Uh, sure," I said. "Just saying there are a bunch of good people who feel that same way I do, who also love the sword."

That seemed to set her thinking. As we were cleaning up the plates after the break, she said, "So rehearsal tomorrow?"

"Yup, but remember, you don't get to kill me till day after tomorrow."

She giggled. "Yeah, I know."

* * *

That night was the final war council for the jousting sequences the following day.

"I need to reshoe Fender," Terry said. "His right rear shoe is not seated well."

"Can you do it?" I asked. We'd nicknamed Defender *Fender* because he was like a car wreck—nobody but Terry could ride him or even handle him much of the time. But the horse loved to run and really liked to play the charging-at-the-other-horse game with Champion.

"Oh yes," Terry said. "I always bring extra shoes and tack. I'll do it tonight." He was smiling like a loon.

"It will help that we don't have to do this in sequence," I said. Joe and Terry would be doubling actors for the joust under helmets. Glick planned to cover the crowd and horse stuff all day.

"Once you guys are unhorsed," I explained further, "I'll come out as Lance, and you and me do our fight." It would be the one we had first showed Devine. We were certainly getting mileage out of that fight.

We broke early, with Terry heading off to reshoe the troublemaker. I went down to take a swim in the pool to clear my head for a half hour. I was confused about my feelings for Anna because they made no sense— bonding over freaking swords—but yeah, I was finally seeing a chance to get a foothold in Hollywood, so I couldn't screw it up.

When I came out of the pool to dry off, I heard Devine yelling in his office. I made my way to just outside the door.

"I don't want you talking to him," Devine snarled.

"How the hell can I work with him without talking to him?" It was Anna.

"You don't have to talk to him every spare minute," Devine said.

"You can't tell me what I can and can't do."

"I can and I will," he said. "I hold your contract—"

"You don't own me," she shot back. "I can walk anytime I want."

"You do, and I'll sue you into oblivion, Anna. Or more. You know I mean it. I've poured a ton into building you up—"

"I never asked for that."

"You never said stop."

I felt dirty listening to their conversation. I almost barged in, but I realized if I did that, it would be the end of my job, and I'd be right back to where I was the week before. I'm ashamed to say I chickened out.

Just then, I heard Candy come into the room. "Knock it off, you two," she said. "Anna has to get some rest for tomorrow. You can deal with all this after the picture wraps."

"Just watch yourself, Anna," Devine said. "I'll fire that stuntman if—"

"Don't you dare," Anna snapped. "If you want your picture with me, you leave him alone to do what you hired him to do."

I heard her storm out and made a quick beeline for my room before she saw me.

It was a long time before my anger toward the producer and my gratitude toward the little actress would let me sleep. What the hell kind of luck was getting this job and now this drama scene to complicate things!

* * *

Day two of stunts comprised the joust sequence and some inserts for battle scenes—close-up one- and two-person fight combinations that Glick could edit into the montage of the big battle.

There was coverage of the reviewing stand with the nobility watching the joust, the scenes of actors mounting and putting on their helmets (at which point Joe and Terry took over), and the joust itself.

The horses both loved the running-at-each-other game, so whenever they turned to look at each other, they were raring to go. Defender was particularly feisty.

It went smoothly, so we finished all that by lunch. Glick moved fast from set-up to set-up and decided he would add some of the two-person battle scenes in the afternoon. They had some dialogue they would do as well, since the Red Wedding set was not quite ready.

"We'll have plenty of time to shoot the burn after the sword fight with Anna," I told Glick when he made the change. "It will not take as long as we'd thought—she's good at this now. If the burn's the last shot of the day, I can break the furniture flailing around and even set fire to some of the table settings."

His face lit up. "I like the way you think, Evan. We'll make that the wrap shot for the picture."

After lunch, while Glick shot other cast members in close-up, Anna and I picked up a little more rehearsal time. She said nothing about the conversation I'd overheard, but I could see she was tense—at least until she picked up the sword. Two swings into the fight, she was grinning.

"Look," I said as we walked through the fight again. "Make sure you don't grin while we're fighting in front of the camera. It's supposed to be serious."

"I can't help it. This is fun."

I laughed. "I do know. If you can't stop smiling, you need to put some evil in your eyes. You know the look, after all, you're a real redhead."

She giggled, "You peeked!" She must have seen me blush because she added, "It might be movie magic."

"Anywhere else, maybe," I noted. She laughed again as we finished the sword session, but when I looked up, there was Devine watching us again, and suddenly, he was the one with evil in his eyes.

I made a point of not sitting near Anna at dinner, and I was conscious that Candy was working subtly to keep us apart. I just had to make it through one more day to finish the job. I felt that every time Devine glanced my way, it was a cold challenge.

The next day, we moved to the Red Wedding set to shoot the climactic sword fight sequence. We did it all in long shots with multiple cameras while I was tricked up in a blond wig to look like Lance. Anna performed flawlessly, so we were able to speed through. They did reversals with Lance standing in for some close-up work with Anna, and just like that, we were done.

Anna ran up, wrapping me in a mini-hug.

"That was the most fun I've ever had," she said.

I found myself putting my arms around her before I realized what I was doing. "Me too, Tiny Terror." Then I looked over to see Devine standing there in his tabard like a low-rent King Arthur and thought, *Shit!*

All that was left was my fire gag.

We broke for a late lunch.

"We got it in the bag, man," Terry told me.

"As long as you don't let me get cooked," I joked. I actually had full confidence in him—he'd be handling the fire extinguisher and would be on me the moment I hit the ground, which was my way of letting him know that I was getting hot. Joe would be on the water-soaked blanket as backup.

It came down to Anna again since her character was supposed to throw the torch at me as I doubled for Lance.

She was nervous.

"I don't want to get it wrong," she said as we were finally ready for the shot. There was an unusual amount of tension on the set, with everyone a little worried. I tried not to let it trickle down to me.

"Easy peasy, Tiny Terror." I was all gelled up, my Nomex underwear hidden under the cotton version of the costume. My only concern was the blond wig coming off or melting to my head—it was the only artificial fiber on my body. I slathered extra gel on it and had them use a lighter coat of the rubber cement so it would not burn hot for too long.

"You can say that," she said. "I'm the one setting you on fire. What if something goes wrong?"

"This is what I do, Anna," I said. "Really, don't worry. We make our own luck, and this movie is lucky for me—I met you, right?"

She brightened. "Right!"

Then we were set, and cameras rolled. Just before Anna lit me up, I glanced over to see Devine in his kingly robes sitting at the dais with the nobility. If looks could kill, I was pretty sure he'd have turned me into ash.

I tried to ignore him, regulate my breathing, and go forward.

Anna threw the torch, setting my back on fire, and I was off and literally running. I had to keep moving forward to keep the flames behind me, as we had no budget for fans. I had to spin—not too tight to keep the flames from my face—but had to keep moving, slamming into things for effect.

I smashed into tables, knocked over chairs, and flailed my arms to make it even more violent.

This was a big stunt for me—the footage from it would lead off my stunt reel—so I wanted to keep it up as long as I could. My maximum time was really only sixty or seventy seconds, and I pushed it pretty hard, even when my back started to feel the heat.

Finally, I dropped to my knees and lay flat, which was the signal for Terry to race in and hit me with the extinguisher.

Joe covered me with the blanket, and the room exploded into applause.

"That's a wrap!" Glick announced to cheers.

"Are you okay?" Anna asked with concern. She grabbed my hand and held it tight.

"Mostly," I said, "just feels like a bad sunburn—I probably went a few seconds too long."

"Just cooked ham," Terry said with a grin. We gave high fives. We knew we'd done a good job on this show.

I looked over and saw Devine walking toward us, a wide smile plastered on his face. He leaned close so only I could hear him and said, "Your luck just ran out, stuntman. For good! You better look over your shoulder from now on."

I smiled and whispered, "Don't you know I make my own luck, pal. I don't like being threatened."

Then I went off to get out of costume. Anna even offered to put some salve on my back. That made Devine seethe.

* * *

## NOW:

"Pull him out of there," somebody said.  Terry jumped past me to grab Fender's head to steady him.  Two more of the crew grabbed Devine's ankles and started to pull him out of the stall.

"Leave him," I yelled. "The police will want to see things as they are."

"But—" someone started.

"He's clearly dead," I said. "Moving him won't do anything."

It was three a.m., and Terry had found Devine when he'd gone to check the stalls to get the horses ready to load later. He'd come to our room and let everyone else know what had happened. And called the police.

The whole cast and crew were a mess, suddenly fully awake and horrified. Anna and one of the other girls had to take a hysterical Candice under their wings.

"What the hell was he doing out here?" Terry asked as he managed to lead Defender out of the stall to a second one.

"It makes no sense," someone else said. "But he was pretty drunk last night after the wrap."

Almost everyone had too much to drink after the wrap.

Now here lay the producer, still in his tabard, the back of his head bashed in with the clear impression of a horseshoe—and there was blood on Fender's back left hoof.

"Why the hell would he come out here to the stable?" was the question everyone asked. Including the police.

The coroner's jury ruled it an accidental death resulting from an inebriated individual who was where he shouldn't have been. Just bad luck.

And that was that.

Since Glick was a junior partner in Divine Pictures and was very happy with the work we'd done on the movie, he paid us stunt guys a bonus.

Glick eventually cut the film, losing much of the adult content and releasing it as *Clash of the Clans* for the general release, and it did pretty well. It was a swan song for Anna's adult film career.

She now works doing stunts, doubling children in films, and is my best sword student.

As long as no one ever questions why Devine would've burned one of his own cricket bats in a pizza oven…or notices that there were nail holes in the shape of a horseshoe at the end of that burnt bat…things are fine.

As for me, I believe a man makes his own luck. If you doubt it, just check the horseshoe I keep nailed up on my wall.

# Stalker

by Jon Lindstrom

Los Angeles can get cold at night. Most people don't know that. It's the ocean. The cool sea air flows in, and during the winter months, it can get down to the forties, even the thirties. That's working in my favor tonight, because that means very few people will be out at this time. Most are indoors, staying warm. I'm out here, in the dark, where She lives.

You're probably wondering why I'm telling you this.

I'm Jason Wright. I'm an actor, and for the last several years, I've been on the daytime soap opera, *Another Time, Another Place*. Maybe you've heard of it? Yeah, it's one of the big ones. Man, if I could only turn back the clock, decide *not* to make my first appearance at the annual fan club convention. But why wouldn't I?

My being cast on that show had been a bit of a fluke, as it was, only meant to be a summer storyline. My character had been introduced as a villain designed to split up a popular couple, and later served as the magnet to pull them back together. Three months, tops, my agent told me. I figured, what the hell? It's not like a soap opera was one of my career goals, but I hadn't worked in a while, and it sure would go a long way to paying off my credit card bills.

By the end of that summer, I found myself in the eye of the perfect storm for Hollywood success: The writers were creatively inspired, and mine had become the most popular story on the most popular serial on TV. And even better, my character was being regularly singled out as one of the most infamous villains in soap opera history.

Given the higher-than-usual ratings, the producers offered me a long-term contract. Three years of steady employment, and with it, a hefty raise, as well as a higher profile than I'd ever known. And as that three years came to a close, they offered me another three. And then another.

Hollywood can be a rocky ride of struggles and triumphs, so I admit I got used to the smooth going of steady work. That was almost ten years ago. Ten ATAP Official Fan Club conventions ago.

That's where She found me.

At my very first appearance.

The events then were always at The Sportsmen's Lodge in Studio City. Built in the 1800s, it was rebuilt in the 1930s, designed to resemble the country lodge it had once been. It had a restaurant and bar, a swimming pool, and a small lake stocked with trout where John Wayne had once taught his children to fish. It was all connected with pathways through trees and shrubs and small bridges over bubbling streams. Kitschy, but kinda cool.

Big gatherings like the fan convention were held in a large banquet room with a raised stage on one end. Every year it's the same. After talking on stage, we would sign literally hundreds of autographs and printed headshots and pose for photos with excited fans. All in all, it was pretty great, getting to mingle with the show's audience. I was pleasantly surprised by the warm devotion they had for the show and for the actors. For the first time, and in the best way, I understood what it could mean to be an actor. We gave, they received, and then they gave back. It really was, and is, a reciprocal relationship.

When She made herself known, she didn't make any real impression at all.

She waited in line for her turn, then handed me an 8x10 color photo to autograph (a network publicity shot of me in a tux, giving my best "bad boy" glare). Then she asked to pose for a picture with me, just like everybody else. I swear, it was so benign, I forgot about her as soon as she was gone.

But a few weeks after that first event, her first letter arrived at the studio.

It didn't even raise any alarm bells when I saw that her return address was from the north end of the San Fernando Valley, only fifteen miles from Burbank, where we filmed. And the letters were fairly typical, just proclamations about my talent and good looks. But within a couple of months, the tone took a more personal turn. She began to admit deep feelings for me, despite our brief, solitary encounter.

Then came the Polaroids.

Not that She was a looker with a gym-toned bod. I would best describe her as "plain." She also couldn't seem to hold a camera still to save her life, but that didn't stop her from sending blurry pictures of herself with her ample cleavage in the foreground, or fuzzy bra-and-panty selfies in the mirror.

I once read somewhere that how a person keeps their house can be a sign of their mental stability. The room behind her was such a mess it looked like someone had lobbed in a grenade.

Then came faceless shots of nipples, and patches of pubic hair above naked crossed legs, along with scribbled notes describing her fantasies of how she would treat me should she ever find me in her bed. Fantasies that I could only describe as "demented," especially coming from a woman.

I reported this correspondence to network security. They seemed bugged that I hadn't alerted them sooner, but, as far as I could tell, they didn't do anything about it. Maybe it was because, as the police later told me, stalkers are almost always men targeting women.

Then things got really bizarre.

She started arriving at whatever venue I was appearing at hours before the doors would open. She would snag herself a seat down front, then *stare* at me the entire time I was on stage. Her eyelids would droop, and her eyes would glisten over this weird half-smile. My colleagues confessed that her presence freaked them out. She once showed up at the house I'd shared with my ex-wife. She walked up and knocked on the door when my ex was home. Now, I've never been one to wish ill on anyone, not even a former spouse, but the moment for action had come.

I called the police.

And…nothing.

And I never knew when she might make herself known again. She would go dark for a few months at a time, and I'd start to hope she had moved on. Like my ex, I wouldn't wish it on my worst enemy, but in truth, I had hoped she'd lost interest in me and found someone else to salivate over. And then, as quickly as she would disappear, there she was again! At different times she had managed to contact, and *convince*, more than one of my friends and/or colleagues that she was either a "soap journalist" writing a profile on me and wanted to interview them for background (but it would be so much better if I was at the interview, too), or that she was an "old family friend" or "distant relative" who happened to be in town and would love to surprise me on set, so could you help her obtain a pass to the studio so she could deliver said "surprise"?

In the end, She found my current home address the old-fashioned way. By lying.

I was tipped off when credit cards I hadn't applied for began showing up in my mailbox. I was suddenly receiving cards from bank branches in places like Fargo, ND, Charlotte, NC, and Wilmington, DE. When I asked the customer service rep at one of them about the origin of the card applications, the woman was helpful, but cautious. Identity theft is a major problem for credit bureaus.

"Let's have a look at your profile," she said.

I felt my brow furrow in confusion. "I've never set up a profile with you."

"Well, you have one here," she said. "I'm looking at it."

I confirmed my personal details by delivering a rundown of my home address, email, and social security number. With enough required accurate identification, she finally read the phone number in the profile back to me. It was a number I didn't recognize…because it wasn't mine, nor had it ever been.

That was the second time I contacted the police.

The Pacific Division of the LAPD was the closest precinct to my home. I said I wanted to file a report of identity theft. Within minutes, I was in the office of an African-American detective in his early forties who went by the name of Gibson.

"I get about seventy of these cases a day," Detective Gibson told me. "But I hardly ever get one so well-documented." He plopped his hand on the stack of papers I'd gathered from the credit bureau and credit card companies. "Kudos on your research." She had left a pretty clear trail. The only hitch was that She hadn't stolen from me. She'd only gotten the cards approved, which meant she already had access to much of my private financial data.

"I'll also put you together with Threat Management," Gibson said.

The Threat Management Unit was the official title of what is euphemistically called the "Celebrity Task Force," a division of LAPD that deals with stalkers and harassers of LA's many higher-profile citizens. Politicians, celebrities. You know, people like me, but more famous.

But, thanks to *Another Time, Another Place*, I managed to qualify.

"And you should file for a restraining order," Detective Gibson added.

"Sounds like a lot more paperwork," I said, dreading the coming bureaucracy.

"It is," said Gibson. "But which would you prefer? Filling out some forms, or having your world turned upside down by someone who won't quit?" He fixed a knowing gaze on me. "Which is how this will go, if you don't do something about it."

"Guess I better find a lawyer," I said.

The next afternoon, I met with a Century City attorney named McAdams. He had come highly recommended, having used his legal acumen to help ensure a famous actress's stalker went to prison for multiple break-ins to her homes in LA, Austin, and New Orleans. He'd also managed to have a stolen homemade sex tape removed from the internet, which was practically considered an impossibility. That really impressed me. Comparatively, my problem would be a simple task, but one that would also cost me $10,000. I gulped…and wrote the check.

Then I started collecting all the physical evidence I could.

With McAdams' guidance, I printed out emails She had sent, copied phone records, and credit card histories. I got statements by everyone from my co-workers and friends, the credit bureaus, anyone I could think of who'd had an encounter of any kind with her. Then I went to the Santa Monica

Courthouse and stood in line to file for a Temporary Restraining Order. It was granted on the spot.

Then, finally, McAdams and I were in court, facing the demon that had dogged my life for the last several years. On the stand being questioned, I could see in my periphery that the judge would literally roll his eyes with each description of her intrusions. I played the voicemails that she'd left on my phone for the court, in which She described the longing she felt for me, and how my life would be better if we were together, and how she would always make her "special lasagna" for us.

McAdams was brilliant when he questioned me. Not so much the opposing attorney.

I've performed many courtroom scenes in my career, and I expected a confrontational approach when I was cross-examined, but this guy's idea of "aggressive" was practically comical. He tried his best to lower his high-pitched voice and contort his bearded, cherubic face into something combative. Instead, he came off like an extra from *Darby O'Gill and the Little People* who had gotten a law degree and hung a shingle.

He approached me on the witness stand, hunched over with his hands stuffed deep into his pockets. "Did she ever threaten you?" he demanded.

"No," I answered, keeping my cool.

"Did she ever once leave you a voicemail that sounded the least bit frightening? Unless you think lasagna is scary."

"No," I replied again. "But Mark Chapman didn't threaten John Lennon before he killed him, either." McAdams had coached me, and with that answer, the cross abruptly ended.

The entire proceeding only took about two and a half hours, during which She declined to take the stand. Instead, She sat, silent, alternating her glare between the judge and my attorney, and mostly at me. This did not go unnoticed by Hizzoner, who looked over the top of his reading glasses and delivered an admonishment.

"Miss, you are going to behave like this man's family died out a hundred years ago. It is *your* obligation to maintain a distance of five hundred yards from him, at all times. For example, if you walk into a restaurant," he said, pointing at me, "and this man is there having dinner, you will leave immediately and find another place to eat. Understood?" She said she did. The judge then formally granted a Permanent Restraining Order, banged his gavel, and court was adjourned.

Shortly thereafter, through the show publicist, I received word from the head of the ATAP Official Fan Club that She had been officially and permanently banned from attending any further fan club events or having any connection to the club at all.

Finally, I had what I wanted—a chance to try and forget this had ever happened.

* * *

I have a policy to never date someone from a show I'm working on, and I've mostly kept to it. But that doesn't extend to someone working on another show. That would just be self-defeating, right?

I met the Beauty at an awards event. I had been nominated again for a Best Villain award (hey, it sounds better than Best Hunk), and we hit it off right away. I admit I was feeling pretty damn good, given the nomination (which I won!), and that my personal life had considerably quieted down. I won't give you the Beauty's name, partly because I want to protect her identity, and partly because she wouldn't see me again after what happened. And I don't blame her.

Our one and only date was at Café Del Rey, a white linen Mediterranean joint down in the Marina with a retro Rat Pack feel. Old-school cocktails, fresh fish, and a great view of the harbor yachts at sunset.

The Beauty was a focused, smart, and ambitious young woman from Illinois. I was really attracted to her, but I fought the urge to make a move that night, feeling it was better to keep a respectful distance. So many guys have been hit with a Me Too moment when they least expected it (not because they didn't have it coming). There was just something about this girl, and I wanted to do everything right. Happily, we talked and laughed the whole night. It couldn't have gone better.

I walked the Beauty to her car after dinner, and as things had gone so well, I had this feeling that *she* was going to make a move. The ladies are so emboldened these days. I say, "Yeah, go for what you want!"

Right when I thought she was about to come in for the kiss, her face shifted to concern when she saw something over my shoulder. When I turned, there was someone dressed in dark clothing approaching us fast, a hoodie pulled low over their head.

The hood opening looked so dark, the person must've had a black ski mask pulled over their face. The gait of their walk looked to me like a woman's.

Whoever it was, they were closing in fast. I saw a glass jar of liquid held in a gloved hand. The approaching person drew back their arm, as if winding up to throw the jar.

I guess my fight-or-flight instinct took over, and I pushed the Beauty away from me, out of the line of fire. She lost her balance and landed on her ass, too stunned to even shriek.

The dark-clad person threw the liquid toward my face, but I managed to duck out of the way. I heard it splash on the car as I grabbed the Beauty by the collar and rushed us across the lot and back into the restaurant foyer. I shut the glass door behind us and held it closed.

"Call the police!" I yelled to the Maître d'.

By the time my vision adjusted to the indoor light, I saw the figure run across the parking lot and disappear. But I knew who it was.

She.

Unfortunately, the Beauty's car took the brunt of the damage. The mystery liquid had seared through the vehicle's paint right down to the metal. The windows were also damaged with what looked like streaks that had melted into the glass. It was later determined to be concentrated Sulphuric Acid. 98%. And it had been intended for my face.

With no positive ID to go on, the police weren't able to make anything stick. Not even the security cameras gave up a lead.

I did pay for the car damage. It was a European job, so not exactly cheap. But I thought that was the least I could offer to make up for what the Beauty had gone through. I just didn't think it was fair that her insurance rate should go up because her date got acid-attacked by a psycho.

On that note, I was almost disfigured. By trying to ruin my face, She tried to steal my *livelihood*. My career is my reason for getting up in the morning. It's my whole identity. Yes, I know Hollywood can seem shallow at times, but let's get real: For an actor, your face *is* your fortune. And She tried to take mine away.

So here I am, hiding in the shadows outside her house. It's amazing what you can learn on the internet, if you look hard enough. And completely anonymous, if you do it right. Is that how She found me all those times? Who knows? Who cares?

Two can play that game.

I got a place for She all picked out in the Angeles National Forest, aka, a legendary dumping ground. It's a spot I found by chance on a hike last year. No trail leading to it, no level ground around it for unsuspecting hikers to stumble over bones. Spent all day digging the hole, so it's deep enough. Just hope no one falls in before I can get back there.

Soon, She'll be keeping company with the victims of drug deals gone sideways, romances gone sour, robberies gone wrong, and serial killers doing what they do. After tonight, nobody will ever be bothered by She again. And I'm still holding out hope for a second date with...well, you know.

I wonder if She made that lasagna she always bragged about. I do like lasagna.

# Actor Sex

by Wendall Thomas

Let's be honest. We've all had it.

If you've lived in Los Angeles more than two months and you've had sex at all, chances are you've had it with an actor. Or a would-be actor. Or a used-to-be-actor. Or an actor turned director. Or a Crate and Barrel Manager who "killed" at the *Glengarry Glen Ross Dinner Theatre* in Winnetka. It's pretty much impossible to avoid. You can't toss a Santa Monica Boulevard "showcase" playbill or a Randy's donut without hitting one. They're everywhere.

Fourteen of them—"25 to 30 and athletic"—were sitting outside my office right now. They were here to audition for Second Groomsman from the Left on *The Sun Never Rises*. I knew my boss would go with the one with the dimple in his chin, because he was about to lose his SAG card, and the part had a line. Blanche Foster was a softy at heart.

I knew this because she was the only one who would hire me. It was a rub-off town. In both directions. Most people rose and fell by the reputations of their contacts. The murder of my casting director boss hadn't been my fault, but it had left me tainted.

Blanche started working in casting in the fifties. She knew the odds of lightning striking twice. So, two months ago, she'd taken pity on me, and here I was, running auditions for soap operas, micro-budget indies, and "disease of the week" movies for the third-place "Might See TV" network.

I looked around at the doomed hopefuls, circled in plastic chairs—an echo of every AA meeting ever filmed. I knew after they'd heard the inevitable, "We'll let you know," they'd head to their actual paying jobs. At the end of the night, most of them would go home with a random Ralph's shopper, dry martini drinker, or pre-menopausal gym rat. With any luck, these encounters would leave both parties with a good story instead of an STD.

As I waited for Blanche to finish up, I checked the front page of the *LA Times*. An accountant in her thirties had been stabbed in her apartment near Larchmont Village. There was a sidebar with a promise from the LAPD that murders were actually down in 1990—only 877 homicides to 11 million residents in the last year—so, it wasn't something I spent a lot of time thinking about.

Until my boyfriend was in a bad mood.

* * *

My currency in the casting world might be declining, but my currency in the girlfriend world was up since I'd met Detective Hanny O'Rourke.

I guess, for a former National Guardsman from Newport News, my seventh degree of separation from Hollywood made me glamorous. For me, the sheer relief of dating someone who wasn't looking sideways into every mirror we passed made up for the fact that he hadn't seen *Chinatown*. He was more of a *Rambo/Dirty Harry* guy, though he had seen *Pretty Woman* three times—only one of them with me.

He was kind, never spent more than ten dollars on a haircut, and I thought I might be in love with him.

But tonight, something was off. He was not usually a man to let his flautas get cold.

"What? Tell me, or I'm taking the rest of that green corn tamale."

He moved the husk out of reach. "There've been two more."

There it was. I'd been waiting for this shoe to drop. He was sleeping with other women. I managed to squeeze out, "Two more what?"

"Two more murders."

"Oh! Oh. Murders. God, I'm sorry."

"Christ, I've only been a detective for a nanosecond, and this has to be my first case? A serial killer?"

"If you want to talk, I'll keep it in the vault." I got up, kissed him on the head, and grabbed two Modelos out of the fridge. I hated beer, but it seemed like a moment for solidarity.

When I came back, he was looking at a stack of headshots on the edge of my coffee table. "Why is this guy wearing a polo outfit?"

"Bad agenting."

"Oh." He took a long swig of his beer and looked around the room.

I took a fake sip of beer. "Is one of the victims that woman in Larchmont?"

He stared at me. "I can't talk about it."

"Obviously. I would never expect you to." My father had been a big one for reverse psychology. I pointed at the flautas. "Are you going to eat those?"

He took a sad, limp bite.

"She was number three. I can't talk about it."

But he did. At least—the "no forced entry" and "they were all killed the same way" part.

I handed him the rest of my beer. "Isn't it usually the boyfriend? Or the husband?"

"None of them were dating anyone. At least not according to their friends. One of them had gone like a year without a date."

"And do you know what they were doing earlier that night?"

"Let me check, F. Lee Bailey." He took his notebook out of his briefcase. "One was at a charity event at the Century Plaza Hotel, one was at a focus group screening at the Cinerama Dome, and one had a meeting at the Bar Marmont."

They weren't the only women who had—at some point in their past—gone home with a bartender from the Bar Marmont or a valet at the Century Plaza. Me, for instance.

"So, basically, you're looking for a possible stranger who these single women probably met when they were out, let into their homes, and had consensual sex with?"

"That's a decent summary."

"Well, that's easy. It's an actor."

* * *

"How do you know?" he asked me.

"Logic. And friends. If these women were single, employed, and even vaguely picky, no matter how drunk they were, they wouldn't go home with a mechanic or a dishwasher or a non-waiter actor. They'd have to be seduced. That's what actors do for a living. It's the fame/charm/looks/headshot combo that makes smart women stupid."

"Headshots? Why did you say headshots?"

"Because actors never miss an opportunity to leave one behind."

His face went white. "I have to go back to work."

He ran out so fast, he forgot his briefcase. It was too tempting. I opened it. I wish I hadn't.

Copies of the crime scene photos were on top.

Three women. Each one had an actor's headshot stabbed into their chest.

They couldn't be the killer's photos, or he'd already be in custody—actor resumes always listed at least five contact numbers.

I grabbed the magnifying glass I used for Leonard Maltin's *Video Guide* and zeroed in on the bloody headshots. Each one was a different pose, but the same grinning face looked out from all three.

It was Jack Nicholson.

* * *

Something pinged in my brain, but I wasn't sure what. I slammed the briefcase shut and put it by the door three seconds before Hanny came back to get it.

He squeezed my hand. "Lock everything. Everything, okay?"

"I will, good luck."

He gave me a distracted kiss and headed to the "unmarked" Lincoln Town

Car that screamed LAPD.

I sat back at the table and took a bite of congealed tamale. It had looked like the Jack Nicholson photos were actual headshots, not the publicity photos actors signed for fans, restaurants, and their dry cleaners.

Headshots were different—they were an actor's calling card. Most had a resume stapled to the back, so they could swap them out if they had a new credit.

There was a definite hierarchy in the headshot world. Extras—also known as "background"—didn't have any lines. They were on the bottom rung. Then there were actors who were used for decoration, who might or might not have dialogue. Just above them were working character actors or rising stars who worked steadily, usually in guest spots. Once an actor had a recurring or lead role in a series or feature, they graduated from the headshot/audition pile to straight offers of work.

Jack Nicholson would have been in the offer pile after his '69 Oscar nod for *Easy Rider* so any actual headshots would have been from the ten years before that. They would be hard to find now. And expensive.

I had an idea about who might have one, but I couldn't do anything about it until morning.

In the meantime, I flipped through the headshots I had on hand. I'd worked on last year's Western, *Guns Ablazin'*, so I had photos for pretty much every actor between the ages of seventeen and thirty-five. I put the ones who had hit on me in their own pile. It wasn't small.

Any casting assistant had their share of romantic offers. On that movie, where everyone wanted to ride a horse and shoot a gun, it had quadrupled. I'd been tempted, but I wasn't delusional enough to think those encounters would be anything but transactional.

My early Hollywood days were another story. Hanny would be horrified to know how many one-night stands I'd had, mostly with some kind of actor hyphenate. It's not like they were intentional. I always thought, *This might be the one*, until they never called, or gave me the number for their answering service, or, worse, their agent.

I read through some of the comments Blanche and I had written on the faces. "Squints too much." "Squeaky voice." "Airbrushed, actually 50." "Too James Woods." "Handsome, terrible."

We saw so many people, we had to find some way to differentiate. Otherwise, they all blurred together. Now that I'd been in casting awhile, it was harder to remember whether I'd slept with someone, or just auditioned them. I guess, in the end, it was the same thing.

The next morning, after screaming the word "cocksucker" a record twenty-three times on the 10 Freeway between my Melrose-adjacent apartment and the Lantana Production Center, I set up for a reading we were doing for an independent feature called *The Condo in the Woods* for a director named Josh Hagerty.

I smiled at the actresses waiting to audition for "Sensitive Drug Addict/Single Mother #3" and went into the inner office to go through more files, in search of what, I wasn't sure.

Blanche arrived fifteen minutes late, like always. She was old school in the best way. First, she loved actors. Second, she loved movies. Third, she knew who she was. Few women in Hollywood, or anywhere, were secure enough to keep the same hairstyle for forty years. It pretty much boiled down to Carol Burnett, Bonnie Raitt, Queen Elizabeth, and Blanche. Her legendary Anna Wintour/Louise Brooks bob with bangs had served her well from her raven-haired days through to her current stylish silver. At seventy-something, she was still slim, favored tailored trousers and designer flats, and wouldn't be caught dead with a digital watch.

We both loved the Lantana lot because of their "Bob Alerts." Robert Redford had an office here, and the woman whose window overlooked his parking spot called the head office whenever his Lexus arrived. The loudspeaker announcement, "Hank, please come to the loading dock," sent the half the building into the hallway for a glimpse. I particularly loved being there with Blanche, as she'd been a casting assistant on one of Redford's first films. He remembered her and always said hello. Suddenly, I understood the value of keeping the same haircut.

Even when the Sundance Kid wasn't around, there was always someone famous there. I'd handed a coffee mug to Micky Dolenz, eaten a piece of birthday cake with Danny Glover—much sexier in person than in *Lethal Weapon*—and held the door open for Cyndi Lauper. I'll admit, when it came to real talent, I was as starstruck as any teenager.

Three hours and one false "Bob Alert" later, I'd repeatedly prompted the actors with the line, "Think of your child. Take the methadone," and Blanche had narrowed the choices down to two skeletal women who looked almost exactly alike. Josh, in a move right out of the low-budget horror playbook, said to make a deal with the one who was the cheapest, and then talk the agent down another thirty percent.

Then he laughed. "You know how desperate struggling actors are."

Heading to the parking lot, I told Blanche I'd follow her home if she wanted to grab a drink.  She lived in one of the Los Feliz apartments Raymond Chandler had rented in the 40s, complete with a turret and louvered windows that overlooked The House of Pies. It was filled with Art Deco treasures, including a Charles Catteau vase in the entryway. We parked in front, then walked down Vermont to Sarno's.

I loved the old school Italian restaurant because they kept a pianist on salary for anyone who wanted to sing opera. Blanche loved it for the cheap Chianti and the chance of finding a budding star.

She'd always had the touch—she'd been the first person to cast Sidney Poitier, worked on the *Smothers Brothers Show*, knew Ruth Gordon, had Sydney Pollack's home phone number, and auditioned anyone who counted. So tonight, I was on a mission.

"Hey," I said, as I offered her the last piece of garlic bread, "Did you ever read Jack Nicholson before he got famous?"

"Jackie! Of course.  I worked for Corman, you know, for a little while." She took a bite. "I gave Jack a ride home from an audition once."

"Really?" I said with as much innuendo as I could muster.

She shrugged. "It was the sixties."

Ah, even Blanche had had actor sex. With Jack fricking Nicholson!  I wondered who else she'd given a ride to. But that was for another day.

"I'd love to see one of his old headshots. Any chance you still have one?"

Blanche's garage had six floor-to-ceiling filing cabinets, all filled with photos and resumes of actors she'd considered over the years. She always said it was as important to remember who someone had been as who they were now. She pulled a step stool to the third cabinet, reached into the top drawer, and yelled, "Ha!"

She pulled out three identical headshots of a very young Nicholson in a corduroy jean jacket, turned sideways, with a bit of devil around his eyes.

I was thrilled. And horrified.

It looked like one of the same photos the killer had used.

While I was staring at it, she came back with a stack of four different versions of "young Jack." I recognized two of them from the crime scene photos. I hoped the killer didn't have all four.

Blanche dug once more through the drawer. "I thought I had more. God knows what I did with them."

I turned one over. It had a few early horror credits. I read down to my favorite part on any headshot: Special Talents. Had Jack lied about fencing, like everyone else who came in our door? No. Under sports, he'd put "backgammon." I loved him.

As we walked to my car, Blanche handed me two of her duplicates.

"Are you sure? These are worth something."

"They're for your collection."

"How do you know I have a collection?"

"Takes one to know one."

I looked up at the windows of her totally noir, totally gorgeous apartment.

"Do you ever worry about them selling the building? Having to move out?"

"Nope. I own it."

"Wow."

"It's my security. And I always keep a unit empty for an actor who needs a break."

Typical Blanche, a sucker for actors.

I kissed her cheek, drove around a little bit to take in the Los Feliz streetlights and Tudor thatching, then headed down Western, took a right on Beverly, and turned up my street.

Hanny's car was outside.

I circled the block looking for a parking spot, wondering what to do with the Nicholson headshots. Funny how it went. I had always trusted Hanny implicitly. But now that I'd gone through his briefcase, suddenly I didn't trust him not to go through my purse.

I spotted a Saab pulling out and floored it. It left just enough room for my VW. If I were an actor, I would definitely include swearing in three languages and extreme parallel parking in my Special Talents section.

I slid the pictures into an old *LA Weekly*, put it under the seat, then got out. Hanny was sitting on the steps.

"Hey," I said.

We hugged for a minute, then I opened the door and hurried us upstairs. When I first moved in, I'd loved that our entryway had been in *Body Double*, but tonight it freaked me out. I closed and locked my door.

Hanny looked exhausted. It killed me to know I had a clue that might help him, and I couldn't share it. I'd just have to keep pestering him until he told me the thing I already knew.

"Any luck?"

"Well, there hasn't been another murder. That we know of. Of course, the other three happened on Saturday nights."

"In a row?"

He asked for a beer, chugged most of it, then told me to sit down. "Look, I know this is weird, but Bogosian thinks you may be right about the actor thing, and he was wondering whether you might help us?"

His partner hated me. They must be desperate.

"To be honest, Callie, I'm not crazy about putting you anywhere near it."

I put my hand on his arm. "If I can help, I want to."

"Great. Okay." He opened his briefcase and reached in.

Thank God. Now I could explain the headshot thing, and he'd never know I'd opened his briefcase.

He laid out six photos.

They weren't from the crime scene.

* * *

They were long lens shots of men in matching jackets, caught in various poses, parking and returning overpriced cars.

"We took these last night at the Century Plaza, where the first victim was last seen. Do you recognize anyone? Any actors?"

I looked at the men, then pointed to one who had his sleeves rolled up.

"This looks like Haley Dupont.  Usually plays a low-level criminal or Anthony Michael Hall's childhood friend.  I might have him here, somewhere."

I did a quick look through my stacks. "Nope. But I know he's with APA."

"AP what?"

"Give me that." I wrote down the phone number for the boutique agency. At this point, I knew them all by heart.

"Thanks, this will help. No one else?"

I looked again.  "They all change their hair a lot.  There's a chance this blonde is Casey Saracen—he had a line in *Eight Million Ways to Die*. I'll check for his newest headshot when I get to the office. What about the places the other victims were seen before they were killed?"

"We have a meeting with the focus group screening company in the morning, and then we're going to hit the Bar Marmont as soon as it opens. We need to talk to the staff there to see if anyone remembers the victim, or saw her talking to anyone."

Years ago, I'd had a fling with one of the Marmont bartenders. I hoped he didn't still work there. I wasn't anxious for my old and new dating worlds to collide. I knew the Chateau was known for its discretion, so they wouldn't offer up names.  Plus, odds were, the bartender wouldn't remember me. I only remembered him because he'd thrown a dozen roses through the window of my car.

"I'm whipped," Hanny said, "Let's go to bed."

* * *

I still thought it was possible to find the killer by tracing the Nicholson headshots, so the next morning, I decided to check the cinema collectors stores. If I found any clues, I'd call in an anonymous tip.

After I set up all the casting appointments for "HOA Captain/Former Navy Seal" for our afternoon *Condo in the Woods* session, I took Melrose to Wilcox. If I parked just north of Sunset, I could walk to the stores I had in mind. I headed to my favorite first.

A week after I got to LA, I stumbled down an otherwise disheartening Hollywood Boulevard into Book City and found a shooting script for *Double Indemnity*. With Billy Wilder's notes.

It was out of my price range, but the owner had taken pity on me, lowered the price just enough to make buying it insane rather than impossible, and gotten a customer for life. The store had every possible book on cinema, signed photos, and endless wondrous and unpredictable treasures— from William Holden's glasses from *Born Yesterday* to Barbra Streisand's microphone from *A Star is Born*.

Matt, the clerk, and I had a quick argument about how the hallucinations were shot in *Jacob's Ladder*, then I asked if they had any original Nicholson headshots.

"Ha! Are you kidding? Since *Batman*? Those ComicCon people are just plain overzealous. Jack stuff is really hard to get now."

I knew it. This was a way to narrow down the suspects.

"Do you have a diehard collector you call first if something comes in?"

"Maybe. Why? Do you have any stuff?"

I slid one of the vintage Jack audition photos onto the counter for a second. He gasped.

"My boss is considering selling a few of these. Why don't you check in with your collector, and I'll give you a call later?"

By the time I got to the door, he was already dialing.

I headed east on the Boulevard past the Musso & Frank Grill to Larry Edmunds Bookshop. It had been around since the late 30s, so I panicked when I saw boxes stacked outside. I stuck my head in.

"You're not closing?"

"Just moving a few doors down," a voice yelled from the back. "I'll be right out."

A tall man with stringy arm muscles emerged from the bookshelves and grinned. "All that stuff on the street is half price."

Like my pal at Book City, his eyes widened at the sight of the Nicholson memorabilia. "Funny. Just had a guy in yesterday looking for one of those."

"Did you have any?"

"One. It wasn't in as good shape as this one, though."

"But he bought it?"

"Yeah. He was kind of a dick about it, tried to jack me on the price."

"Is he a big collector?"

"Just Nicholson stuff. He said his Mom always told him he was going to be the next Jack Nicholson."

"Does he look like Jack Nicholson?"

"You might think so if you were his mother. And nearsighted."

"Ouch."

"Yeah, I mean, maybe a little. Let's just say he's no Christian Slater."

"If he comes back, will you let me know? I'll see if I can dig out more in the meantime and we can figure something out."

"I'll take that one now."

"Not a chance." I gave him my pager, work, and home numbers.

Was this collector the killer? Could someone who revered Jack use him as a murder weapon? Or did he actually hate Nicholson? Actors left their headshots at auditions. Were these murders auditions for something worse? That was fricking terrifying. The psychology didn't quite line up for me yet, but I still felt there was a connection.

The annoying thing was I felt like I knew this person, but I couldn't remember how. I had a flash of sitting in a booth somewhere and hearing, "I like it. I like breathing through it." Then it was gone.

In the meantime, I decided to head to Hollywood Division Station. The Desk Sergeant waved me back to the bullpen. Hanny and his partner, Mel Bogosian, hovered over a pile of plastic bags.

Hanny was shaking his head. "He wouldn't have left the knives if they could help us, right?"

"What kind of knife is it?"

They both whipped around. Hanny smiled.

Bogosian didn't. "Steak," he said.

"I mean, what brand. Can I see?"

Hanny picked up one of the bags and held it out to me.

"Miyabis," I said. "They use these at the Chateau Marmont."

"How do you know what kind of steak knives they use at the Chateau Marmont?" Hanny asked.

"Because I've had steak there. And I got a fricking dissertation on those knives. Go ahead, roll your eyes. But when the studio's paying, you always get the most expensive thing on the menu to make up for all the posturing crap you're going to have to endure."

Bogosian shook his head. "They posture about knives?"

"Yes. And watches. And stocks. And real estate. And Wagyu beef. And in extreme cases, the wonder of Jean Claude Van Damme. Hanny doesn't posture about anything. That's why I like him." I grinned at him. "Have you been to the Marmont yet?"

"Later. We did meet with the focus group." He handed me a list. "Recognize any of these? They're the people who worked the screening."

I speed-scanned the pages. "This woman was a murder victim on *Matlock*. I don't recognize anyone else. Where's the list of attendees?"

"What are you talking about?"

"Tons of broke actors sign up for these free screenings. And they have to turn in score cards, so the company will have a record. The victim could've sat next to the killer."

"Dammit," Bogosian said. "Call them, Hanny."

Hanny took off to find a phone. That left me alone with his grumpy partner. "I could probably help more, Detective, if I actually knew how the women were killed. The details."

"Nice try. You know we have to hold some information back."

"Okay. Fine. Tell Hanny I'll see him tonight if he isn't working."

Since I was a block from Sunset, I decided to take the scenic route west today. Maybe I'd get lucky and hit stop-and-go traffic in front of the Beverly Hills Hotel. I could look at that thing all day. I did hit traffic, but in front of the Rainbow Room instead.

It reminded me of the roses guy. I'd been stuck in my non-air-conditioned car on Highland on a Hollywood Bowl night, inching along for ages beside a cute guy in a Camry. We'd honked simultaneously at a Mercedes that passed us on the right. Then, at the stoplight at Highland and Sunset, he tossed a bunch of red roses through my window and yelled, "Have coffee with me!"

I told myself I pulled over just to keep him from following me home. But the truth was, I was starved for romance. Who wasn't? So it turned into more than coffee. For one night at least. Thinking back, it had been stupid and reckless. The flowers were clearly his go-to pick-up technique. It would have worked on almost anyone. Trapped in our cars on the streets of LA, we were all ugly sitting ducklings.

But, there was something else that had drawn me in. Not just the flowers. What had it been? Oh shit. It was that he reminded me of Jack Nicholson.

I pulled over in front of the Hamburger Hamlet and put on my hazard lights.

Had I slept with the Headshot Killer? I hoped not, but one of the things I did remember was that he bragged about how many stars he had met working at Bar Marmont.

I was so distracted by the time I got to the Lantana lot, I almost created a "Bob Emergency" by practically dinging the Sundance Kid with my car. He did a *Legal Eagles*-esque sidestep out of the way and smiled. I loved him.

I rushed down the hall to the office. Blanche was standing outside with a dark-haired man. He turned around with what might be considered a devilish grin.

"Callie? Do you know Nick Reason? He was spectacular as the young *RFK in LBJ: The Early Years*. I decided at the last minute to bring him in for the HOA Captain part."

Yes. I knew Nick. I had once left him sleeping in my apartment. Beside a dozen wilting roses.

* * *

Nick Reason.  How could I have forgotten that name?  Why hadn't his headshot been in Blanche's stack? Did he remember me? I couldn't tell. We were about to shake hands when his beeper went off. He apologized, saying he'd just make a quick call and come back.

Blanche and I headed into the office, where Josh, the director, was waiting. As usual, he was dressed too young for his fifty-odd years, complete with perpetual baseball cap—whether it hid hair loss or was an homage to Ron Howard, it was hard to say.

"I told you I'm looking for a *Shining* vibe in this guy. Are you sure Christian Slater was a hard pass? Can we go back to him?"

Blanche shook her head. "No. You're due to shoot in three weeks. I've brought in the best actors I could find in your price range.  Why don't you give them a chance?  Maybe you can be known as the director who discovered the next Christian Slater."

She was a genius.

I heard the office phone.  It was Larry Edmunds Books, saying they definitely had a buyer for as many headshots as I could get. I said I'd make arrangements later and headed into the session.

There were five actors waiting, including Nick. All of their mothers, or high school girlfriends, or both, had probably told them they were the next Jack Nicholson. Cripes. So all of them were trying to do the actor's inflection, to varying disastrous degrees. Were all of them potential suspects?

Nick was last. He sat down, legs akimbo, and grinned. I tried to keep the sides from shaking as I read the "Furious Condo Owner" part, with feeling.

It wasn't the first time I'd read lines with an ex.

It was always humiliating to see someone who'd rejected you, but in an audition, they needed you, so the shoe was on the other foot, Cinderella-wise. The possible serial killer thing added a whole new dimension.

I'd been lucky enough to work with several smart directors who knew how to inspire actors. Josh was not one of them. He kept asking Nick for "*Shining*. More *Shining*," which wasn't that easy with dialogue about condo improvements. I actually felt for the guy. There was only so much you could do with the line, "The gutters are filthy." He tried, adding an occasional "man," but it was an uphill battle.

After Nick said a polite goodbye to Blanche and Josh, he proceeded to invade my personal space. "We had a date once, didn't we?"

"Of sorts."

"Yeah. I remember. You lived on Sycamore, right?" Shit. "I have to run an errand," he said. "But you want to grab a coffee or a drink later?"

And be stabbed? No, thank you. But if he was the killer, it would keep him from picking up anyone else. And maybe I could get some evidence.

I gave him my pager number and headed back to Larry Edmunds Books.

I spent a long time in my car, looking at Jack Nicholson's headshot. Then I went inside and put it on temporary consignment. I was headed out the front door when I saw Nick Reason squatting on the sidewalk, going through the half-price boxes in front. Holy shit. Should I run?

Too late. He'd seen me.

He stood up. "Are you following me, or is this just kismet?"

"Hard to tell." I pointed at Musso's. "Want to come?"

He held up some photos and a book. "I'm going to buy this stuff. Save me a stool."

Was he there for the Nicholson shot? It was too weird of a coincidence, wasn't it?

I sat at the end of the bar and ordered the requisite martini. Nick showed up when I was a third of the way through my drink and waved at the bartender. "Hey, Ruben!"

Ruben grinned, and about two seconds later, another martini appeared.

"Come here often?" I asked.

"Ruben and I go back."

"What did you get at Larry's?"

"Presents for someone." Oh God, was that what he called them? "And this." He pulled out *The Richard Burton Diaries*. "You can learn a lot about the craft by reading memoirs."

After two more martinis and a one-way conversation on Brando's feelings about the Method, he leaned in and whispered, "You want to get out of here?" This was it. I looked at my watch. It was eight. Hanny usually showed up at my apartment around now.

"Sure. Want to follow me?" I said. "I just need to make a phone call." I left a message for Hanny that I thought I might have been propositioned by the killer and was bringing him home.

When I got to the street, Nick was standing by his Camry. He gestured me in.

"I'll drive us. We'll come back and get your car after." After what?

What was I doing? I hoped Hanny had gotten my message. I got in.

He pulled out and headed east on Franklin, away from my apartment.

"Where are we going?"

"My place. I've got to drop something off." I spent the next fifteen minutes trying to work up the nerve to drop and roll. Finally, he stopped the car.

In front of Blanche's building.

"What the hell are we doing here?"

"Blanche didn't tell you? She's letting me stay here." He held up the headshots. "These are for her."

What was going on? Was Blanche harboring a serial killer, or had I gotten everything wrong? Should I go upstairs with him? Or flee to a clean, well-lighted place—i.e., The House of Pies?

Then I noticed the garage door was up. The filing cabinet drawers were open, headshots thrown everywhere. We both swore and ran for the front door.

Nick let us in. We could hear the soundtrack to *Little Shop of Horrors* and someone yelling, "I never even got a call back! I deserved a fucking call back!"

We flew in to find Josh, the horror director. He was standing over Blanche, naked except for his baseball cap, Jack Nicholson headshot in one hand, Miyabi knife in another. I hoped Blanche would forgive me when I bashed him over the head with her Carl Catteau vase.

I let Nick restrain the unconscious Josh while I went to untie Blanche. She was shaken, but okay. "Christ," she said. "What an asshole. He was wrong for the part, goddammit! I made the right call."

"Yes, you absolutely did."

I called the Hollywood Station, and ten minutes later, Hanny and Bogosian were there to arrest the real Headshot Killer.

Later, when questioned, Josh, the psychopath, admitted the other women had been "auditions" for the main event—Blanche. "All you have to do is tell a woman you're a film director and you're in."

At least I'd been a little bit right. He had been the "buyer" at Larry Edmunds and Book City. The knives were from his personal collection.

The next day, Blanche forgave me for the vase, but not for suspecting her protegé, Nick. Even a softy has her limits, and for her, actors always came first. At least she let me go, so I could get unemployment.

That night, Hanny left a message about a celebratory beer at Boardner's. He'd had more than a few by the time I arrived. I told him Blanche had fired me and I'd decided casting wasn't for me.

He got a strange look on his face and grabbed my arm. "What? You can't quit! The *Flatliners* premiere is in a month! You promised Blanche would get us in. How am I ever going to meet Julia Roberts, now? Dammit!"

Wow. Okay. I took his hand off my arm. "I completely understand the feeling. I prefer actor sex myself." I paid for his drinks on the way out.

Like I said, it's rub-off town. In both directions. I'd lost a job and a boyfriend, but I'd sold the two Nicholson headshots to Larry Edmunds for five grand.

Highland was wide open. I swore in three languages at a Mercedes that cut me off on Willoughby, then parallel-parked in front of my building with one hand. That night, I left the windows open.

# About the Contributors

**Paul Awad** is a filmmaker and writer. He is author of the IPPY award-winning science fiction thriller *When Earth Shall Be No More*. His short story "Touch of Grey" is published in *Friend of the Devil: Crime Fiction Inspired by the Songs of the Grateful Dead*. Recent films include *Bicentennial Bonsai: Emissaries of Peace* (PBS) and *A Savage Nature* (Gravitas Ventures). www.paul-awad.com

**Eric Beetner** is an 8-time Emmy nominee for editing competition reality shows. His work as editor, producer and writer has been viewed by tens of millions across the world for nearly three decades. A slightly smaller number has read his 30-plus novels and over 100 short stories. For more, visit www.ericbeetner.com

**Tiffany Borders** is a Carolinian by birth, a Californian by choice. First Hollywood job? Assistant to a celebrity publicist. First industry sale? Zombie movie. As a professional ghostwriter, Tiffany's written/co-written four published books and two produced films, one of which is pretty darn good. She's also a 10-year judge for The Page Awards, an international screenplay competition. Her most recent project was with screenwriter Robert Towne and his family. You cannot conclusively prove she has been linked to any murders.

**Ellen Byron** spent many happy days—and not-so-happy late nights—working in the Wilder Building on TV shows produced by Paramount Studios. Her TV credits include *Wings, Just Shoot Me, Still Standing,* and *Fairly Odd Parents,* pilots for all the networks and several major cable outlets, plus many series that disappeared after a season—or less. Ellen is a bestselling author, Anthony nominee, and recipient of Agatha and Lefty awards for her multiple mystery book series.

**Teel James Glenn** worked as a stuntman/actor on over 300 soap opera episodes and network shows like *Spenser for Hire* and many low budget flicks. He has stories in over 200 magazines including *Weird Tales, Cirsova, Mystery Magazine,* and *Sherlock Holmes Mystery Magazine.* His novel *A Cowboy in Carpathia* won best novel 2021 in the Pulp Factory Award. theurbanswas hbuckler.com

**Matt Goldman** is a New York Times Bestselling author and Emmy Award-winning television writer. He has been nominated for the Shamus Award and Nero Award. Matt's television writing credits include *Seinfeld, Ellen, The New Adventures of Old Christine,* and *Dirk Gently's Holistic Detective Agency.*

**Jon Lindstrom** is a 4-time Emmy©-nominated actor, bestselling author, award-winning filmmaker, and occasionally a drummer. By most accounts, he is also a pretty nice guy. He lives mostly in Los Angeles, where he writes about the good people, the bad people, the business of show, and the experience of living in sunny, seductive, corrupt LA. Credits include *True Detective, Bosch, General Hospital,* and *Must Love Dogs.* www.jonlindstrom.com

**Adam Meyer** is a writer/producer and a Derringer Award-winning and Shamus Award-nominated fiction writer. He has scripted several TV movies as well as written shows for Fox, CBS, National Geographic, Tubi, and others, such as the long-running *America's Most Wanted* and the Emmy Award-Winning PBS series *Made With Love.* His short fiction has appeared in many anthologies including *Best American Mystery and Suspense 2023.* He is also the editor of *In Too Deep: Crime Stories Inspired by the Songs of Genesis* and author of the novel *The Last Domino.* www.adammeyerwriter.com

**Alan Orloff** has published thirteen novels and more than sixty short stories.

His work has won an Anthony, an Agatha, a Derringer, and two ITW Thriller Awards. He's adapted two of his novels into screenplays, and, man, is he desperate to make it big in Hollywood. And yes, he would do just about anything to help his thespian son make it big, too. www.alanorloff.com

**Stuart Orloff** is a multi-talented actor, writer, and director based in Los Angeles. He is thrilled to be making his literary debut co-writing with his father. He is desperate to make it in Hollywood, but not desperate enough to commit murder. Yet.

**Kathryn O'Sullivan** is a writer and filmmaker. She is author of the Colleen McCabe mysteries (Malice Domestic Best First Traditional Mystery winner) and the IPPY award-winning science fiction thriller *When Earth Shall Be No More*. Her short stories and plays have been published in numerous anthologies. Recent films include *Bicentennial Bonsai: Emissaries of Peace* (PBS) and *A Savage Nature* (Gravitas Ventures). www.kathrynosullivan.com

With roots in the Texas Hill Country and the Mississippi Delta, **Gary Phillips** must keep writing—short stories, comics, novels, scripts, cereal box copy...to forestall his appointment at the crossroads.

**Robert Rotstein** is a USA Today bestselling author. His most recent novel is *The Out of Town Lawyer* (Blackstone Publishing), which Kirkus Reviews calls, "A highly original courtroom drama ripped from the headlines and then some." His latest novel, *A True Verdict*, was released in January 2025. He practices law in Los Angeles, representing clients in the entertainment industry.

**John Shepphird** is a Shamus Award-winning author, two-time Anthony Award finalist, and writer/director of television films. Novels include *Deception Specialist* (Jack O'Shea series book #1) and the Hollywood-themed whodunnit thriller *Bottom Feeders*. John's short fiction has appeared in *Alfred Hitchcock's Mystery Magazine* and various crime fiction anthologies. As a director, his films include *Jersey Shore Shark Attack, Chupacabra Terror, I Saw Mommy Kissing Santa Claus,* and *Teenage Bonnie & Klepto Clyde.* www.johnshepphird.com

**Shawn Reilly Simmons** worked as a movie-set caterer on many projects, including THE INVASION, starring Daniel Craig and Nicole Kidman. She's a multiple Agatha Award winner for Best Short Story and Anthony Award winner for Best Anthology, with over thirty published short stories and nine novels to her credit. She is also the President and Managing Editor of Level Best Books. www.shawnreillysimmons.com/

**Phoef Sutton** is a New York Times Bestselling author. The winner of two Emmy Awards for his work on *Cheers* and a Peabody Award for *Boston Legal.* His novels include *Fifteen Minutes to Live, Crush, Heart Attack and Vine, Colorado Boulevard,* and *From Away.* With Janet Evanovich he has co-authored *Wicked Charms* and *Curious Minds.* He also does a podcast with Mark Jordan Legan about weird and unusual cinema: *Film Freaks Forever.*

**Wendall Thomas** served as the casting assistant and director's assistant on *Young Guns,* was an entertainment reporter for MTV, and has written and developed projects for Disney, Warner Brothers, Showtime, RKO, PBS, A&E, and NBC. She writes the award-winning Cyd Redondo screwball travel mysteries and short crime fiction about Los Angeles and teaches in the Graduate Film School at UCLA.

**Stacy Woodson** is an *Ellery Queen's Mystery Magazine*'s Readers Award winner, a two-time Derringer Award winner, and a Macavity Award and Thriller Award nominee. Her fiction has also been adapted for animation and appeared in the *Best Mysteries of the Year.* When she's not writing, she works as a Background actor. Past projects include *Homeland, Jack Ryan, The Walking Dead: World Beyond, Wonder Woman 1984,* and *Terminal List: Dark Wolf.*

# About the Editors

Adam Meyer is a writer/producer and a Derringer Award-winning and Shamus Award-nominated fiction writer. He has scripted several TV movies as well as written shows for Fox, CBS, National Geographic, Tubi, and others, including the long-running *America's Most Wanted*. His short fiction has appeared in many anthologies. He is also the editor of *In Too Deep: Crime Stories Inspired by the Songs of Genesis*.

 Adam: www.adammeyerwriter.com

Alan Orloff has published twelve novels and more than fifty short stories. His work has won an Anthony, an Agatha, a Derringer, and two ITW Thriller Awards. He's also been a finalist for the Shamus Award and has had a story selected for Best American Mystery Stories 2018. He's adapted two of his novels into screenplays, and, man, is he desperate to make it big in Hollywood. www.alanorloff.com

 Alan: www.alanorloff.com

SOCIAL MEDIA HANDLES:

Adam:
 https://www.facebook.com/adam.meyer.9693

Alan:
 https://www.facebook.com/alanorloff
 https://twitter.com/alanorloff
 https://www.instagram.com/alanorloff
 https://www.threads.net/@alanorloff

# Also by Adam Meyer and Alan Orloff, Editors

<u>**Adam**</u>

**Novels**

*The Last Domino,* 2005, Putnam

**Novellas**

"Two Shrimp Tacos and a .22 Ruger," published as part of Guns+Tacos, Down & Out Books 2022 (winner of the Derringer Award for Best Novelette)

"Fast Cars, Dirty Diapers," to be published as part of Chop Shop series, Down & Out Books 2025

**Anthologies (as editor)**

*In Too Deep*: *Crime Stories Inspired by the Songs of Genesis,* to be published February 2025, Down & Out Books

**Notable short stories**

"The Fourteenth Floor," appeared in *Crime Travel* and was nominated for a Shamus Award

"Mr. Filbert's Classroom," appeared in *Magic is Murder* and was reprinted in *The Best American Mystery and Suspense 2023*

**Selected television projects**

*Kidnapped by a Classmate* (TV movie/writer)

*My Life as a Dead Girl* (TV movie/co-writer)

*The Other Wife* (TV movie/co-writer)

*The Monkey's Paw* (TV movie/story by)

*Italy: Made With Love* (PBS documentary/co-writer, 2023 Emmy Award winner for Outstanding Educational and Informational Program)

**Alan**

## Novels

*Diamonds for the Dead*, Midnight Ink 2010 (Agatha Award Finalist)

*Killer Routine*, Midnight Ink 2011

*Deadly Campaign*, Midnight Ink 2012

*The Taste*, 2011, self-pubbed

*First Time Killer*, 2012, self-pubbed

*Ride-Along*, 2013, self-pubbed (trade paper: 2014)

*Running From the Past*, Kindle Press/Amazon Publishing, 2015

*Pray for the Innocent*, Kindle Press/Amazon Publishing, 2018 (ITW Thriller Award Winner)

*I Know Where You Sleep*, Down & Out Books, February 2020 (Shamus Award Finalist)

*I Play One On TV*, Down & Out Books, July 2021 (Agatha Award Winner, Anthony Award Winner)

*Sanctuary Motel*, Level Best Books, October 2023

*Late Checkout*, Level Best Books, October 2024

**Notable Short Stories** (50+, including one in five consecutive Best New England Crime Stories anthos)

"Rule Number One" appeared in *Snowbound* and was selected for Best American Mystery Stories 2018.

"Dying in Dokesville" appeared in *Malice Presents: Mystery Most Geographical* and won a Derringer Award.

"Rent Due" appeared in *Mickey Finn: 21st Century Noir*, Vol. 1 and won an ITW Thriller Award.